Argent: Wanderer
By Wayne A. Delk

This work is dedicated to the three great earthly lady loves of my life, the three ladies who presently and forevermore will hold my heart: my mother, Barbara Virginia; and my two daughters, Kayla Simone and Madison Elisha. The first taught me of love while the others continually remind me of love's beautiful and enduring consequences.

More than four years ago I began in earnest to write this story. It had been in my mind for a brief time prior as little more than that: a story. I had but two characters in my mind: an older, harsh loner with a sad background and a young manchild with his own mysterious history. As I began to write, the story slowly began to develop and grow beyond any confines I sought to give it. My own personal life made the writing extremely difficult and I found myself binge writing for a few days and then going days, weeks, even months without writing anything.

Life sometimes needs to give the one living it a swift kick in the arse to get things in motion. So my swift kick came (that being its own dramatic tale!) and I got to shaking and got to moving (on the writing, anyway). What has been so very amazing is that the characters waited patiently for me to return to them and their story.

The story grew to be so very large that I found myself in the midst of what has potential to become a multi-volume tale. This first volume is to be part one of what appears to be a two-part telling. Maybe. I have already jotted notes for a pre-story which may well come into being if the characters continue speaking to me and telling me more of themselves and where they've been. And where they wish to go.

I hope you enjoy reading nearly as much as I have enjoyed writing as they continue telling me their stories.

A

1 The Meeting

Evan awoke with a start. He had fallen asleep while waiting for the Wanderer to arrive. He knew it was dangerous to sleep alone in the open. Evil men still roamed the land, and he knew what fate awaited him if they found him. He was unable to defend himself against those who chose to ravage the innocents left in the world. The Wanderer was late. He normally arrived within minutes of Evan settling into his small hiding place near the dumpsters behind the shell of what had once been a large Wal-Mart. Guided by his ever-present muse, Evan always knew when the stranger was coming. Evan's muse, that internal voice he often heard and imagined as a beautiful woman, spoke to him only briefly but was never wrong. He thought of it as his subconscious, that part of him that remained alert and kept him safe even when he was unaware.

The Wanderer had a stash of supplies inside the gutted store. Evan didn't know how to get to it. It was very well hidden. On only one occasion had Evan dared to venture inside the massive store, and he had come upon a large, dying dog in the rubble. It was wild and covered with bloodied, matted fur. Impaled through its midsection by a long metal stake upon which it had fallen, it lay in a pool of its own blood. It stank of its own recently loosed bowels. Even mortally wounded the dog had uttered a low growl, bared its considerable teeth, and lunged attempting to bite him. Only the metal stake had kept the dying pooch from making one last meal of Evan. He had not returned to the interior of the store since.

He wondered what could be delaying the enigmatic figure. The man would be leaving this area soon (his inner voice had said so). Evan planned to go with him. The man would lead him to a better place. Somewhere peaceful and serene. Safe. He had seen it in his dreams. The Wanderer led the way, and he followed. He and another. The other a shade he could never clearly see. When he tried to look directly at this specter in his dreams he saw only a dark, empty space. It seemed to be a nothingness that traveled with the Wanderer. He did not see this shadow during the times he actually spied the Wanderer coming to the store for supplies. Only in his dreams. The shade was not large. In fact it could very well have been a child. Boy or girl he could not tell. He hoped to find out soon though.

The sudden pop of a small caliber handgun in the distance quickly returned his thoughts to the present. Something was going on nearby and he hoped it was not headed his way. He had seen a small band of rogues headed to the Outlands while he had been headed to the store. He had hidden from them in a gutted office park as they passed within nearly 100 yards. They were very confident and brazen, traveling in the open, not attempting to hide from anyone. They were Marauders, come from some distant part of the land to pillage and take whatever could be found. And to kill anyone they found for nothing more than sport. Evan had witnessed it before. He had lost the one human friend he had ever known to a large band of Marauders two springs prior.

Evan and Greg were playing in the clean fields on the north end of their village. There weren't many clean places near the village to play. Most of the clean space was used for living quarters or food storage (what little food could be gathered or grown for storing). But the adults had

6

seen fit to leave a small lot available for the few surviving children in the village. Greg, though more than a year older, was nearly six inches shorter than Evan. He was slim and somewhat frail. But he had the wild heart of boy beating in his breast and strove to keep up with Evan in all things. On this day they had been playing with an oblong ball, playfully throwing and kicking it as Archer had shown them. Archer, the keeper of the books, was knowledgeable about a great many things. He had told them the ball was a football.

"What you have there is a treasure of Boyhood Americana," he said in his most serious and austere voice as he beheld the ball in Evan's hands. "That, my young lads, is a football. A Nerf football, to be exact." Evan and Greg looked at each other and burst into peals of boyish laughter. "What is so funny?"

Both boys stopped laughing for a moment then looked at each other again and began snickering until they were once again laughing uncontrollably. Archer couldn't help but smile himself. He rarely heard laughter in the village; so much of their time and energy was spent just working to stay alive that the simple sound of laughter seemed to have become less than an afterthought for some. But in actuality it was a wonderful thing to hear: the laughter of children, the recharging of one's soul. He continued to smile at them, patiently waiting for the laughter to cease.

Evan gathered himself enough and said, "Nerf. That's funny. Nerf." Greg was still giggling as he tried out the word. "Nerf. Ha!" Both boys again giggled as Archer began to show them how to hold and throw the ball. Evan caught on quickly and within moments was throwing tight spirals at a good distance. Greg wasn't nearly as athletic but tried twice as hard. After a few minutes Archer said his goodbyes and went back to work in his small library of books within the pull-behind trailer in which he lived. The boys went off to try their new toy.

It was an overcast day, as most days had become in the new world. Those days that weren't overcast were either filled with a light fog, which smelled of sulfur, or a mist that stung the flesh of those exposed for too long. The sun made brief and scalding appearances these days. The boys walked out beyond the regular boundaries of the village proper, itself nothing more than a small town of shanty structures protected by some of the few good men with weapons known to be left in the land. Many of them former law officers or military, others good men who knew how to wield a weapon and dedicated to protecting the last vestiges of civilized life as it had been. There weren't a great many of them, but they were enough to keep the majority of marauding Marauders at bay. The Marauders hardly ever traveled in groups larger than five to ten. The protectors of the village numbered more than 20 total and always patrolled with at least half their number on duty at any given time. The remaining number were available at a moment's notice if the alarm were to sound. There had been no contact with any marauders for more than six months and the last contact had gone without so much as even the thought of a threat from the traveling rogues. The protectors made a show of force upon sighting the small band of men and they moved along quietly. No others had been seen since. They had thus become complacent.

The two boys found their way to the clean lot and began to throw the ball to one another. Evan continued to work on his technique, throwing the football in tighter and tighter spirals, zipping it to Greg with greater speed and accuracy. Greg tried to emulate his friend all the while, though he couldn't quite get the hang of it. Evan caught a pass from Greg and held the ball for a moment. He looked at his friend and smiled.

"Move back. I'm going to throw it far."

"How far you gonna throw it, Ev?"

"Far as I can. Just back up a little, and I'm gonna see if I can get it to you."

Greg moved back near the edge of the lot. He looked questioningly to Evan. "Is this far enough?"

"A little more."

He moved to the edge of the clearing. Beyond him lay a copse of dense desert shrubbery, the only thing (aside from different varieties of deformed trees and cacti) left growing outside the tended greenery planted by the villagers in their makeshift greenhouse. The desert shrubbery was spongy and thorny. Not really green, but dust colored. With only tiny needles for leaves the shrubbery was better described as a mass of thorny sticks and twigs interlaced amongst the dusty landscape at varying heights from less than a foot to more than six feet. It grew in patches of varying sizes, some as large as small forests, others small enough to be uprooted and used as hedgerows. The patches dotted the known landscape. Some 20 yards behind Greg was a fairly large and low-lying patch. Archer called them mutant cacti. Whatever they were, they were all over the place.

Greg yelled to his friend, now nearly 40 yards distant, "You can't throw it that far, Ev! That's too far." He smiled and awaited the throw. Evan smiled back. "You just watch. I can and I will!" He looked up into the sky and noticed a multitude of birds soaring almost directly overhead. They were large. He could tell even from his vantage. He had seen such birds before though not so many at once. He looked back at his friend. Greg waited impatiently. "Come on, Ev. Throw it!"

Evan then had a great idea, at least great in the mind of an 11-year-old boy. He would throw the ball high and far and then run to a nearby hiding place in one of the secret tunnels. The protectors had built them long ago in the event the village needed to escape into the lowlands.

They were not now, nor had they been for some time, used by the adults. The entrances were hidden from the sight of any searching eye. Evan had found almost all of them and had followed several of them down to the lowlands on his own. He had not told anyone about this. He had somehow felt that it was important to keep this knowledge to himself, though he could not understand why. He had not even shared his knowledge of the hidden tunnels with Greg. He knew of a nearby tunnel around a low half-wall to his left. It was concealed by three barrels of used oils. The oil was recycled, as was everything in the village that could be, and used to fuel lamps and other tools adapted to run on fuel. The barrels were quite large and behind them, against the low wall, was a well-hidden trap door leading to one of the escape tunnels.

He smiled a crooked smile, the left side of his mouth turned upward, and Greg tensed. Evan cocked his arm back and then it was gone, the ball now a rocket headed to the sky. As it climbed Evan began to run toward the wall while Greg tried to track its path and get under it. Evan skirted the edge of the wall and took cover behind it as the ball landed in the thicket of desert growth far behind his friend. Greg went in to retrieve their new, prized possession, and as he reached out for the ball he was gripped by a hand that appeared seemingly from the earth itself. Fear and panic enveloped him as the outlander took form. He had been lying in wait in the thick desert growth. Greg was able to let out a brief, startled cry before another hand roughly covered his mouth and pulled him down to the hard, dusty earth. And still another hand tightly squeezed his testicles as a bearded face nestled against his own and whispered, "Make another sound and I'll rip off yer balls and shove 'em down yer throat." Greg went still and quiet at that, though silent tears began to roll as his bladder released a small flow of urine into his trousers and his captor's hand. He could make out at least four of them, *and whichever was holding his boyhood seemed quite pleased with the warm wetness and began to slowly rub and squeeze Greg's crotch.*

*Evan watched with boyish delight as his friend entered the copse of bushy growth to retrieve the ball. He had not known how far he could throw it. It appeared he had mastered the football and could add that to the list of things he could immediately learn to do. The list was seemingly daily getting longer. He saw Greg bend down and then he was gone. He heard him yell out briefly and then nothing but some slight movement of the thick growth. He stood and began to make his way around the wall when he heard it. The voice. It spoke clearly and distinctly this time. Not whispering as it had before. **Stop. They will kill you if you go out there. You must get away.***

Evan hesitated. He stood looking into the desert shrubs, thinking desperately of a way to get his friend to safety. Then he saw him. Greg was up and struggling fiercely to make it out of the copse. The large forms of the marauders appeared almost as quickly and overtook Greg just as he reached the edge of the shrubs. He screamed aloud then. It was a scream of pure terror, and if Evan had been able to find his own voice he would have joined in. The scream was cut short as one large hand grasped Greg around the throat while the companion hand plunged a long blade into his back. Evan watched in horror as the blade pierced the slight body of his friend. It protruded several inches from the front of his shirt. Evan watched as the outlander picked up his small friend using the blade embedded in his back. Greg's eyes widened and his body stiffened then went limp. They were all coming out of the desert growth now. Shots were being fired from small arms near and far. He could hear gunfire from the far side of the village as well.

*   **Go now!***

Evan ducked behind the wall and disengaged the hidden lock, opened the small door, and entered the small tunnel. He quickly closed the door behind him and sat in total darkness. He heard the sounds of gunfire, screaming, and the guttural laughter of the marauders as they killed any and all villagers they found. The screams resonated in his ears, burning into his memory along with the image of Greg being pierced. He held his hands over his ears and wept silently.

Another gunshot, this one noticeably closer, brought Evan from his brief reverie. He felt the light touch of panic begin to caress his nerves. He felt an overwhelming urge to leave, but the voice whispered, *Wait. He will come.* Evan remained hidden, watching and waiting. Only moments later did he notice movement as the Wanderer approached the back entrance to the store. He wore a large hiking pack on his back along with two long guns. Evan was somewhat familiar with firearms having seen different types of weapons carried by the protectors in the village of his prior life. He had never used one but he had seen the damage they could inflict.

The Wanderer carefully entered the store and disappeared from Evan's sight. Long moments passed. He was taking much longer than he had the previous times Evan had spied. Something must have gone wrong. Evan could hear voices in the distance as the marauders he had seen earlier made their way closer to him. Closer to the Wanderer. He wondered what was taking so long. Had something happened inside the store? He hadn't heard anything, but that didn't mean the man hadn't fallen to some quiet, unknown danger. Evan decided to investigate. If he remained outside he ran the risk of being discovered by the marauders. Going inside the store he would definitely expose himself to the Wanderer, but that had always been an inevitability. He moved cautiously toward the rear entrance. Another gunshot, followed by rough laughter, sounded nearby. Evan paused just outside the entrance listening for any indication of movement within. Satisfied that no one (or nothing) was lurking near the entrance he quickly stepped inside.

He remained crouched just inside near the doorway, a large hole where the back door had been, waiting for his eyes to adjust to the gloom. Debris was scattered throughout the interior. Not much had changed since his last venture inside the large store. Innumerable shelving remained overturned throughout. Everything of apparent usefulness appeared to have long been taken. Some small wildlife had taken refuge in various nooks and crannies. Rats' nests abounded and he made sure to steer clear. He was in what had been the shipping and receiving area. Broken wooden pallets and useless handcarts lay all about. Cardboard boxes of varying sizes were strewn about, some opened and long since missing their contents, others somewhat intact with unknown contents awaiting a future time when they might prove useful again. A dim light shown through the doorway into what had been the store proper. He stepped cautiously forward, stirring the ever-present dust that covered everything, leaving footprints in his wake. He stopped at the doorway and listened. This time he could hear movement farther within. His curiosity got the better of him and he moved through the doorway and farther into the store. He crept slowly through ragged aisles of toppled shelves and now useless items until he felt he could go no farther without being discovered.

He peeked over the top of the mound before him and saw the Wanderer leveraging a large slab of broken concrete using a metal pole. After just a few moments he seemed satisfied. He walked out of view and returned without the pole. Evan noticed a holstered handgun on the Wanderer's hip before he slipped into a large duster. He retrieved his pack from the floor, placing it on his back. He picked up his rifles, shouldering them both. Then he stepped over to a large wagon loaded to capacity with two big Igloo coolers, three duffel bags, and several military-style ammunition boxes. He grabbed the handle and began to draw the wagon away from Evan's hiding place toward the front of the store. His other hand held a battery-powered electric lamp emitting a blue phosphorescence. Evan's heart beat loudly and fast in his throat. The Wanderer was leaving. He was going away. He had not ever removed so much from his cache before. Evan knew it was now or never. He had to go with the man. He had to leave. He could not survive much longer on his own. Too many marauders were entering this part of the land.

Marauders! He had to warn the Wanderer. There were marauders nearby. He had forgotten about the gunshots while inside the store. The Wanderer would be killed and his bounty taken. One of the wheels on the wagon hit a large stone and a duffel bag was dislodged, falling to the floor. The Wanderer stopped and sighed, not turning around. He remained facing forward, seemingly waiting for something.

"Well, boy, I don't have all day. Are you going to skulk about forever or come over here and give me a hand?"

Evan ducked down, his heart in his throat. His pulse raced and a slick sweat immediately covered his entire body. How had he known? Was the Wanderer magic? A sorcerer? Evan had hidden well. He had been quiet. More quiet than a mouse. He thought he had been, anyway. He tried to calm himself. A few deep breaths and he steeled himself to look over the mound again. The Wanderer had turned to face him but had made no move to advance.

"It is time to go now, boy. It is no longer safe. If you want to live, come with me now."

Evan stood up slowly. He looked intently at the strange man standing fifteen yards away. He made his way

14

slowly toward the Wanderer wondering all the time what he would look like. The Wanderer turned away before Evan could get a good look at him. Speaking softly, yet urgently, and pointing towards several items in the rubble the Wanderer said, "Hurry and use those straps to tie down my supplies." Evan quickly picked up the tie-downs and began to use them to secure the supplies. He was so intent that he didn't realize the Wanderer was gone until he looked up. He was face to face with two strangers. Marauders. They wore ragged clothing and were armed with handguns.

"Lookit what we got here, Billy. A little bit of fun just tyin up a present for us. Whatcha got there, young fella?"

Evan stood slowly and looked about for the Wanderer, but saw no sign of him. Where had he gone? He couldn't have left him here to die at the hands of these rogues. Could he? Evan didn't know what to do. He had been careful to steer clear of marauders for the past two years, yet here he was faced with the two disgusting men before him. He stepped back and slowly looked over his shoulder toward the way he had entered and saw another pair creeping toward him. No going back the way he came.

"He ain't thinking 'bout leavin now, is he?" The second of the two in front of him grinned as he began to move to Evan's left flank. With only the natural light entering through the broken front windows there were several dark areas inside the store, though Evan was well lit by the lamp sitting on the floor near the wagon. The marauders moved into and out of the lit areas as they encircled him. He knew he would not be able to escape them, but he would not go down without a fight. He slid one hand into his shirt and the other into his pocket, preparing to use his best weapon. He began to turn and track one of the rogues circling him. The slingshot was out of his shirt, loaded with the ball bearing from his pocket, and on target before the marauder was able to react. His shot flew to its target and struck the marauder just below the left eye, breaking the cheekbone instantly with an audible crack. The marauder went down screaming, and Evan moved quickly to hide behind a nearby pile of debris automatically reloading his slingshot. The downed rogue fired a shot in Evan's direction, though it was well high.

"Motherlovin son-of-a-biscuit-eatin whore! Arrrrgh!" He was thrashing about on the floor, making far too much noise.

"Shut your hole, Billy!" The first marauder snapped at the downed one. He was moving farther away from his injured cohort. Tracking farther into the darker areas of the store. Evan moved quickly and found a crevice through which he could see the hurt Billy. He saw him attempting to sit up. He was holding his rapidly swelling face with one hand and attempting to sight in on Evan with a small handgun in the other. He was looking in the direction Evan had been. Evan sighted in on the filthy man and fired another shot of his own. This time he caught Billy on the side of his head in the temple. The crack was even louder and there was no scream at all. Billy slouched over to one side. He was out of the fight. Evan briefly wondered if he had killed the marauder. He didn't have long to ponder Billy's fate as he felt the tip of a knife slightly break the skin on the back of his neck.

"Drop your toy, boy. I won't tell you again."

Evan dropped his weapon and was roughly dragged to his feet. He was turned about quickly then was face to face with the smelly ogre who had entered the front with Billy. The large man smiled wide, showing the few rotting teeth left in his head. Then he licked Evan's face, seeming to savor the taste.

"Mmmm. Yeah, boys, we got ourselves a good one here. Jojo, check on Billy. We need to get these goodies and get the hell out of here." He held onto Evan with an iron grip, the knife held at the ready in his other hand close

16

to Evan's midsection. Jojo knelt at Billy's side briefly then stood up shaking his head.

"He's dead, boss. Damn boy killed him. What the hell? I thought you said this kid would be easy.'

"Shut up, Jojo. Is there anybody waiting back home for you, boy?"

Evan was still trying to think of a way to get out of this. The sharp knifepoint in his side brought his focus back to the rogue, the boss.

"You got any friends that might be waiting for you? Anybody headed this way to meet you? This seems like an awful lot of booty for one little boy to be carrying." He began to look around the store suspiciously. Evan shook his head quickly. The boss glared at Evan, then smiled. "Jojo, go check out back again. Slim, you go to the front. Both of you, hurry up and get back here to help get this stuff."

Both men scurried off to their assigned locations. The boss squeezed Evan's arm tightly, painfully. "Tell me who's with you. You can't be alone. No way, no how." He was shaking Evan with each sentence, glaring at him. He slowly looked around the store again. Slim returned from the front of the store shaking his head.

"Nothing out there, boss."

"You sure? Did ya look good?"

"Yeah, boss. Ain't nobody here but us and this boy. I'd bet my life on it. We're alone."

"You better hope so, Slim. I'll kill you myself if we get ambushed out there." Evan noticed the look on Slim's face. Apparently he took the boss at his word. "Where the hell is Jojo? How long does it take to scope out the back of the store?"

Out of the shadows of the rear of the store Jojo slowly came into view. He wasn't alone. Walking slightly behind and askew, the Wanderer accompanied the marauder. Jojo looked at the boss, fear registered on his face. He also wore a fresh bruise on his cheek. Apparently the boss didn't immediately notice Jojo's new companion.

"What the hell took ya so-?" His eyes then focused on the stranger and he pulled the boy close, the knife seeming to materialize at Evan's throat. "I'll kill him, man. Let my man go and I'll give him back to you. We'll part our ways peaceful-like. No harm done, right?"

Evan watched as Slim quickly moved into the shadows, attempting to skirt around and get an angle on the Wanderer. He looked back at the Wanderer, noticing that he appeared focused on the boss. He hadn't moved. Neither of his hands was visible: one hidden behind Jojo, the other behind his back. He cocked his head slightly then spoke.

"If you want to live, call your man off. The one trying to come about and get at me from the side. I'll kill him and then you if you don't. All I want is my supplies and then I'll be on my way. As far as the boy goes...he ain't mine. You can keep him for all I care."

The boss hesitated just a moment, considering. Then, "You trying to pull one on me, ain't ya? Of course the boy is yours. Why else you coming in here, risking your life? Ain't nobody stupid enough to go one on three for supplies. A basket o' goodies." He glanced briefly at the wagon and noticed the boxes of ammo for the first time. He looked back up at the stranger and thought he saw a smile. "Slim, get that son-of-a-whore!" he yelled as he shoved Evan, hard, towards the stranger and Jojo; then he turned and bolted for the front of the store. Everything else happened quickly, though Evan's mind absorbed the images with the clarity of slow motion.

The Wanderer looked to his left as he brought up his left hand. The semi-automatic handgun fired two shots in rapid succession as it was extended toward Slim who had raised his own handgun. He had been lurking in the shadows, slowly approaching the stranger. He was hit once in the chest and once in the face, the second round shattering the lower left half of his mouth. Teeth and bone fragments exploded along with a fine spray of blood as the round ripped through his jaw. He had been advancing on the Wanderer, and his momentum carried him face forward as he fell onto the dusty floor. The blood started pooling around his head and Evan could hear gurgling as Slim's body tried to breathe. He wouldn't live much longer; the first shot had severed his pulmonary artery from his heart. Another pool of blood was spreading from his chest area as well.

Jojo took the brief moment the stranger's attention was diverted to make his own move. He had never seen Teddy run from anyone before. But here they were. Just one guy and Teddy had taken off running. What the hell? When the stranger's gun fired on Slim, Jojo spun around and swung a wild elbow at the stranger's face. He missed entirely as the strange man leaned back and punched him in the stomach. Doubling over and dropping to a knee he instinctively put his hands over his stomach and felt warm wetness flowing out of himself and onto his hands. He looked down and saw his own blood slowly staining his shirt. He looked up in time to see the barrel of a large handgun pointed at his face. He hadn't been punched.

"Please, mister. Don't-" The report echoed throughout the store. The gun in the Wanderer's right hand was definitely a larger caliber. Evan saw the back of Jojo's head open in a pink spray of brain matter and bone chips. His head rocked back and he immediately fell over onto his side, lifeless. Evan stared at the newly deceased Jojo, the gaping wound in the back of his head oozing blood and other fluids, no more than five feet from him. The Wanderer stepped past Jojo and made his way to the front of the store. Evan watched in wide-eyed wonder. The Wanderer was a giant as he stepped slowly beyond. Evan could see the tiniest particles of dust as they were thrust into the air by the Wanderer's boots. Everything seemed to be moving too slowly. His ears were ringing from the gun blasts.

The Wanderer had holstered both handguns as he calmly walked to the front and was now readying the long gun he had removed from his shoulder. It was a scoped, bolt action .308 caliber rifle. He reached the front of the store and took a knee, bringing the weapon up to fire. He looked briefly through the scope, the stock up to his cheek. He fired one shot. The blast from the muzzle seemed louder than the three handgun blasts combined. Evan was still staring at the canyon that had been Jojo's head when the shot rang out. Then everything went dark.

He must have passed out for a short time. When he came to, he was lying on the floor, his face in the thick dust, with the smell of gunpowder still hanging in the air. He sat up and saw the three lifeless forms in the dust. Hungry flies were already buzzing about the open wounds of Slim and Jojo. Evan looked into the open head of the latter and thought the brain matter looked a little like the maggots that would soon hatch there. That was if the scavenging animals of the land didn't get to the bodies first. Coyotes and such seemed to always come in the wake of the marauders, feeding on what carrion remained. Not to mention the vultures. He turned his head at the sound of squeaky wheels moving across the dusty floor. The Wanderer was moving his wagon toward the front of the store, preparing to leave. Evan stood and took a quick second to be sure his legs were steady. Though he had seen death (and a fair share of it for one so young) he had never been so close as to be able to reach out and touch the dying as they gasped their last breaths. It was somewhat disturbing and unnerving, but the thing that resonated most in him was that he felt a little thrilled as well. He had killed a man today. And though he had always known it to be a possibility in order for him to continue surviving, he had not before known if he would be capable. And even though he greatly valued life in general, he felt the slightest hint of pleasure at the thought of taking the life of a marauder.

As he walked toward the enigmatic figure waiting near the front of the store, Evan thought about the day's events. He had come to the store to await the arrival of this strange man, the one the voice had led him to, the one who would lead him home. He wasn't sure about the last. He didn't know where they were going. He had been hiding and surviving alone for the better part of two years, but now he was not alone. He was with the Wanderer. He was afraid, but he did not know why. He couldn't know that he was now in the care of one of the most dangerous men left in the land. He couldn't know it, but he felt it. It both frightened and thrilled him. He stopped just behind the Wanderer and waited silently.

"It'll be getting dark in a couple of hours. We need to put a little distance between us and this place before then." The man spoke without turning to look at Evan. He stood ready to travel, having donned what appeared to be an old, dusty Stetson to go along with the old duster he wore. He looked every bit the cowboy. An ancient gunslinger. All he needed was a hand rolled cigarillo and the picture would have been complete. "I'm sure you know there are worse things roaming the land than these bandits. The smell of blood will bring some of them here." He turned slightly and Evan caught a hint of the steely grey eyes boring into him. He almost looked away but was too intrigued by the man to do so, even though his natural inclination was to avert his eyes. The Wanderer smiled wryly and looked forward again. "You're a brave boy. I didn't believe you would be until I saw it myself...." He trailed off as though he might have more to say but shook his head slightly and sighed softly through his nose.

Evan's breath caught in his throat and his heart skipped a beat. He wanted to say something, anything. But his mouth wouldn't cooperate. His brain wasn't helping much either. He couldn't think of anything seemingly appropriate to say. "I think I killed one of them, mister." He heard the words come out without really knowing he had spoken them. He immediately wished he could take them back. Of course he had killed one of them. He was exhibiting his uncanny ability to state the obvious. Of course he hadn't had anyone to talk to for a while, so his conversation skills were a bit lacking. The stranger seemed to take little notice of his small companion's anxiety. Instead he motioned to the wagon.

"There's a can of oil in that bag. Put a good amount inside the wheel joints. We don't need the cart bringing any unnecessary attention to us before we get there."

Evan did as he was told, thinking, Where is there?

The Wanderer seemed to hear Evan's thought, and looking directly at him stated flatly, "We've a long way to travel, boy, and I don't mean to walk the entire distance. You'll have to keep up for the next few days until we get there, and you better hope my transport is still there waiting for us. If not...well, let's just say you and I will get to know each other much better once the winter storms arrive." He glared at Evan while he spoke and for a few more seconds once finished. Then he gave Evan that wry smile, somewhat sly and utterly chilling at the same time. He apparently hadn't had very many dealings with children. Evan was almost certain he didn't have any of his own.

Evan finished his task and repacked the oil canister in the bag, making sure all the gear was still secure on the wagon. He stood up and looked out the front of the store toward the rolling cascades on the other side of the useless interstate. Rusted carcasses that had once been automobiles littered the weed-covered roadways and even more were on the interstate several hundred yards beyond. The two travelers exited the store and began to make their way across what had been a parking lot. Evan noticed a figure seated on the pavement at the front of what used to be a four-door sedan. The occupants of the vehicle had long since turned to dust. As they got closer he realized the figure to be the marauder the others had called boss. Twenty yards before reaching the man he noticed the first large spattering of blood on the dusty ground. He then saw drying droplets and finally larger drops culminating in large smears of blood leading to the seated man with a small pool growing in his lap. The Wanderer's round had pierced the upper right back and exited out the chest. The exit wound was a lot larger than the entrance wound. More blood was coming out the front, although there was a considerable amount vacating his body from the rear as well.

The Wanderer stopped Evan a few paces from the downed man. He then moved forward alone. The marauder's lips were pale and he was struggling to breathe as his right lung continued to fill with blood. He coughed up blood and mucus. He dazedly gazed up at the Wanderer and the coughing momentarily increased. He seemed to be trying to speak. Evan couldn't make out what he was saying, but he thought he heard one word: dead. No kidding, buddy. Yes, he was damn near dead. Evan watched as the Wanderer stooped down and removed the handgun from the dying man's waistband. He looked at it briefly before storing it in the small of his back. He then removed some loaded magazines from the rogue and the Bowie knife with which he had held Evan hostage. The Wanderer turned the knife this way and that. He pointed it to the dying man and said plainly enough, "We are going our way now, friend. You'll likely be paid a visit by some furry-" he looked briefly in the sky, "-or winged critters pretty soon. I'm sure you would have liked the ability to defend yourself with your pistol, but I don't think I'll allow it. I will, however, leave you with the knife." He then leaned forward, tossed the knife deftly in his hand, and brought it down in a quick stabbing motion deep into the man's left shoulder.

"ARRRHHH!" The scream seemed to go on for an eternity. When it stopped Evan thought the man would lose consciousness, and he almost did. His entire face had gone pasty white. The Wanderer wouldn't allow him to pass out. He squatted in front of the marauder and slapped him severely across one cheek, then the other. The critically injured man stared into the grey eyes of his executioner. His breath was ragged, labored, filled with more blood. "Arrrhhh." He moaned weakly as he vomited blood and mucus onto himself.

The Wanderer stood and looked up into the sky again. "You better ready that knife soon. I think the first diners have arrived." Evan looked up along with the slowly dying man. The birds he recalled from his childhood circled above. At least a dozen. He remembered them very clearly: the winged carrion feeders, unequaled at stripping the flesh from their meal. Opportunists extraordinaire. Evan looked back at the marauder, the murderer. He saw death and fear. The man had pissed himself. His bowels had loosed. He tried to reach up for the knife with one hand and then the other, each time screaming in agony. Even if he could get his hands upon it he probably lacked the strength to pull it free. There would be no way to fight off the birds. The buzzards. They would eat him alive if he did not die before they began their meal. Evan hoped he would still be alive when they started. He felt the beginnings of a smile growing on his own face before he caught himself. He looked away somewhat ashamed. He found himself looking into the eyes of the Wanderer. There was no smile there. No hint of emotion at all. Or maybe there was. He just couldn't tell which.

The Wanderer motioned for him to come along, and Evan began to follow. They trekked beyond the parking lot, across unused roadways, over the interstate, and to the beginning of the rolling hills beyond. They traveled that distance before the first few buzzards began to land in the

Wal-Mart parking lot. Several of them gathered at the front of the store, scenting the meat lying within. They hesitated, apparently not wanting to risk the confines of the store's interior just yet. A few of the large birds ambled and jockeyed for position as they began approaching the dying man in the parking lot. His name had been Hinton. Theodore Hinton. In a previous time, a better time, that would have been the name he would have been known by. But in this age, he became Teddy. A boy who grew up in a town of rejects and was prone to violence early on. A young man who learned quickly that in order to get what you wanted in life you had to take it. And in order to keep what you took you needed to kill. And in order to kill and stay alive afterwards you needed a crew to back your move. Now, his crew was dead and he was nearly there. What a day this had turned out to be!

He started crying when the first few buzzards landed in the parking lot. They were closer to the entrance, over fifty yards distant. But he saw them beginning to move toward him. He tried to yell at them, but he could barely take a breath. He was drowning in his own blood. The only problem was that he had not drowned yet. He was still alive and about to be eaten by damn birds. Eaten alive! His mind was spinning at the thought. He tried again to reach for the knife, already knowing it was no use. Grey spots immediately appeared at the edges of his teary-eyed vision. His hand dropped painfully into his lap. He didn't have any strength left. Nor did he have enough blood to sustain him for much longer. He glanced down at the incredible amount of blood on him and on the ground. How much blood did a person have inside anyway? He had no idea, but if he was a gambling man he would have bet all he had on the probability that he had bled most of his onto the thirsty, dusty, God-forsaken ground on which he sat. He looked up into the face of what was clearly the ugliest bird he had ever had the misfortune of meeting.

Well, fuckface, what the hell are you waitin--. His thought was cut short as the first buzzard plucked his right eye out of his head, quickly devouring it. He had only the briefest moment to register the incredible pain before a multitude of additional large, sharp beaks began to tear the flesh of his exposed face, neck, and arms. They dug into the gaping wound in his chest. He felt the rending of his flesh and tried to scream as his lips were torn from his face. His brain registered the texture of a feather on his tongue just before the tongue was itself pulled out of a newly renovated hole in his throat. They were doing all kinds of fun shit to him and he was alive for a good bit of it. Finally his heart gave out and his brain quit working. It was just as well. They made their way to his heart not long after. And the brain...well, they could save that for later. They still had some goodies below the waist to attend to

2 A Gift

The Wanderer and boy walked for a long time in silence. Evan was still processing the day's events. He was excited and leery all at once. Happy, yet strangely reticent. He looked from time to time at the profile of the enigmatic man beside him. The Wanderer walked with a purpose, taking surefooted steps as though he were following an unseen path. They were entering a low-lying area with a small stream flowing through its heart. The land here had some modicum of plant life growing. Each year it seemed to grow a bit hardier, spreading ever so slightly outward from the valley that cradled it. The two approached the stream and could hear various sounds of life nearby. The chirping of birds and insects was clearly audible. The sun had begun to set as the Wanderer stopped twenty yards from the stream. Though not the strongest flow of water passed through it, the stream carried cold water from the foothills to the west and north. Many in the flatlands considered the area beyond the foothills to be cursed, hexed, magic. The Wanderer removed several items from one of the coolers and one of the duffel bags and began to set up camp. Evan followed directions as quickly as possible to help, and soon the camp was prepared. Evan lay down in blankets provided by the Wanderer and was asleep sooner than he thought possible. The Wanderer noticed the slight smile on Evan's sleeping countenance before closing his own eyes. For some reason it troubled him. He closed his own eyes for a time and rested briefly, once attuned to the normal pulse of the valley. Once convinced that they were safe he drifted into a light, restful sleep.

The heat seared his exposed flesh. He sat up and found himself on a child's bed, in a child's room. A girl's

room. The bedroom was adorned with the stuff of female
prepubescent adolescence. Stuffed animals strategically
placed on furniture, on the bed, and on the windowsill
stared accusingly at him. Their black, soulless eyes
admonished him. Each in turn as he looked upon them
silently screamed its reproach until he was forced to look
away. Posters on walls of pink and fuchsia and rose began
to discolor and then curl at their ends. As he absently
wiped sweat from his eyes the first of the posters began to
burn. Images of kittens, puppy dogs, and unicorns all began
to follow suit. He stood and quickly made his way to the
door, passing a mirrored dresser. In the reflection he
caught a glimpse of a child on the bed with arms
outstretched, reaching for him. His heart in his throat, he
turned around and watched the empty bed slowly go up in
flames.

There was no one else in the room.

The heat became unbearable. He ran from the
room, the door opening to the outside world. He sprinted
blindly into the early evening, passing beyond a forested
hillside and into a broad expanse of open countryside. He
continued running until his lungs burned, his ribs ached,
and his legs became numb. He passed over creeks and
through fields. His muscles and lungs began to scream
their own silent but painfully persuasive arguments for him
to stop. He ran on until he could run no farther. Doubled
over, he stood gasping in a garden of myriad of colors.
Flowers bloomed all about. The setting sun settled softly
upon the horizon lending amber hues to a beauty he would
be unable to describe though his life might depend on it.
The cool evening air caressed his roasted face, neck, and
arms. He wore only denim blue jeans and a t-shirt. He
walked the garden slowly, passing over soft grasses to leafy
overhangs from willows, birches, and trees he knew not the
names of. He touched them to remind himself their texture.
His bare feet fed on the sustenance offered by the buoyant

carpet of grasses. After many long moments of wandering he settled beneath an aged oak, seated with his back propped against the strong tree. He looked upon the gardens in awe. He was struck dumb. Closing his eyes he felt wetness streaming down his face. Silent tears came upon him suddenly.

He thought about all he had lost, all he had been unable to save, all the beauty he'd had in his life that he had taken for granted: his family, his friends, his faith. They were all gone from him now. Only distant and haunting memories remained. The beauty of the Earth was no more. There were no more gardens outside the home he had abandoned. He knew it, but his mind could not pull him away from the image he found himself within. Rich, luscious verdure blinded him when he again dared open his eyes. He took deep breaths of fresh, clean air. He could smell the various aromas of rose, lily, oleander, chrysanthemum, hyacinth, lilac, and gardenia. They intermingled on the air, forming an intoxicating scent that filled his senses.

For a time unknown to him he sat beneath the old oak and basked in the sights and scents, the light touch and sweet sounds, the imagined taste of verdant life all around him. The sun had dipped over the western horizon yet a distant glow remained. The evening air remained cool. A meandering breeze blew caressing kisses on each of his cheeks. Eyes closed, he recalled faces of those he had lost over the years. He saw his wife, Angela, the love he had given himself to only to have her taken so violently from him. She had been so vibrant, so full of life and energy, though distant before the end. He felt he had begun losing her long before she was actually gone. He could recall her smile and the sound of her voice when she called to him, the scent of her hair as she lay sleeping beside him. Lilacs.

(And smoke?)

He felt warmth grow on his cheeks as the sun's rays touched him again. The smell of the garden grew stronger, urgent. It was nearly overpowering. From behind his eyelids he could see the orange glow growing brighter. The sun calling to him, urging him, demanding of him: Get up!

He opened his eyes to a conflagration burning voraciously in the near distance. The plant life in the great garden cried out to him with its beauty. It screamed within the chiaroscuro of its newfound dance with the coming flames. The flames advanced unchecked, gaining ground, feeding freely on all living things in its path. The sights, sounds, scents of the garden bade him save it. Save us! The plant life about him cried in its varied ways. As in times long past he felt unable to help when it counted.

He began backing away from the flaming vision before him. In ever-increasing steps he retreated until he tripped and fell to the carpeted earth. He immediately came to his feet and looked at the duffel bag he had fallen over. Old and dusty and entirely out of place. Though it did not belong in this place, he recognized it immediately. It had been a gift given him long ago. He looked at its familiar shape and coloring. It was his bag. He knew what was within without looking. Slowly he unzipped and reached inside feeling the familiar, cool metal of his own personal talisman. His breathing slowed along with his perception of time. The advancing flames faded to the background of his thoughts, the increasing heat losing its touch upon him. The garden's call lost no potency, but it became less a shrill scream and more a melodious plea.

He breathed deeply and savored the aroma, the sweet and sustaining scent of the garden fighting to hold the frenzied flames at bay. His hand gripped the handle and he smiled. This tool he knew well. He held death in his hand. He remembered himself now. He was a harbinger, a herald. In his wake were a great many of those who had found the release they deserved. He had not necessarily

chosen this path as much as it had chosen him.
Circumstances had led him to this. And he had accepted it
for his part. In some instances he had relished it. He had
never been one to shirk his duty. This duty had been set
before him, a path laid open. He remembered now that he
walked it and, more importantly, why he walked it. Death
does indeed come to all, but some need it much sooner than
others. Slowly and deliberately he stood erect, pulling
about himself his duster and placing his Stetson upon his
head. He strapped on his gun belt. He then holstered the
only thing left that offered him comfort: his Colt 1911. He
faced the wall of flames closing on the edge of the defiant
garden. An odd inclination of one eyelid accompanied his
smile as he walked purposefully forward. Within the flames
awaited his destiny.

Leaving the relative safety of the garden and
entering the sparse surrounding woodland he felt the full
blast of the heat emanating from the encroaching flames.
He paused briefly, feeling the heat flow over his body,
fingers probing for chinks in his newfound armor. He took
a final deep breath and strode into the inferno.

The Wanderer awoke silently, slowly opening one
eye ever so slightly. The sun had just cleared the rim of the
valley, the warmth of its rays only just touching his face.
The boy had already gotten up and was away from the
camp. Opening both eyes fully and looking about their
small campsite he saw no signs of trouble. The boy had
awakened and moved from their site on his own. That was
not nearly as bothersome as was the fact that he had done
so without the Wanderer awakening. The Wanderer got up
and broke camp, replacing all his gear in the bags and
loading them back on the wagon. Evan strolled back into
camp as the Wanderer was placing the last of the gear on
the wagon. The Wanderer did not look at him or pause even
the slightest.

"Get your things ready to go. We're leaving." He spoke evenly. Evan moved quickly to his small number of belongings and packed them together. He glanced nervously at the man who stood waiting for him. The Wanderer stood facing the direction in which their path lay. He was frowning and staring intently, peering into the new day.

The two travelers walked throughout the morning eating from pre-packaged meals the Wanderer recovered from his pack as they moved. They did not stop until near midday. Evan was tired but remained excited. They had traveled the length of the valley before they rested for a true meal. The Wanderer kept a watchful eye on the stretch of forest in the distance. Their path led directly into a vast growth of stunted trees with oddly shaped, dull brown foliage. All that was the slightest greenery was behind them. Evan took time as they ate an actual meal to steal several glances at the strange man leading him. Once he began to get over the fact that this man was a killer (and apparently one much better than the marauders and protectors he was accustomed to) he started to pay attention to much less noticeable qualities. There was a distinct sadness that hung about him. The Wanderer's eyes held many secrets and showed just as much. To Evan at least. He saw great loss and regret in those eyes. There was a cruelty there as well. He had felt it the day before. But now he could see it lurking just beneath the surface. The Wanderer enjoyed inflicting pain. Yet there was something else, something good there as well. The infliction of pain was of a retributive sort. Justice. Evan could feel the concept though he knew not the word. The longer he thought about the Wanderer the more intriguing and enigmatic he became. The more Evan wanted to learn.

"How did you beat them? Those marauders back there? There were more of them, but you beat them. Killed them like--" Evan's mind began to relive the event again. He saw the rounds from the Wanderer's guns tear into the flesh of the attackers. He saw blood, tissue, and brain matter all being ripped from those men. The images replayed in his mind's eye with distinct clarity. He knew he would never forget the day he actually met this strange man even were he to never see him after this moment. The images of the men the Wanderer shot were burned into his memory. And he saw the metal bearing crack the skull of the man he himself had killed. That image was there as well. It too was crystal clear. He had killed a man. He was a killer. It hurt, that knowledge. But it also excited him.

The Wanderer remained looking into the distance, letting the boy drift off into his own thoughts. Finally, he turned and looked at Evan. The boy had looked down at his hands while caught in his reverie. The Wanderer felt the slightest bit of pity. He knew the boy would not understand much of what was happening.

"I did what I had to do. How is not so very important. Besides, those men deserved no better." Evan looked up into those eyes and his blood went cold. There was no regret, no empathy, no feeling of remorse anywhere to be found in those steely orbs. "They would have done much worse to you or me if given the chance." A chill ran down Evan's spine as he was forced to look away, back down at his own hands. "One day you will understand better my ways. Perhaps. At any rate it was necessary for us to get out of there. If you want to go on living you will have to accept certain truths about life. One such truth is in death's certainty. All things die. Some much sooner than they should. Others, not nearly soon enough. Either way, we leave this place, this life. The struggle matters, not the end." Evan glanced up again and saw that the Wanderer had again turned to look to the distance. "I will do all in my power to keep your death at bay. You are needed here and far from here. You are...fated--"

Evan saw something else in the Wanderer's eyes, but before he could discern it the Wanderer abruptly stood and walked a short distance. Evan again was intrigued. He was perplexed as well. What was he speaking of? He thought of the voice he sometimes heard in his head, the voice that led him to the Wanderer. The same voice that had saved him on more than one occasion throughout his young life. Fate? He frowned at the thought. He was familiar with the concept. He was uncomfortable with the prospect.

He was about to stand when a sharp hiss stopped him. He looked up into the urgent glare of the Wanderer.

"Don't move. We are watched." Evan heeded the words and remained seated on the small mound of earth upon which he had consumed his meal. Their eyes locked briefly as the Wanderer nodded. "Stay here." He maintained eye contact until Evan nodded in return. He turned then and walked back into the valley proper. The wagon remained but the Wanderer still had his weapons.

Evan sat with his heart pounding in his chest. He felt blood coursing through arteries, his pulse almost audible in his ears. The voice was not there, telling him to run or not to run. He was alone, the charge of a strange man who had left him alone in the open land. He was afraid. Death hung above the air, near to him but not for him. He felt panic begin to caress him, stroking his hair, whispering in his ear: *Run away run away go after him don't let him leave you run run run!* But the Wanderer was near also. As near as the death hovering in the air. He had not left Evan totally alone. The Wanderer would not allow anyone to hurt him. Evan knew it without really knowing it. He felt it. That realization had a strangely calming effect on him. His heart slowed to a more manageable pace. The panic drifted away silently and he regained himself to a degree. After a short while he forced himself to eat some of the MRE given him by the Wanderer. The bite went down slowly having not been fully chewed. Evan quickly chased it down with some water. He managed to aspirate a bit of water and began coughing uncontrollably. He finally regained the ability to breathe normally and as he stood and cleared his watering eyes he saw a strange man standing some twenty feet before him. The man, head askew, stared evenly at Evan. Evan stared back.

Evan still held the MRE in one hand and a canteen in the other. The stranger was armed with what appeared to be a crude crossbow, held at the low ready, bolt already notched. Moving slowly, Evan placed his canteen and Meal Ready to Eat on the ground before him. He briefly thought about retrieving his slingshot from inside his clothing, but thought better when he looked again at the stranger and noticed the crossbow trained on him as he bent over. Slowly he straightened to his full height. The man was not a marauder. Evan noticed the stranger's gaunt physique. Moreover, he felt an anxiety about him. He was dressed poorly, but clean in appearance. He continually glanced at the foodstuffs Evan had been eating from then back in the direction of the stunted forest.

Evan felt waves of desperation emanating from the strange man. Beads of sweat appeared on the man's forehead and his breathing increased. His heart rate was near that of Evan's earlier when the Wanderer had walked away. Where had he gone, anyway? Evan glanced back over his shoulder into the valley but saw no one. He looked back at the strange man and saw him visibly shaking. Evan felt himself begin to shake as well. He closed his eyes and felt the heartbeat of the strange man in his own chest. His own breathing matched the man's also. His anxiety rose to a fever pitch. He forced it all down. He concentrated on his breathing and his heart rate too. Calming himself completely, he reminded himself that he was no longer alone. He was relatively safe now. Taking several deep breaths he opened his eyes and saw the strange man looking upon him in astonishment.

"How...what...who are you?" The stranger was staring at Evan, the weapon hanging loosely at his side. He was walking forward slowly, his steps tentative. "How did you do that?" Evan was not sure what "that" was so he only shrugged.

"I...I don't know." He stepped back instinctively as the man came forward. He began to sense some urgency in the man as he approached. Evan almost turned to run as the strange man came forward, but he could feel the quiet desperation flowing off him in waves. He paused and spoke very directly. "You need my help. I want to help you, but you are scaring me." The man stopped moving. "Will you please put your weapon down? I will give you food and whatever help I can. I mean you no harm. You know that, don't you?"

"Yes." The man assented, nodding slowly. The man looked at his crossbow and hesitated only for a moment before placing it on the ground. He looked pleadingly at Evan. Evan felt his own heartbeat, his breathing, his entire disposition matching that of the stranger. He maintained his own calm in the face of his amazement at this phenomenon. The man looked again at the food and back at the forest edge.

"Who is it you are worried about?" Evan asked softly. The stranger looked for an extended time at the forest before turning to face him. "How many are you?" Evan asked.

"There are but three left: my son and daughter and me. My wife...she fell to a sickness not long ago. My daughter is sick now. She...she can no longer walk. I seek food for us all. We are...we are...will you help us?" Tears were forming at the rims of his eyes.

Without thinking Evan spoke: "I will help you." He moved forward and reached for the stranger. The man hesitated, then he took Evan's hand in his own, shaking it weakly. The tears flowed down his face freely now. Evan removed three of the MRE packets from a duffel bag on the wagon. He gave them to the stranger. The stranger took them eagerly and started to walk away. He retrieved his weapon after storing the food in a pouch he wore at his side. He strode away from Evan quickly but stopped after covering half the distance to the forest. He turned and waved. Evan returned the gesture. The man continued on and disappeared into the dusty tree cover.

Evan stared after the man long after he had vanished. He stared in wonderment. How? How had he felt what he felt? He had been a part of the stranger for a brief time. He had felt what another person felt. The fear, the uncertainty, the urgency. He had felt all that and more. He knew the man was with two others before he had been told. He had felt it. How was that possible? What was happening to him? He was deep in thought when the Wanderer returned. Without a word he walked up to Evan and asked about the stranger. Evan did not hear him at first, so deep in thought he was. But eventually he registered the Wanderer's presence and looked at him.

"How did you do that?" The Wanderer asked evenly.

"I don't know. I can't explain it. I could just feel what he was feeling and then all of a sudden I made him feel better. He was afraid of me. I could tell he didn't want to hurt me. He needs help. He's not alone. He has kids like me."

"Hmm." The Wanderer was looking at him questioningly. He stared at Evan for a time, peering into him. Then he looked away toward the forest.

Evan continued to look at him for a time. He could see the Wanderer's mind working, could see him thinking about what had just happened. Evan wondered what he thought. He closed his eyes and began to concentrate, reaching out to find the Wanderer's heartbeat. He felt nothing for a time, his concentration fading after nearly a full minute. He opened his eyes and found those gray orbs trained on him. The Wanderer was looking at him reprovingly.

"Don't waste your time, boy. I am...I am different." He turned and walked to the wagon of supplies. Grasping the handle, he began walking in the direction the stranger had gone.

He turned and walked to the wagon of supplies. Grasping the handle, he began walking in the direction the stranger had gone.

"Where are we going?" Evan asked as he followed. The Wanderer did not answer. He walked in silence, his focus forward. Evan became more than a little apprehensive as they entered the forest. He felt a purpose about the Wanderer, and the sense of death had returned to the air tenfold.

They traveled for a brief time, making several twists and turns into some severe undergrowth. Eventually they found what they had been seeking. A small clearing opened before them and within was the stranger. He stood before two small children, one of whom was laying on a makeshift cot of old cloth, the other seated beside. The father held the crossbow leveled at the Wanderer. Evan stepped into view and made eye contact with him. He immediately lowered the weapon.

"I don't know what to do. She is getting worse." He stepped aside and looked imploringly at Evan and the Wanderer.

"What's wrong with her?" Evan asked as he walked forward. He looked down at her face. She slept fitfully, her light brown hair damp with sweat clinging to her head. He looked upon her olive countenance and felt a strange sense of recognition.

"She fell ill five days ago. It is the same sickness that took their mother. It is a sickness that has stalked the land since the Great Fall." He was looking at his children as he spoke. He turned and looked into the eyes of the Wanderer. Each held the other's gaze for a short time, an unspoken message passing between them. The Wanderer walked forward, his eyes not leaving the father. He then looked down at the young girl. He knelt down opposite her brother, who had been silent since he and Evan had arrived. Evan remained standing as the Wanderer placed a hand on the girl's forehead.

"How long has she had the fever?" The Wanderer looked up at the father.

"Three days. Before that she complained of headaches and body aches. She's been in and out of consciousness all morning."

The Wanderer stood up slowly and retrieved a canteen and a clean cloth from the wagon. Wetting the cloth with water he returned to the girl. He placed it on her forehead and face. He dabbed briefly before handing the cloth to her brother. "Don't move her from this place." He was looking at the father again. "She will not survive any more travel."

"But we cannot remain here in the open! I cannot protect them through the night...if we should be attacked. There are things out here. You don't understand..." He stopped himself, locking eyes once again with the Wanderer. There was a passing moment as the father looked upon the Wanderer that Evan thought he saw a flash of recognition. It passed quickly enough as the Wanderer stood up from the girl's side.

"We will stay with you this night." Evan was surprised at the words of his companion.

"Will you keep us?" the father asked.

"Just for the night." The Wanderer glared at the father.

"No longer?"

"No longer."

The two men again locked eyes before the father acquiesced, nodding slowly. He looked at Evan for a time before speaking.

"Thank you. We have nothing to offer in repayment. Nothing but our gratitude, worth next to nothing in this age. But I give it nonetheless." He looked again at the Wanderer as he spoke. "Please forgive my manners. I have not given my name. I am Terran. My son, Finn and daughter...Kiran."

"I am Alex. And we seek no payment." The Wanderer spoke as he returned to the wagon. He retrieved a small vial from a pack, and then he motioned the father over. He handed the vial to the father and whispered into his ear. Evan watched as the father dropped his head, nodding quietly. Though he had not heard what was said, Evan had an idea. The two men spoke in quiet tones for a while longer, walking a short distance farther from the children.

"What is your name?" the young boy asked quietly.

"Evan. And you are Finn?" Finn nodded and looked at his sleeping sister.

"Kiran is very sick. Father tries but he cannot help her." He moved closer to Evan and lowered his voice. "He cries and prays at night when he thinks I sleep. She will die soon. He is very sad. She will die like mother died."

Evan noticed Finn crying. He was remembering his mother, remembering her death. He was now seeing his sister die the same slow and agonizing death. Evan closed his eyes and mentally reached out to the boy. He was amazed at how quickly he was able to touch Finn. His mental assurances immediately calmed the boy. When he opened his eyes the boy was smiling at his sister. Finn stood and looked at Evan.

"Will you keep her company for a while?" Evan nodded. "I'll be back soon." Finn ran quickly from the small clearing without a word to his father, who only glanced curiously at Evan when Finn darted past. The Wanderer (Alex!) and Terran were still having a private conversation out of earshot. Evan felt the dark presence of death hovering closer. He looked into the eyes of the Wanderer and for a moment death looked back at him. Fear washed over him as the Wanderer began to walk toward him. Evan noticed the vial returned to the Wanderer's hand and then the syringe in his other. A complete and thorough understanding of what was about to happen came upon him. Darkness enveloped his sight and all that remained was the darkly glowing form of the Wanderer. He was death incarnate. And he was coming for the girl. He was coming for Kiran.

Evan watched him come and felt himself stand. All was slowed to a crawl. He looked into the Wanderer's eyes and saw a determination he would not be able to deter. He saw justice there. He saw severity. He saw anger. And he saw the last thing he ever expected to see: compassion. The darkness began to fade all about him and the Wanderer became human again. They stood before one another, neither of them moving. Evan fidgeted before the tall figure, wondering what to say, what to do.

"Out of the way, boy." The Wanderer spoke softly. "She suffers and will not last the night. Her body is ravaged by sickness and will not recover. She will die horribly before the eyes of her father and brother. I will do what I can to end her suffering. To end their suffering."

Evan looked back at the sleeping Kiran and for the first time actually looked at her. He could see the pain throughout her body. Her mind was trapped in a seething and roiling abyss of fevered agony. He knelt beside her and gingerly laid his palm atop her head, allowing himself to open to her. He immediately went rigid as he was drawn into her fevered delirium. She was adrift in a vast internal storm. A small, rudderless vessel caught in a full-blown hurricane. Pain wracked his body and mind. For a brief moment he lost himself in the pain, the sickness. It was all-encompassing and overwhelming. He screamed aloud.

Darkness shrouded his vision. Every nerve in his body was stretched to its limit by the searing pain of fever. His mind coiled upon itself seeking relief from the sudden impact of delirium. Evan lost himself to the girl's plight. Glass flowed through his veins and spiders crawled in his head. His heart labored in his chest as his mind fought against him. The full impact of her straits was overwhelming. He fought against the effects of the sickness as best he could but it was to no avail. He had become her in sickness. And the specter of death loomed near. He was but a mote in so potent a force. What could he do against such a thing?

Panic tried to creep into his heart. It pushed at him. It nudged and cajoled. It gnawed and whispered. It caressed. And he recognized it and refused.

Evan remembered himself. He calmed his breathing, his heart, his mind. He envisioned a great storm all about him and then pushed it back out of his mind, out of his being. The storm violently resisted for some time, lashing out with sickening virulence, but in the end it faded from view until it was nothing but a memory.

Evan opened his eyes. Sweat covered his body. He was lying prostrate on the ground, and every muscle in his body ached. He tried to sit up and found he could not. Dark spots immediately converged from the corners of his vision and he fell back into a blanket of bedding.

"Be still, young one." Evan recognized the voice of Terran. "You need to rest. Please, be still now."

Evan's sight cleared and he noticed that darkness had come upon the land. How could that be? It hadn't been much after midday. He fought off a wave of nausea as he turned his head to look about the campsite. Terran and Finn tended a fire in the center of the camp. They cooked a stew over the flames. Its aroma filled the small clearing. Evan's vision blurred briefly as he turned his head further, looking for the Wanderer. Alex. He remembered he had given his name as Alex. His sight cleared again and he saw a form kneel before him. Kiran! The girl smiled at him and he felt his heart skip a beat. Never before in his brief life had he seen anything more beautiful.

"Sleep Evan. All is well for now. We are safe. We are all safe. Rest."

Evan smiled back at Kiran as his eyes closed. He was almost immediately asleep again.

Alex Sloane, the man known to many as the Wanderer (and to others as Dark Wanderer), watched Evan and Kiran from the far side of the small campsite. He had just finished a helping of hare stew. Terran had cooked the meal after Alex brought the meat back from a brief hunting expedition. He watched the boy and girl intently. He wondered what he had gotten himself into. He knew what was expected of him, but this boy... How could this boy know what was before him? How could this boy be expected to do what was needed of him? He shook his head and looked off into the foliage outside camp. Feeling a glare upon him he turned to look into the eyes of Terran. The father was looking at him with the same look he had become accustomed to over many long years. Fear and hope intermingled. Terran and all other innocents had nothing to fear from him, but he was the embodiment of that which all feared. He brought death in his wake and those who knew of him felt it. Terran was aware of the old world. He knew of Alex and his kind. Alex didn't blame

Terran or any others he had saved in the past. He meant death to far too many.

Alex looked away, back into the darkness outside the ring of light from the fire. He could not understand the powers at work in Evan. If he had not seen it himself he would never have believed it. He had come across people who had spoken of magic, witchcraft, demonic powers. He had never believed any except that evil he had seen in his own past. The only magic he had ever seen was the magic of fear. The fear of death. The fear of pain. The fear of starvation. The fear of all the bad things in the world. Fear could make people do things they would not otherwise do. Fear could change the course of the world. Fear had already changed the course of the world and continued to do so. He had seen it. And he had to an extent become it.

Alex stood and exited the campsite. He had much to think about. Things had changed forever. Again.

Evan awoke to an overcast morning. Clouds hung low in the sky as the sun tried to break through. The threat of rain loomed close. But it was only a threat. Terran was certain that there would be no rain. He and Finn were gathering their sparse belongings and preparing to break camp. Evan, remembering his failed attempt during the night, sat up ever so slowly. He took his time and finally sat completely upright. His body ached, but not as severely as before. The nausea was not there, though his head ached. And he was hungry. Terran and Finn both greeted him gaily, smiles on their faces. Father and son glanced at one another conspiratorially then looked back at Evan before continuing their work. Evan wondered what was so humorous. He thought to ask them when he noticed the bedding beside his own.

Kiran lay sleeping beside him. Evan looked at her and felt something stir within him. He felt peace steal over his body. His entire being was calmed by her presence. And awakened at the same time. Her face was aglow. He could feel the health restored to her. He took note of her breathing, its evenness. Slow, steady breaths. He closed his eyes and felt out for her. A bright yet soft light filled his senses. Its warmth flowed over him. He felt comfort. It was as if the light was holding him. No harm could come to him now. He was safe and empowered by the light. It would light his path whenever he needed as long as he needed. He felt this immediately. But he could go no farther. There was no way around the light. He could not get farther into Kiran's presence. The light would not allow it. He opened his eyes.

Kiran was awake. Her smile was more beautiful than he imagined. He looked upon her and felt himself becoming lost in her presence. Her eyes held secrets of life, of love, of eternity. He wanted to learn more about her, learn more about those secrets. He found himself staring at her, into her soft, green eyes. Green eyes flecked with gold. Her dark hair held hints of auburn. He was smitten. She batted her eyes a few times and sat up, still looking at him.

"I hope you are feeling better."

He heard her but found it difficult to reply. He was dumbfounded by her mere presence.

"I'm...I'm better."

"Good." She stood quickly, retrieved some breakfast, and returned to him. She handed him some dried meats. "You will need to regain your strength. The dark one says you must leave soon." She lowered her head then and turned to walk away. She turned back to him, forcing herself to look him in the eye. "Thank you, Evan. You have saved my life. I don't know how, but somehow I knew...I don't know. Anyway, I just wanted to thank you." She turned and walked away before he could reply. He could only watch in silence. He ate a brief meal then made his own preparations to break camp.

As he gathered his belongings he sensed her looking at him, but each time he tried to make eye contact she looked away. Terran and Finn seemed anxious as well. And Evan had no idea where the Wanderer had gone. When asked, Terran only said that he had left the camp sometime during the night and had not yet returned. Evan wondered if things could get any stranger.

The Wanderer strode into the camp in a flurry of motion. "We are leaving now." There was no questioning his words. Everyone began to move with more purpose. Evan had the wagon moving and Terran and his two remaining family members followed carrying their belongings. The three stayed close to the Wanderer. He was moving purposefully through the forest. He had not spoken for a time since breaking camp.

Evan felt the apprehension all about them as they walked. There was something out there that frightened the Wanderer. Evan didn't need to ask what it was. Obviously it was something none of the others needed to see. They eventually slowed and then came to a stop. The Wanderer turned and looked at them all, one by one.

"We cannot stop for long. A large band of rovers moves nearby. We need to be gone before they get deeper into the valley. Before they come upon our campsites." Alex was more concerned than Evan thought he should be regarding the marauders. There was something else. The Wanderer saw the question in his eyes and gave a quick, almost imperceptible shake of his head. Evan took the hint and kept quiet. All of them drank water and snacked briefly before moving on. The Wanderer led them completely out of the valley and into a broad forest.

Three hours later the small group exited the forestland and stood at the fringe of a vast desert hardpan. Evan stopped in his tracks. He felt himself regressing, becoming a smaller boy, and losing himself to memories better left forgotten. There was darkness in the desert of his past. It loomed behind and now just ahead. The Wanderer and the others stood near him, watching the blank, faraway look on his face. But Evan no longer saw them. He had gone back to a place he had run from ever since the death of Greg. The murder of Greg. The desert was no place to live. Only the marauders had been able to maintain a livelihood out there. And they did that by murdering and taking everything they needed or wanted. Evan looked into the Wanderer's eyes. The man noted the pleading, frightened look coming to the surface. He felt a twinge of pity, but their survival was at hand. The desert held some darkness for Evan, but it was their only escape from the thing that was now after them. The marauders behind them were not alone. The thing with them was worse than anyone they might encounter in the desert before them.

The Wanderer walked over to Evan and gently placed both hands on the boy's shoulders. He pulled him close and spoke into his ear. "We have to keep going. There is an evil back there. With the men coming behind us. Evan, you have to go in there."

"I can't. I can't go back." Evan was speaking so softly that Alex barely heard him.

"If we don't go in there, they'll get her. They will get Kiran and take her away." The Wanderer pulled away slightly and looked into Evan's eyes. "You know what they will do to her, don't you?"

Evan looked over at the girl. She was tired, covered in a light, sweaty sheen from their forced march. She saw him looking and smiled, worriedly. He took a deep, steadying breath and looked back into the eyes of the Wanderer. The man saw the determination there and knew he had reached the boy. Following a brief meal and more water the five companions walked into the desert

3 A Town

Holden sat at the table, looking at his mug, thinking about his current situation. He was out of food, water, and every other necessity. He was also nearly out of other trading items. His partners, Craig and Stenny, had deserted him after those damn protectors at New Hope Township had caught Loomis. Idiot people were actually trying to rebuild the world the way it had been. They had even held a trial before they hanged Loomis. It was a foregone conclusion that he was guilty, but the damn people in that town had decided to try to reinstate what they called real justice. Holden didn't buy it. There wasn't any real justice left in the world, if there ever had been. That blind bitch had died a long time ago. Real life was what was left in her place. And in real life the strong took from the weak. And sometimes in order to survive you had to steal by using strength of intellect, especially if you weren't one of the physically strong.

Loomis had gotten cocky and overconfident. He had started stealing in broad daylight without doing a really thorough job of casing his potential victims. He got caught in the act. When the wannabe lawmen had caught him he was nearly two miles from the little township. He had run away with only the clothes on his back and the loot he had taken: six coin from some old lady who had been more observant than Loomis had thought. Holden and the others were lucky to slip out of town while the chase was on for Loomis. They found out about the trial and subsequent hanging two days later from a traveling clan of gypsies who had passed through the town the day of both events. The gypsies had stopped near their campsite and had been kind enough to sell them some day-old bread and a skin of ale. Holden knew enough from previous dealings with their type to give as little information about himself as possible, but he did barter important information. He told the gypsies about marauder movements in the south flatlands and the gypsies gave the same regarding the north.

That had been three days ago. He, Craig, and Stenny had come to this large trading town hoping to score some loot. But they had not been greeted very well. An obvious band of marauders had been in the camp and seemed to have control of the hired guns paid by the traders to guard the town and its various enterprises. Craig and Stenny had promptly disappeared, leaving Holden without warning and with nothing to trade. They had taken his belongings. All his belongings. He didn't even have a change of underwear. He had spent almost all his coin on food and drink, the vast majority on drink. He was nearing the end of his rope. He didn't know what he would do after this day. He had hoped the marauders would be moving on soon. It was extraordinarily unlike them to be seen in any settlement, let alone remain like regular folk.

Holden looked up from the table, his mug now empty. He looked toward the door just as a trio of marauders entered. Loud and boisterous, they made their way to the makeshift bar and seated themselves. Holden wondered how this had come to pass. Marauders were seen as the lowest form of human existence on the planet. Even lower than thieving scavengers such as he. Most worked hard to avoid them, or to defend themselves against them. Protectors of villages and towns were paid and fed to repel them with force of arms. It was even rumored that there were men who walked the land in search of them for the sole purpose of killing them. Known as walkers in the northland and wanderers in the south, these men were rumored to possess dark magic. Magic used to kill evil men. Many believed them to be walking devils, seeking out the most evil men in order to take them to some horrible hell. Holden wasn't sure if the walkers existed, but if they did they weren't devils taking evil men to hell. Evil men and good alike now existed in the hell left behind by those who had sought to rule the world.

It was that same old story of power corrupting and absolute power, blah, blah, blah. Holden just wanted to make it through the day and come out on top again. He could not care less about power. He was just about to push away from his table and head for the door when he heard a bit of conversation from the marauders.

"We need to be ready when the caravan gets here, tomorrow. There'll be enough coin for all of us for a long while." The speaker was a burly, bearded fellow with a bald head and a patch over one eye. A peg leg, parrot, and a big hat would have completed the picture.

Holden immediately readjusted himself in his chair and upon noting one of the three glancing his way he put on his best drunk performance, head bobbing forward slightly with eyes appearing closed. He even managed a small trail of spittle forming at the corner of his mouth and leading to his chin. The probing eyes returned to the discussion. The marauders paid him little attention after that.

"We need to make sure everything is in place by nightfall. We can't screw this one up. The B-man will have our asses for sure if we don't get him what he wants." The pirate was still speaking. He seemed to be in charge of this small group. The others were mumbling, just beyond the range of Holden's hearing. One fellow leaned forward speaking urgently to the others. Holden couldn't make out his words.

"Shut the hell up, Irving. Bar keeper's coming." The pirate glared at his cohort as the proprietor walked to the end of the bar and took the marauders' orders. They remained quiet until he returned with their drinks. Irving, dark-skinned with nappy, black hair cut short and a bad case of acne, looked nervously around after the keeper had left their end of the bar. He leaned forward again and said so quietly that Holden almost missed it.

"Since when do we take a woman back to HQ without having our way with her? I mean, come on man. I'm still wondering why we spent so much coin to buy these dumbass guards. We coulda just come in here with some muscle and taken this place. Mr. B got himself a big enough army now he coulda took this place easy." Irving sat back and shook his head slowly. "Something strange about this whole deal, man. Something real strange."

The others seemed to briefly share in his thoughts. They mumbled some agreement for a brief moment. At least until the pirate spoke again. "You blockheads seem to have forgotten who butters your bread. You ain't paid to think, just do what the man tells us to do. He pays us to do what he wants done. Don't start asking questions about things that don't matter."

He was looking at each of them in turn as he spoke. Making sure they were on board. Marauders were, after all, a tricky and self-serving lot. Holden was spellbound by the conversation itself. Marauders were not known to plan out heists; usually they roamed and pillaged whatever they felt they could. If a band of marauders made its way to a town too large or too well defended to successfully pillage they would move on until they found a smaller, less-defended one. It had been that way for as long as Holden could remember. Their number had never been so many in any group until now. Holden had never known more than six to eight marauders to form any sort of unit. Their cutthroat nature kept them from getting too large. Once they grew in size they usually killed one another in power struggles or split to form independent divisions. Yet somehow there were at least two dozen in the town now. And there were possibly that many guards in the town. Guards that had been bought by someone. Who could afford to buy that many guards?

Holden eventually made his way back to the hovel he had made for himself just inside the walls of the traders' camp. He had bought a cheap, tattered blanket and had made a small lean-to of scraps of discarded wood. It was currently the best he could do. He had told himself that he would find a way to get back on his feet soon. Less than an hour ago he had given up on getting anywhere near to back on his feet. But fate had dropped a golden egg in his lap. As he lay in his bedding he thought about the remainder of the conversation he had heard in the small tavern. He let the information seep into his mind, relaxing as he did so. The past few days had been hard on him. The loss of his small yet effective crew. The lockdown of the traders' camp by the marauders. The death of Loomis. But now he had something to look forward to. There was indeed a light at the end of the tunnel. He fell asleep with a slight smirk on his face. He slept peacefully for the first time since coming to this place.

Early the next morning Holden awoke hours before sunrise. He gathered his few remaining things and made his way out of the traders' camp. He began his way north. He kept an even pace. He was determined to reach the crossroads before midday. He could not help but smile as he felt the change in his fortune. Lady luck had returned. The reward would be great. He would foil the plans of the marauders before the caravan ever made it to the town. He would stop the caravan at the crossroads and inform them of the marauders' plan. He would tell them about the guards being compromised and how many marauders were there and so on and so forth.

Holden kept walking and thinking, smiling all the while. He was so caught up in his good fortune that he failed to notice the figures coming up on his rear. By the time he thought to turn around to check his six the three were within a few hundred yards. A cold chill ran down his spine as he recognized the men as marauders. They were walking with a purpose directly after him. He began to run as best he could, but he was tired. He had already been walking for several hours. He had not eaten much the day before. And he hadn't had much water either. His running quickly became a slow trot after less than a quarter mile. He continually looked back at his pursuers. They ran when he ran and walked when he walked, all the while gaining on him. Holden could see the crossroads within half a mile in the distance. The marauders were within 200 yards behind. He increased his pace as best he could. He had to make the crossroads. This particular crossroads was the only way the caravan could come and he had to get there to warn them. To get his reward.

Several buildings remained standing at the crossroads. If he could get there he might be able to hide or find a way to defend himself. He continued to run, pain burning in his legs and lungs. A stitch pulled at his side, and his head began to pound. He willed himself to go on, knowing what they would do to him if they caught him. He had to keep moving. He could not stop for a moment or they would have him. He had seen the aftermath of several marauder attacks. Their disregard for human life transcended the understanding of most who inhabited the lands. But he understood their cravings. They simply gave into the evil residing in all people. Holden understood human psychology better than he could explain it. All people have a dark side. For most it is kept in check by the ability to reason and a sense of duty to family and community. But there are those whose ties are broken. Those who have no family or community to hold them to the rest of humanity. Those who are swept up in their darkness. Those who answer the primal call of self. Those who answer the twisted call of depravity and make it part of them. Marauders.

Ignoring the pain and lack of oxygen Holden maintained a good pace until he reached the first buildings of the crossroads. He turned quickly around a corner and kept running. He made his way around several other buildings, leaving the roadway farther behind him. It was less than an hour before noon. He had to hurry. He slowed to a fast walk after several more turns through small alleys, attempting to listen for signs of pursuit. He found himself in an abandoned strip mall. Many of the shops had been boarded up, and those that hadn't had windows broken out. He checked several doorways until he found what he was looking for. The roll down door covered the door and window of the business. Holden had several talents, one of which being the ability to pick locks quietly and efficiently. The tools were out of his hidden interior pocket and in his hand as soon as he found the door lock. He fumbled with the lock for a moment, dropping his tools several times in the process. His heart was racing, pounding in his ears. His breathing was ragged, and his hands were shaking. He took several deep breaths with his eyes closed. He envisioned the tumblers in the locking mechanism being manipulated by his tools. When he opened his eyes and reapplied himself to his task he was able to work.

After only a brief moment he got the lock open and pushed the roll down door to its up and open position. It was far too loud. That could not be helped. He tried the door to the business: Owen Pawn. It was locked as well. Again he worked on the lock. He was much calmer this time. His heart, though still beating too fast, was slowing. The pounding in his head was still there. He felt as if he might vomit. Sweat coated his hands and arms, and the salty wetness dripped from his brow and pulled his clothing tightly to him. The lock opened and he entered the store. Amazingly the store's interior was intact. A light coating of dust covered everything, and heat hung heavily in the still air. Many of the items had been taken but not by scavengers or marauders. Apparently the owner had removed many necessities before the end of the good old days. But there were plenty remaining. Holden eyed a Remington 12-gauge shotgun behind the counter. It, along with several other more expensive makes, stood within a glass case. The case was of course locked. He made his way behind the counter and began to work the lock. Then he heard the single gunshot from nearby.

"To hell with this," he muttered to himself. He put his tools in the hidden interior pocket. He picked up a small display standing on the counter and threw it into the glass case. It shattered loudly and he reached inside and took the shotgun in his hands. He worked the action, pumping the fore end back then forward. It was unloaded of course. "Shit!" he hissed. He began pulling open drawers and looking under shelves. Pocketknives, semi-automatic handgun magazines, and other accessories filled his vision. He found another locked cabinet beneath a shelf. He started kicking it until the door slid off its track. Getting it open he found several boxes of ammunition: handgun, rifle, and shotgun. Several other gunshots sounded even more closely, and he heard voices yelling for him.

He hastily grabbed and opened a few boxes of shotgun ammo. A gunshot sounded almost just outside the door he had entered. He promptly dropped the open boxes, spilling ammo onto the floor behind the counter. He bent down and grabbed another box from inside the cabinet and emptied several rounds into his coat pocket. He also picked up several of the rounds from the floor. He didn't notice the different colors of the rounds. Green from one box and gray from the other. He began loading the magazine tube. He could only load four rounds in the tube. He racked the weapon and chambered a round and then loaded a fifth round. As the fifth round clicked into the magazine tube he heard the front door open.

"Woohoo. Look at this place. I think our little buddy came in here to hide." Holden didn't recognize which voice, but he was almost certain it was one of the marauders from the bar.

"Damn, man. Some good stuff in here. Let's hurry up and take care of his ass and get some supplies before we get to work."

Both voices were moving as they spoke, coming farther into the store. Holden could hear his own breathing coming in ragged gasps. He closed his eyes and tried to calm himself. A shot rang out in the store louder than he could have imagined. He was jerked out of his self-calming state as if he had been slapped across the face. He stood up quickly and leveled the shotgun at the nearest marauder. Before any of them could think to say anything he pulled the trigger.

Holden knew a little about weapons. He had stolen and sold enough of them to become acquainted with their operation. He had come across a wide variety of small arms and had made sure to learn enough of their operations in order to sell them to lone traders and travelers in need. He had on one occasion had the fortune of getting his hands on a Remington 870 twelve-gauge shotgun less than a year before this day. After stealing it from an unsuspecting rancher in the far western plains, he had become very familiar with its workings. He had known to depress the action bar release at the front of the trigger housing in order to rack the first round. He knew the spread pattern at such a close range would not be very great, so he had attempted to point the weapon directly at his target. He also knew that the weapon would be louder than the handguns he had heard. He knew that it would have a more violent recoil as well. The one thing he had not expected was for absolutely nothing to happen when he squeezed the trigger.

Both marauders stood facing him, handguns at their sides. They looked at one another then at Holden. He felt panic begin to rise within him. Both marauders smiled at him, and began to raise their weapons simultaneously.

Holden saw it all happening in super-slow motion. His mind raced. What had he forgotten? The weapon was loaded and charged. He had done everything he remembered to get it loaded, charged, and ready to fire. The handguns continued coming up on target. The barrels of each would blaze away and he would die here. All because he had forgotten...the safety! In one deft motion he pushed the safety from right to left with his trigger finger and immediately pulled the trigger. The blast almost ripped the shotgun out of his hands. The marauder nearer him took several steps backward as he dropped his weapon. He tripped and fell over a display of sunglasses. Holden maintained his hold on the weapon and brought it up to his shoulder as he racked a fresh shell into the chamber. The spent shell tumbled through the air, bouncing off a nearby counter and onto the floor.

As he turned to train the weapon on the second marauder, Holden felt a searing hot pain pierce his neck. The suddenness of it caused him to raise the weapon slightly as he pulled the trigger. The recoil seemed greater than that of the first shot he had fired. As he began to rack a third round he noticed the second marauder drop to the floor in a heap, his head tilted backward. He kept the shotgun trained on the downed marauders as he skirted the counter and walked over to check them. The first lay on his back. Holden noticed red wetness growing beneath his clothing. It appeared as though almost all eight 00 Buckshot pellets had found their mark in his chest. The marauder was still alive and trying to breathe. He looked up into Holden's eyes. Holden saw wide-eyed fear in the dying man's eyes. Likely the same fear the marauder had seen on the faces of the countless number of innocents he had killed. Holden bent over and picked up the dropped handgun. He placed the barrel of the pistol to the dying man's head. The marauder closed his eyes.

"Pow!" Holden snapped, smiling slyly at he marauder. He shook his head at the dying man and stood up, placing the handgun on the counter. He looked over at the other marauder. His head was tilted back at a strange angle. Holden walked over to him. He was not moving and for good reason. When Holden stood nearer the body, for that was what it was, he noticed the left eye missing and a large opening at the back of the head. Brain matter oozed out into the rapidly expanding pool of blood at the back of the dead man's head. Holden reached into his pocket and removed several shotgun shells. He then noticed the two different colors: green and gray. Eight-pellet buckshot and one-ounce slugs. He also noticed a small amount of blood on his left hand. It was then he recalled he had been shot. The adrenaline began to subside and he also started to register the pain at the base of his neck, at the point at which his neck and shoulder meet.

As he looked down at himself he noticed more blood staining the front of his shirt. Though not a great amount there was enough to immediately alarm him. Glancing at the dead and dying men on the floor, Holden noticed that the first marauder had stopped breathing. He stared at them and thought about how he would make it back to the actual crossroad before passing out from blood loss. He realized how lucky he had just been. He very easily could have been killed by the two men lying dead on the floor. Those two had come here to kill him. Two versus one. The odds definitely had not been in his favor.

He walked over to the front door and was about to open it when he remembered: THREE! There had been three marauders chasing him. Where was the third one? He stood still at the front door, looking out at the dusty parking lot through dusty glass. He could not see any movement but thought going out the door into the open would prove a fatal mistake. He retreated into the store and hurriedly loaded a rucksack with more ammo and as many supplies as he could locate. Noticing the blood staining his clothing he found the bathroom and bandaged himself as best he could. It was a rush job and the bleeding was not completely stemmed.

Within the bathroom Holden sensed his time had run out. He put the sack on his back and held his weapon at the high ready as he walked slowly out into the store again. The two bodies remained as he had left them. The front door was still closed. Dust still covered all except that which he and the now dead marauders had disturbed. He looked long and hard at the front door and beyond. Fear crept into him. He knew there was another marauder out there, somewhere. Most likely waiting. He would have heard the shooting. He would have come to the store. He was probably waiting somewhere just outside the door. Holden's heart began to race and he felt a strange sensation come over him. He stopped thinking about escape. He closed his eyes as he had done a few minutes before when the first two men had come into the store. This time his mind went blank and drifted into emptiness.

It quickly filled with images unbidden.

He was exiting the store. A few rusted automobiles sat useless in the parking lot. He noted one in particular, a large Chevy pickup truck with one door open. It was near the far end of the lot, nearly 100 yards from him. It was completely covered in dirt and dust. It was too far away and the interior too covered in shadow to actually see inside. But he knew the third man was there. He looked at it for a long moment then turned away and began to walk in the direction of the crossroad. He made his way around the strip mall and began to walk faster through alleyways. He passed what had been homes but were no more than empty shells now, some burned and fallen, others broken and ransacked. He continued on, passing through a small graveyard he had seen before while running from the marauders on his way to the pawn shop. Most of the markers remained. He thought it peculiar that the respect for the dead remained into this age of mankind while the respect for life seemed to have passed into extinction.

Holden slowed and finally stopped after passing through the graveyard. He heard a slight noise behind him.

"Real slow now. Put that damn scattergun down. I ain't gonna say but once." The marauder spoke evenly through gritted teeth. Holden put the shotgun down and began to turn around. "Slowly, you scavenging piece of shit." He found himself staring down the dark, gaping barrel of a Desert Eagle. Big damn barrel. Holden knew that he would not get out of this one. The marauder would kill him now. His luck with the other two was only luck. And it had run out. A broad smile spread across the marauder's face. Holden watched the finger slowly pull the trigger to the rear. The round exited the barrel and the rapidly expanding burning gases followed.

Holden never heard the bang.

He opened his eyes, blinking rapidly. He stood at the front door of the pawn store. Backing away from the door, he unloaded the shotgun and separated the buckshot from the slug shells. He then loaded a slug into the chamber and four more into the magazine tube. He took handguns and ammo from the bodies on the floor. He wasn't sure of what was happening, but he meant to survive it for as long as he could. His heart began to pound and the pain in his neck grew. His head hurt and he could feel the surge of adrenaline coursing through him.

It was time to act.

He stepped out the door and stood in the bright sunlight. He breathed deeply and looked out into the parking lot. He saw what he was looking for and started walking that way. He held the shotgun at the low ready as he moved. He walked down the sidewalk beside the entrances to the other stores. He was strangely calm. His heart pounded, his head ached, the bullet wound in his neck throbbed intensely, yet he could see everything with absolute clarity. He stopped in front of what had once been a Payless Shoe Store. He closed his eyes again, took a deep cleansing breath and turned toward the dirty Chevrolet pickup in the parking lot. The driver-side door was open. The windows were gone and within the shadows he made out the figure of the third marauder. Holden was closing the distance quickly. The shotgun was no longer being carried in the low ready. It was up and ready to be fired.

At a distance of 30 yards Holden fired the first round into the cab of the truck. He racked another slug into the chamber, the empty shell of the first hitting the ground as he let loose with second shot. He continued firing thusly as he closed the distance to the truck. The shotgun fell empty to the ground and a pistol was in his hands as he reached the door to the pickup. He fired six more rounds from the 9 mm Glock as he stood at the open door. Looking inside the truck he saw the bloodied body of the marauder. He sat inside the cab, his back against the opposite door. Three of the five slugs had found their marks. One in the chest, one in the shoulder, and a third had removed the lower left half of his jaw. The blood continued to pool in the front seat of the extended cab pickup. Holden stood looking at the man dying horribly before him. The marauder's eyes were wide and staring at him. Blood poured from the ragged hole ripped into the lower left half of the man's face. Holden watched the tongue work to no avail as the marauder gurgled on his own blood. The wounds to the chest and shoulder were bleeding freely as well.

Holden watched for several more moments until the man took several erratic breaths followed by one deep inhale with a slow, rattling exhale. He was dead. Holden reached into the pickup and removed from the front seat, beside the body, a .50 caliber Desert Eagle.

Holden sat at the crossroads. In the middle of the roadway, legs crossed, sweat dripping from his sallowed face, he tried not to think about his gunshot wound. The flow of blood had slowed, but he was still losing too much. His clothing and skin was slick with it. He was hot and tired, and every bit of him wanted to just lie down and fall asleep. He thought about how within the last 24 hours his life had so drastically changed. He had never imagined he would be in his current position. But then he had never imagined many of the situations he had found himself in before either.

He wondered how the two other members of his now defunct crew were faring. He hoped those thieving bastards were in some way suffering. Not as he was, but at least struggling to make it day to day. He had hooked up with them out of necessity. They had tried to steal from him the day he met them. He had been in a traders' camp looking for work to trade for food. Craig, Stenny, and Loomis had looked like any other scavengers. But Holden had known them for what they were as soon as he saw them. He had been struggling to find anyone in need of his skills. Struggling and failing. No one really had a need for very many electronics or mechanical items in need of repairing. Some small jobs fell into his lap from time to time but not with much frequency.

He thought about some of the adventures they had had in the short time they had been together. A brief smile graced his face before he fell over to his side. He passed blissfully into unconsciousness. He never heard the hooves and vehicles coming toward him. He never saw the men dismount and approach. He didn't feel their rough hands remove his weapons and place him out of the roadway. And he did not see the young woman exit one of the motorized vehicles and look gravely upon him.

"Get him to the physician." She spoke to one of the armed men who stood near him.

Holden was lifted and taken to another large vehicle. His wounds were tended and he was given new clothes. He slept for a while and dreamt of fields of myriad of flowers. Bright hues of yellow and blue and red and every possible variation abounded. He ran through field after field, feeling the textures, smelling the aromas, and reveling in the glory of nature as he had never imagined. As he lay in the makeshift ambulance a smile spread across his face and remained there for a long while.

An old man tended the bullet wound, his face grim and determined. The young woman sat beside Holden and gently held his hand. She did so for quite some time as her mother's men searched the area surrounding the crossroads. She watched the smile set upon his face at her touch. She smiled along with him as she sensed the goodness within. She closed her eyes for a time as the physician worked to close the wound. She felt the man stiffen as the wound was properly cleaned and then stitched. He calmed again and relaxed in her presence as she prepared to leave. As she released his hand he quickly sat up and looked her in the eye. He whispered two words and fell back onto the cot, unconscious. The young woman (no more than a girl, actually) stared blankly at the man lying before her. She exited the truck slowly and called for the captain of the guards. The two words echoed in her mind as she watched him approach: Marauders. Ambush. The crease in her brow, which her mother always teased her about, sat heavily upon her face as Captain Girard walked toward her.

The captain reported the findings of his men: three dead marauders. The girl's frown deepened. She relayed the words spoken by the unconscious man in the truck. Captain Girard thought only briefly before asserting that the man had likely been commenting on the three dead men they had found.

"He was likely speaking of the others we found." Girard's face seemed impassive. The girl, however, knew that he had his own doubts.

"Perhaps." She spoke as she looked at the truck, the man recuperating within.

"Lady Heather?" Girard was looking on her questioningly. She cleared her face and regarded him briefly. "We mustn't delay. Your mother--"

"I know, captain. I know." Heather sighed heavily. "I know too well the importance of our mission." Indeed she did. She shook her head and looked at the captain. "Let us carry on then."

As she began to walk toward her own vehicle Captain Girard called after her, "And what of this fellow?"

Heather turned about and thought but a moment. "He comes with us."

Five minutes later the caravan began to move towards the marauders' trap.

Bradley stood at the window looking out at the townsfolk as they went about their daily business. Most were traders of some sort or other, scratching out a living by bartering services and goods for any and all essentials. Some were actually homesteaders. They remained in this sprawling town, making a home of it. They owned homes and businesses. The town was larger than any he had previously been in. He had seen some to rival it, but even then only in passing. Yet there was something special about this one. He had known it the moment he had stepped off his horse and met the armed greeting party three months prior. He had been relieved of his sidearm and taken to the mayor.

Walter Taylor had seemed a judicious fellow. He had greeted Bradley warmly enough, but Bradley wasn't fooled. Taylor was shrewd and, more importantly, a believer in the old concept of community. He had explained why the armed guards had met Bradley just outside of town. Not many men traveled the open country on horseback, and of those who did almost all of them had companions. A lone rider was an anomaly. Bradley had listened and watched. He spoke when spoken to, offering no interruptions to the elected official before him. He wore his own warm and inviting demeanor. When asked his business, Bradley took his cue and explained his reason for traveling solo.

He had told Mayor Taylor of his narrow escape from Newcastle Township, a town a scant 35 miles west of their present location. Marauders had attacked two nights prior and had managed to overrun the defenses of the town guards. Twenty armed fighting men had not been able to repel the organized attack. Bradley had been a very successful trader. He had made a considerable amount of coin in Newcastle. The night of the attack he had barely managed to ride out of town with the clothes on his back and as much coin as he could get into his satchels and saddlebags. He knew of "Mayor Taylor's trading town" (he actually referred to it as such) from the traders he had done business with as they passed through Newcastle. He had come this way, slowly and as safely as possible, being careful that he was not being followed.

The mayor had leaned back in his chair at his desk in his office as Bradley relayed the story. At its conclusion Taylor sat forward with his elbows resting on his large desk, his fingers steepled before him. He had seemed to be considering the tale with much interest before he leaned forward even farther and asked what Bradley's intentions were now. Bradley noticed Taylor's eyes glance ever so quickly (almost imperceptibly) upon the satchels and saddlebags on the floor just within the door of the office. Bradley's belongings had preceded him to the mayor's office. Bradley had offered his warmest smile yet and replied most earnestly that he intended to relocate at Northern Alley Trading if they would have him. Taylor had smiled broadly at that, stood, and offered his hand across the desk. Bradley had stood and with two solid shakes he had become a new permanent fixture in town.

Within the last three months he had managed to purchase land, building permits and operating licenses (from the mayor), and building materials. He had hired laborers to build his small, yet effective, shop. He had started trading from the small place he rented (from the mayor) two days after arriving. He was an excellent haggler and was known to buy almost anything of any apparent value to anyone. And he either had any need or was able to get whatever anyone needed within a few days. He began to turn a profit after only a few weeks of operation. His permanent shop was completed three weeks after his arrival and it rivaled all other trading shops in the town. He had quickly become an important fixture in the ever-growing settlement.

He had also learned a great deal about the town's hierarchy (even supposed democracies had them): the mayor, council members, business leaders, outspoken homesteaders, et cetera. He had learned them and gotten close to them in one way or another. Some without them ever knowing it (it was always amazing the loyalty of friends or family could be purchased by a few coins or trinkets). After three months he had his finger on the pulse of the entire town. Nothing happened here without his knowledge of it long beforehand.

When the first few marauders arrived two weeks ago he knew the time was fast approaching. He needed to start the ball rolling, as Brickman sometimes said. He had made a late night call to the sheriff of the guards. They spoke but briefly before Bradley left the sheriff's home. He had gone carrying a heavy satchel on one shoulder. He returned to the home at the rear of his shop empty-handed.

He whistled a tune he had never heard except as whistled by his mentor. He wouldn't have known who The Police were anyway.

On this day, as he looked out his window and watched the townsfolk mill about, he thought about all that was coming. The end was nigh. And with it a new beginning. All good things must come to an end (another of Brickman's salient offerings--the man was full of euphemistic quips). The future was Brickman's and, by extension, all those who followed his lead. Brickman was the answer to all the wrongs in the land. He would bring about a lasting peace. Stability. He had saved Bradley years before and had taught him a great deal about life. And death. Today there might be death for some, for quite a few most likely. But the resulting good would outweigh the means necessary to get there. After all, making an omelet did require the breaking of a few eggs. Brickman yet again.

It was early in the morning. Sunrise had only just broken. He had not had a customer yet. He was still looking out the window when the front door of the shop opened. The bell over the door jangled softly. He turned and watched the hooded figure enter his establishment. The man walked toward him and stopped less than a foot away. Pale hands reached up to pull the hood back and Bradley looked into the deep blue eyes of his mentor, his teacher, his sensei. Brickman looked back upon his prized pupil and smiled. Brickman held his arms open and Bradley embraced the man to whom he had pledged his undying service. Brickman's arms closed about him gently.

"You have done well, my boy. Very well indeed." Brickman spoke gently, his voice barely above a whisper. "I see all preparations are in place."

Brickman pulled away slowly from his pupil and looked him squarely in the eye. "What resistance will we have?"

"Very little. The guards are ours. The mayor may prove a nuisance, but without the guards he will be but a small thorn in our side, an irritation." Bradley spoke thoughtfully. He was replaying in his mind the calculations he had made over the past few months. "Some of the landowners may prove more of a hindrance. A singular example might be necessary to get the others to come around to our way of thinking."

Brickman regarded the young man before him. He smiled and once again complimented, "Well done."

Mayor Taylor sat at the desk in his modest office. He thought about the growth the town had experienced under his leadership. Northern Alley Trading had been little more than a well-defended stopping point for traders from north and south. It had been born out of necessity some 20 years prior. He had been elected mayor only two years ago and had made very aggressive strides to reach even farther to the North for support and alliances. The past year he had found himself in the presence of an envoy from The Northern Kingdom. The only recognized monarchy in the land. Far to the north, the Kingdom (as all who knew of it in the south call it) was its own separate land. There were almost none known to have traveled there, or at least none that came back to the south. Since his life in Northern Alley Trading began as a boy of six he had known of only one old-timer who claimed to have been to the southern boundary of the Kingdom. He could recall great tales of the beauty and exquisiteness of the lands to the far north and the great people who live there.

The previous mayor and the then-current town council had struck an agreement with several other towns in the southlands to form a loose federation of towns. This federation had proven to be very good for the growing township. Trading between the included southern towns had increased tremendously since the pact was struck.

Taylor, however, had seen an even larger opportunity in the distance. The North was the true prize. If he could help engineer the reconnection of the desolate lands of the south with the Kingdom-- He looked wistfully upon the portrait of his father that sat above the mantel across the room from his desk. The portrait had been done by an artist traveling through some years before. Taylor had been a member of the governing town council at the time. His father had retired from the mayor's office following three 4-year terms and had told his son to take his mantel and make something more of it. His father had died during his campaign for mayor, just prior to the election. Taylor had won convincingly and had inwardly sworn an oath to do just as his father had instructed. He was going to make his town, his community, the entire southland better.

Bradley had been correct in his impression of Taylor. He was a very shrewd politician. He had made deals with a great many businessmen and landowners to further the growth of the town (and he had profited as well, but nothing considered illegal by any living in the world of long-moved-along). But the danger in Taylor was his belief in the community. The community small, the community large, the community grand. Taylor would work tirelessly to see the community grow, and his fervently altruistic beliefs coupled with his charismatic personality could bring a great many people to his cause. If there were a cause over which to choose sides. Might there be sides?

Brickman said there were always sides. Some people were just too chickenshit to choose one. After today there would be sides and if the people of Northern Alley Trading didn't choose wisely they would find themselves on the losing side of the coming war.

Bradley was also sitting at his desk in his office. His office was not so very modest. A large, oversize oak desk was framed by the equally large bay window behind him. The heavy drapes were pulled shut and only an oil lamp lit the interior. A large tapestry hung on one wall and several paintings adorned the others. He too had had a fireplace built in his office. He sat in silence, eyes closed, meditating. A slight smile (a smirk, actually) was on his face. He was seeing. Seeing all Brickman's plans come to fruition. Seeing all his preparations fall in place like the brickwork of his grand place of business. Seeing the people of this town fall in line with the greatness of the real New World. He was a part of something so great that he at times was in awe of it. In awe of its architect. Brickman.

"Are you ready?" Brickman sat across from him.

Bradley, although not shocked by his sudden appearance, still wondered how Brickman did it. He opened his eyes and looked into the cool blue orbs across from him. Brickman wore the hooded robe, hood pulled back. Although he smiled, his eyes held within them an unconcealed cruelty and vengeance. Bradley loved Brickman as any son could love a father. He had never known his own and was just out of boyhood when Brickman had plucked him from the dirty city streets. Few people went into the ruins of the big cities. Most still believed the cities held the creeping death. But a few truly desperate and starving individuals chanced it. Bradley hadn't even known the name of the city he'd been wandering. Brickman had told him the name. Atlanta.

"I am indeed ready." Bradley involuntarily returned a smile. He looked at the atomic clock on his wall. "We have a brief time before it begins. Would you like to walk the town for a while?"

"Why not? You can show me the sights, the hot spots as it were." Brickman smiled at his pupil as he spoke. Bradley knew the sarcasm for what it was and smiled back. After all, what sights were there in this dusty town? The only sight had not yet arrived. And they had been preparing for her arrival for some months.

The two men rose, walked outside, and stood in the roadway. Many of the other townspeople were going about their day, running their shops, buying and trading goods. Walking amongst them, Bradley pointed out various points of interest and, more importantly, people of interest. He knew that Brickman was taking in everything. Even the things he failed to make mention of. Brickman would have the layout of the town and a good idea of all the major players before the event began. He checked the sun's current position in the sky and calculated they had a few hours left.

They walked on as any two old friends might, the one leading the other about as if all were right in the world.

The early evening bell rang in the town common. It was two hours before the sun would drop below the horizon. Dust settled in certain areas of the town while stirring in others. Homesteaders, the wealthier ones, flowed slowly out of town from their businesses to their sprawling homes in the nearby plains. They owned hired hands, some with weapons (all registered with the town council of course). While the town was awake and alive with all its inhabitants during the course of the trading day there were almost twice as many guns present. The homesteaders entered at staggered and overlapping intervals throughout the day, bringing with them their hired hands and hired gunmen. But during the evening and night there were only the town's guard left. Even knowing this fact was not enough to make anyone foolish enough to attack. Of the guards' number, one in four was armed with a semi-automatic rifle.

Mayor Taylor and his politic elite had built an enduring remnant of the old world. To the best of their ability they had recreated an image of the old town, resplendent in its recent antiquity. And well protected from those who would raze it to ruin. He retired to his home, walking amongst those in his charge as he did so. Standing upon the threshold of his front door and looking back upon the few who remained in the streets and their byways, he smiled in contentment. His father would be proud of the progress achieved thus far.

He entered his home and closed the door behind him. After a bath and a change of clothes he would be better prepared to welcome the envoy from the North. Royalty in his home. His father could not ever have dreamed. He stood with his back against the closed front door a moment, a smile upon his face and his eyes closed as he savored the sweetness of the thought. All would be well for his people. He would guide and lead them forward. Progress would be his legacy. Progress and prosperity. He would be remembered as the one who initiated the rescue of all from the wastelands and the marauders. Those scourge would be nothing more than petty nuisances and individual rogues ere the age was done.

Taylor had plans far beyond Northern Alley Trading. He would see the great city of the North before long. He would bring it south in all its glory and become part of its hierarchy in his homeland.

He opened his eyes and breathed deeply. He moved toward his bathroom and the warm bath that awaited him. All was well and all would soon be better

4 A Trap

*A*nd *who might you be, pleasant one?*

Holden turned at the soft voice. Sitting in the midst of a kaleidoscope of colors, flowering buds effusing him with giddiness, he was startled but slightly. He sought out the speaker but saw no one.

How do you come by here?

Melodic, beautiful, enticing. He sought the voice that questioned him but could see nothing within the large meadow nor amidst the elms or willows at the nearby forest's edge. The voice came much as sweet lyrics from some long forgotten song.

Without realizing he'd done so Holden stood and looked about, searching. His heart quickened.

"Who's there?" he asked, almost at a whisper.

I did not call you, pleasant one, yet here you are. Come to me of your own. Strange that this should be. I do see you, however, and see some purpose.

The voice seemed to be carried softly on the wind. It came to Holden from no discernible direction but filled his senses with warmth and comfort. He was transformed to the child he had been some many years before. The young boy huddled close to his mother's breast as she sang him softly and gently to sleep on so many nights in the roaming survivors' caravan. He remembered not the words of the song she had sung to him all those many years before, but the soothing comfort of her voice and the feel of her filled his memories. He became lost in the memory for a moment and felt an utter and immense peace take hold of him.

His eyes now closed, he felt a stirring in the wind as it caressed every bit of his exposed skin. A kiss on the wind touched his cheek. A distant melody sang to his ears as a smile came to his face. His breathing deepened and slowed.

He saw his mother's olive complexion and huge brown eyes. She smiled at him, silently telling him that all would be okay. He was safe.

Though I am glad to see you, glad that you have come, you have to go now, pleasant one. Now that I see you, I see you have important work to do.

Holden opened his eyes and felt wetness on his cheek. Tears filled his eyes and blurred his vision. The meadow, the forest, the clear blue sky, and even the aromas carried on the wind began to fade from him.

"This is all just a dream. A dream before the end. Am I dying?"

It is a dream. She spoke slowly, fading away as well. *But not just a dream. You've a special gift that brought you here. It will lead you to him.*

The tears flowed more freely. "Lead me to who? I don't understand."

Seek first the knight. Find the Wanderer.

The last words were but a whisper as Holden's eyes fluttered open from the living dream. The smell of floral sweetness remained in his nostrils. Mingled with the childhood memory of his long-dead mother and her loving embraces were the sights of the meadow and the voice of the wind. Her words stayed with him and so did the sadness at the thought of all he had lost.

He wept in earnest, the tears traveling paths previously carved in his sleep.

Outside the ambulance, an unusually silent night gripped the town he had fled earlier in the day.

Captain Girard sat alone in the cell. He felt the swelling coming in earnest on his cheek and around his left eye. He was bruised on almost all his body. And two of the fingers on his right hand remained at odd angles. They were definitely out of joint and possibly broken. He reached over with his left hand and snapped the index and middle fingers back into place. He felt more than heard the snap as they went back to a normal position. Gritting his teeth, he grunted loudly then continued to breathe deeply until the pain and nausea passed.

He closed his eyes and thought about his current predicament.

They had walked into a well-designed and even better executed trap. He had felt that something was wrong. Prior to making the journey south he had been wary, and upon finding the injured stranger on the roadway his hackles had been up and calling for attention. He just couldn't figure it out until it was far too late. He replayed the events over in his mind.

The initial meeting with the mayor had gone much as he knew it would. They met with him alone in his office. The mayor, Lady Heather, and Girard had met in private. No other townspeople had been invited or allowed. Girard had positioned his own men outside and in for security. Nothing seemed obviously out of place, but a gnawing suspicion grew within him. Something did not feel right.

That meeting had gone for nearly an hour, the mayor speaking about himself and his town, about the past, about the future. He was a most magnanimous host and an even better statesman. He was definitely wasted on this place, but then again he was probably exactly what the people of the south needed. Someone to get them back into the fold, someone to connect them to the greater Kingdom, someone to pull them up from the hell they were so close to falling into.

After the meeting the mayor had led the way to the council. The meeting proper had been called. All the council members had assembled. As the mayor and Lady Heather (followed by Girard and six of his best men) entered the chamber, the council members quieted and stood. They remained standing and silent until the Lady had taken her seat. Girard was afforded a seat at her right. The mayor had made his own way to a lectern erected before the raised arc of the council dais.

The mayor waited for all the members of the council to get an eyeful of the stately entourage before beginning his speech. He had prepared for this moment his whole life. This was the beginning of the greatness he had hoped for his town, for his people since he had decided to follow in his father's footsteps. An envoy from the North was here, in his town, at his behest. And the council was on the verge of forming a pact that would bring Northern Alley Trading into the folds of the only organized national government known to exist in the land. The only one since the last had fallen.

Girard and Lady Heather had been listening intently to the mayor when the man in white had come in. Tall with short-cropped grey hair, the older man had been accompanied by a slight young man, well dressed with dark curls and pale skin. They had walked purposefully to the very center of the council hall. The mayor had been speaking in earnest about the growth of the town and the trade routes to be added to the Kingdom. Girard had again noticed how eloquently he spoke (reminding Girard of some of the more powerful barons he'd had the chance to hear as they spoke at court in the palace).

The mayor had faltered in his speech as the two interlopers had entered. Many of the meetings held in the council chambers were open to members of the local population, but this meeting had been closed. Guards had been posted within and without the chamber. The mayor finally stopped speaking altogether as the pair reached him.

"Bradley? What's the meaning of this?" He spoke to the younger of the two men. "What...how did you get in here?"

Bradley whispered something into the mayor's ear and pulled him firmly but gently aside. The older man in white looked at the assembled council with what appeared to be the slightest smile at the corners of his mouth. He looked at each of the members seated before him until his eyes came upon Lady Heather. Girard's nerves had been humming since the two had entered and now they were nearly afire. The old man smiled broadly showing unnaturally white teeth.

"My lady," Girard spoke urgently into her ear, "perhaps we should retire until a later time."

Then he saw the eyes change. The old man's smile remained, but the eyes gleamed with malice. He had seen that look before. He had seen it in battle, fighting during his early days of service to the North. He had likely worn the look in his own eyes as he dispatched those men who wore it in their eyes as they faced him on the battlefield. Bloodlust, eager and determined. With the intensity of berserk.

The look within the old man's eyes spoke to the warrior in him and warned of something greater. Girard had never been much for spirituality, but he caught a hint of evil in the eyes looking upon his greatest charge. And it would not be until later that his memory recalled a ripple, a slight change in the face of the man in white. As if another face lay just beneath the surface. Lady Heather had begun to rise at the slight pressure his hand gave to her elbow. She had learned to trust in his instincts over the past year. As the two got to their feet, four marauders entered the chamber.

Pandemonium ensued.

Girard's pistol was in his hand immediately and he had instinctively moved Heather behind him.

Two council members tried to run from the room. Both were pistol whipped by two of the marauders. They crumpled easily to the floor, unconscious.

Shots rang out. One of the council members clutched his abdomen after standing. Pulling his hand away he regarded the bright red stain in disbelief before looking into Girard's face. Girard looked away, searching for a target, not even taking time to mark the fall of the council member who had just been shot.

The marauders moved through the fray. He could not get a clear shot at them. The town guards within the chamber were firing at random, taking great care. His own soldiers were engaged in the battle as well. They fired shots of their own.

"Captain!"

Girard turned at the call and noted a young soldier (Edward, he would recall later in the cell) making his way toward him from some ten yards away. He was but a boy. Clothed in the red tunic of the royal guard, with fiery red hair, and fierce green eyes, Edward bore intensity and excitement upon his countenance. He even smiled as his eyes met Girard's.

God bless the young and stupid. Girard saw all this with absolute clarity and an uncontrollable slowing of time. He marked the way the soldier (Edward) properly held his weapon at the ready as he approached. He noted his eyes scanning as he approached. And he noticed the town guard approaching at an angle from his (Edward's) rear. He saw in absolute, perfect slow motion as the guard raised his weapon to fire. His instinct registered the danger before his mind could. He didn't want to believe what his soldier's instincts saw clearly.

Betrayal.

The guard brought the weapon up and fired a mere tenth of a second before Girard got off his own shot.

Edward's left eye exploded out of his head in a red and pink mist as the round fired from the guard's 9 mm pistol exited his head. After taking one additional step his momentum carried him face forward to the floor. His feet continued moving. An awful, repeated moan escaped from him as he lay there dying.

Girard's own round found it's mark, hitting the murderous guard to the left of the nose, punching through his cheek, tearing through a sinus cavity, angling down through the roof of his mouth, ripping through his larynx before coming to rest between two cervical vertebrae. Girard didn't take the time to note the guard's descent to the floor before seeking out additional traitors.

He kept Lady Heather concealed behind him. He saw two more of his men go down at the hands of the guards. They all were shot in the head at close range. Their faces became seared into his memory almost immediately. He fired one more shot before it all ended. Again, he found his mark, hitting another of the guards. The round struck the shoulder, turning the guard as he attempted to murder another of his men. The guard's shot went wild, and Girard's man was able to get his own shot at the same guard, hitting the guard twice in the chest.

Girard's man was killed almost immediately afterward by a marauder who had flanked him.

The marauder fired one round at the base of the soldier's head and ducked immediately behind the concealment of a chamber chair. Girard could not get a clear shot as council members continued to attempt to flee the chamber.

He watched as the last of his men were killed by marauders.

He then realized he had backed himself and Lady Heather into the northern wall of the chamber. He stood with his weapon pointed at the last marauder to have fired his weapon. He was taking up the slack in his own trigger to fire when he felt a most unnatural compulsion to drop his weapon.

He paused.

"Hold, Captain." The voice spoke evenly and with compelling authority.

He watched in astonishment as his finger released the trigger and the weapon began to slowly lower from its target. He fought against his body, his mind battling intensely. A vibration went through him, a tremble gaining in intensity. His breathing intensified while all else about him stood still. Every eye in the room seemed upon him, and as he looked around he noted the faces of marauders, council members, Mayor Taylor, town guards, the slight and pale one, and then his eyes settled upon the glare of the white haired one.

It was he who had spoken.

Girard focused on that gaze and rebelled. His arms, now weighted down as with lead, began to rise to acquire the old man as his new target. The man smiled a smile without humor. A smile of evil. Girard felt ice upon his heart and knew that it was here that he could not fail. Not in this. He hardened himself and brought all his will to bear. He trusted in himself and his training and his commitment. He did as he had done so many times before. He envisioned himself acting and followed it with action. He saw himself on target and saw himself pulling the trigger smoothly and surely. And he acted. But nothing happened.

He never pulled the trigger.

"Drop your weapon, captain. It is grown too heavy a burden for you."

The .40 caliber fell to the floor of the chamber with a loud clatter. All was silent for several moments. The old man approached Girard and Lady Heather slowly. No one else moved. He stopped, his face within mere inches from Girard's, and he regarded him with keen interest.

"You will be a most interesting addition."

It was then that the hand of Lady Heather struck out, slapping the face of the old man with a resounding smack. The marauders moved hurriedly forward and Girard began to come out of his trance. The old man's hand came up suddenly and the marauders stopped in a semi-circle around them. He turned back to Lady Heather, the smile no longer evident.

"You will learn to appreciate me and all I stand for before all is said and done. You above all others." He regarded Girard, who was visibly shaking the cobwebs from his head. "Take her away, and break this one," motioning toward Girard, "but keep him alive."

As he walked away he remarked, "I have work yet for him."

Marauders placed hands upon Lady Heather and she screamed and struggled. Girard broke his trance completely and as he moved to protect his charge he was struck from behind. He fought to defend himself and reach the Lady but a large, heavy thing struck behind his right ear and another hit him on his left cheek below his eye. He lost his balance and fell to his knees. As he struggled to regain his feet he caught a boot to his midsection and doubled over. Several intolerable moments passed as Lady Heather was whisked out of the chamber. He looked up into the face of the slight, pale one.

"Oh, captain, my captain." Bradley looked down upon Girard, regarding him with what appeared to be genuine sadness. He looked at the men around Girard. "Stand him up."

Rough hands pulled Girard to his feet. Those same hands held his arms out away from his body and kept him off balance.

"Give me his hand. His weapon hand."

Girard tried to struggle but a punch to his ribs and another to the breadbasket took all the fight out again. Bradley now held the first two fingers of Girard's right hand out before him. Looking Girard in the face he snapped them both in rapid succession. The pain tore through Girard with white-hot intensity. He did not realize he had screamed until afterwards. All else blurred into a haze of pain as he was beaten into unconsciousness.

He awoke some time later in the cell. He was alone. He had lost his men (not sure of the fate of the others left outside the chamber and within the town, but he assumed they had been captured or killed). He had lost his charge, the one he was bound to protect unto his own death. Lady Heather was lost. He had failed and now he was prisoner. And he was broken.

He attempted to stand and fell to the floor of the cell in pain. His left knee had been badly damaged. It was swollen, and the pain was excruciating. His head ached inside and out. He felt several lumps beneath his hair. His left cheek below the eye was bruised and swollen. His torso hurt so badly that each breath was a painful chore. He was loath to raise his shirt to look at the bruising. He did so anyway and gave himself a cursory assessment. He reckoned he had one, possibly two broken ribs, but he did not think there was any true internal damage. He hoped so anyway.

His nose also ached. He touched it with the fingers of his good hand (his left hand, dammit!) and noticed it at an odd angle. Broken for the second time in his life. (The first time had been in a bar fight during his early days as a young soldier.) He placed the palms of both hands on either side of the crooked, bloody mess at the center of his face and pressed together while turning his nose back toward center. His slight grunt belied the sharp pain that flowed into his throbbing head. He sat on the floor and blew out a large amount of blood and snot from his fairly straightened nose.

He stared at the bloody glob of mucus on the floor between his legs and began to harden himself.

One step at a time, soldier. Get your bearings and wait for the next move to come. No matter what he needed to stay calm. He began to fold his mind into himself, shutting off his mind's perception of the pain his body was experiencing. Each bruise, bump, broken bone became a

84

distant thing. He sat on the floor for several moments, slowing his breathing and his heart rate, gaining control of himself. It took him longer than it had in times past, but he eventually reached a state of true concentration without internal distractions. But he had no control over external ones.

"Hello, Captain Girard." The old man stood outside the barred cell door, looking down upon him.

Girard's eyes opened and the pain tried to creep back in. He fought it back down.

The old man smiled.

"You are a strong one, a real fighter." He emphasized the last word with a slight swing of the fist. Girard only looked on. The strain to keep the pain out was immense.

The old man showed extreme agility, squatting deftly outside the cell.

"You will have to learn that there are some things in this world that simply cannot be fought. Some things are without equal. Invincible. Inevitable." He was silent a moment before standing slowly.

Girard's breathing had quickened along with his heart rate. The pain in his extremities was now more intense. The superficial bruises began to speak again. His right hand hurt like hell. And his ribs and knee began to enter back into his conscious.

Oh hell! Girard was starting to lose his control.

"I will teach you." The old man spoke those last few words and then snapped his fingers. The pain flared throughout every inch of Girard's body from each injury, old and new. For nearly ten seconds Girard's screams echoed in the cell. Another snap of the old man's fingers and the pain went back to the barely controlled ache.

A thick sheen of sweat covered Girard's entire body as he sat on the floor staring into the eyes of the devil on the other side of his barred prison door. The old man stared back.

The smile was gone.

After a few moments of hot tears and deep, heartfelt weeping, Holden began to regain control of himself. He looked around and saw that he was lying in the rear of a large vehicle. An IV was in his left arm. The bag of plasma hanging beside him was empty. The vehicle was quiet, and he could see no one else around. Darkness greeted him as he sat up and peered out the vehicle's windows. A sharp pain in his neck reminded him that he had been shot. He reached up and felt the clean bandage.

Almost immediately he remembered everything else.

He tried to reach for the handle to open the door and became entangled in the IV. It took him a few moments to remove the tape from his arm and then slowly pull out the IV. Just as he finished and reached for the handle, someone opened the driver's door and dove into the vehicle. An opaque partition separated the front seat from the rear. Interior lights came on when the door opened, but Holden could not see clearly who had entered the vehicle with him. The driver's door closed and the lights went out as the new passenger fumbled about.

"Shit, shit, shit!" He was hissing under his breath as he searched for something. Holden moved closer to the glass partition and tried to peer into the front cabin. He saw an indistinguishable figure bent over and groping on the floor for something. The shrouded image sat up quickly.

"Thank God." He had found a key. The key.

He started the engine on the vehicle and the barely perceptible hum of the electric engine became audible.

A shot rang out in the night and shouts soon followed. The vehicle began moving forward slowly at first. Several more shots were fired in the near distance.

Holden looked out and saw more men making their way to other nearby vehicles. The men wore red tunics. They were but a few in number, half a dozen at most. They were being pursued by twice as many. Though their retreat was orderly, with two continuing to fire at the marauders giving chase as the others fled, the enemy simply overwhelmed them with the amount of rounds being fired.

Holden watched helplessly as the marauders cut down the valiant guards one at a time. The guards fought fiercely. For every guard killed, three marauders fell, but it did not matter. The number of marauders continued to grow. Only one of the guards reached a parked vehicle. As he opened the door a round struck him in the back. He continued inside as several more rounds hit him.

The vehicle never moved.

Rounds began to hit the vehicle in which Holden sat. He could hear the shots continuing and the subsequent sound of the rounds hitting windows and metal. But none penetrated. Something exploded nearby. The vehicle picked up speed and soon began moving too quickly to see exactly what was happening at the edge of the town. He was moving away. He looked forward through the partition and saw that the vehicle's headlights opened onto a clear road. No marauders blocked their path.

Holden sat back and remained quiet. He thought about rapping on the glass separating him from the driver of the vehicle and making an introduction, but he did not want to chance an unwelcome reply. So instead he just sat back and wondered about what was to come. And as he sat there he remembered the dream. It remained fresh in his memory.

Seek first the knight. Find the Wanderer.

He rode on in the rear of the vehicle for some time, hours likely. He lost track of the passage of time. The speed had slowed to something more manageable for night travel. Holden looked out the window as his mind wandered. After some time he closed his eyes and recalled the voice on the wind, in the wind. He smelled the flowers of the meadow. He felt the embrace of his mother. Shortly thereafter he drifted off to sleep.

The vehicle drove on into the night.

5 A Violence

The small band of travelers trekked through midday, following a path only the Wanderer seemed sure of. Little was said by any of them. Occasionally, Finn would ask his father something in hushed tones. He was as curious as any child might be, but his father's patience seemed worn thin. He began to tire of Finn's questions and after a time responded sharply, quieting the boy. Finn fell back in their column near Evan, who walked at the rear behind Terran who carried his daughter cradled in his arms after she had grown too tired to walk.

The Wanderer was intent on moving and would not risk a stop just yet. Evan was tired but was compelled to push on, knowing that whatever was behind them was indeed worth fleeing if the Wanderer chose to seek escape rather than face it head on. He followed head down, battling demons from his past, so did not notice Finn fall in step with him.

"Who is he?"

Finn's question brought Evan back to the present. He glanced forward at the straight back of the Wanderer. He looked for some time before responding.

"I don't know, for sure."

Evan frowned and shook his head, thinking hard about an adequate description of the man he knew as the Wanderer. Alex. Who exactly was he?

"He's like the scary bogeymen father told us about." Finn whispered conspiratorially.

"Father said he's like them but better. Father said he's a good guy." He paused and looked at Evan, slowing his step a bit more to drop back from the group. "He's scarier than any bogeyman I ever imagined."

His voice was even lower as he said the last.

"Why are we following him?"

"Don't be afraid of him." Evan spoke evenly, holding the same low volume as Finn.

"He is a good guy and he is here to help us."

The two maintained a slowed pace for a while more, walking on in silence for a brief time.

"So, he ain't gonna hurt us, is he?" Finn asked at last, an earnest appeal in his eyes. Evan felt a release within and a lightening of his spirit as he thought of all he knew of the Wanderer and all he felt about the small group now traveling in the cloud covered desert.

"He is not going to hurt us, Finn. Even better than that I think he is going to protect us."

Evan smiled at the boy warmly and was encouraged to get a return smile.

"Good. But I still think he's scary."

Evan looked at the back of the Wanderer and thought to himself, *You have no idea.*

"Yeah, I think he is a little scary, too."

Ahead of the column, walking intently forward, the Wanderer plotted their course. They were headed west, across a rather large swath of midland desert. Whatever was behind them might or might not have picked up their trail. He hoped not. He had stopped a few times throughout their march to check the horizon at their rear but had seen no signs of pursuit. He trusted his eyes and other senses, but he also knew to trust his instincts even more. His instincts told him to put as much distance as possible between them and the enemy. The marauders were one thing. But they had not been alone.

The thing that traveled with the marauders was a thing of evil. It was a perversion of man, a thing bred by evil men, borne of madness and twisted science from the old days. It walked on two legs, had two arms, a head on top, with a large enough brain to be considered human-like. But it was not human. A genetic perversion, fed by its

90

insanity and the flesh of men, it was used by some marauders to hunt men. It had tiny slits for eyes but heightened olfactory senses. It could smell prey (human or otherwise) at great distances.

Some years before, Alex had been hunted by one of these creatures. It had been in the care of a trio of marauders. They had pursued him for two and a half days through rough terrain before Alex had grown tired of running. Having set a trap to snare his pursuers, he had had to fire thirteen rounds from his M4: one round for each marauder, ten for the hunter. The tenth round had been a head shot. It had been the only shot to stop his demented pursuer. The thing had not registered any of the other shots to its torso. And the speed at which it had moved. That concerned him because of the small group he now found himself attached to. If he were forced to face another of those things, would he be willing to sacrifice any of Terran's family in order to save himself and the boy? He did not want to have to make such a choice. So he pushed on, taking them farther into the desert and, hopefully, away from the monster at their backs.

Some time after the sun's noon passage he stopped for a small meal break. After providing Terran and the children with foodstuffs from his supply he seated himself near an outcropping of rock, facing backward down the path they had already traveled. Alex stared into the distance as he snacked on some dried meat product. After several moments he turned and looked at the small group before him. Terran sat huddled with his children, making sure they were eating and drinking enough. He fawned over Kiran especially. The Wanderer noticed the constant glances the girl directed to Evan. He looked over at the boy.

Evan stared back at him. He wore a look of deep concentration, a crease parting his brow. Seeing the Wanderer looking at him, Evan dropped his own gaze and turned his face aside. The Wanderer thought he saw dissatisfaction on the boy's face and possibly consternation. He smiled to himself. The boy squirmed briefly then took a bite of his own jerky before stealing a glance at the girl. Their eyes met briefly, long enough for each to smile at the other before their mutual embarrassment took hold.

Finally, Evan stood and walked over to the Wanderer. Alex watched him approach, making no effort to mark the approach or subsequent arrival. He continued to eat his small meal and sip from his canteen. Evan sat beside him carefully. He sighed audibly.

Silence from the Wanderer.

Evan glanced sideways at him. He sighed again.

Still nothing from the man. He remained a chewing statue, seemingly taking no notice of the boy beside him.

Finally, Evan could take it no longer.

"So where exactly are we going?" Evan spoke timidly. His voice was just above a whisper. The Wanderer did not immediately answer. Instead he took another bite from his own jerky, chewing slowly. He looked at the boy and the others. They were all staring. Apparently the question burned in all of them.

"Look westward, beyond the haze on the horizon." Alex pointed in the direction he mentioned and all eyes turned there. "There are survivors there. A town. We go there." He paused. "For now."

None of the group could see anything beyond the haze. They all looked back at the Wanderer, but he was already chewing another bite and looking back in the direction from which they had come. A grim determination was set upon his countenance and held Evan at bay for a moment before he spoke again.

"Who...who is back there? Who is it that you are afraid of?"

The silence was thick on the air. The Wanderer turned after taking a deep breath and spoke loud enough for all to hear.

"There are men in this world, men of evil. They do evil to other men, their hearts are full of malice, they think only of themselves. They plunder, rape, murder. They are not so many, but their violence, their savagery make them a force indefensible to many."

He paused, returning his gaze to each of them in turn. Settling upon Evan, he continued.

"These men flourished during the anarchy which followed the Great Fall all those many years ago when the world fell to ruin. Long before you children were born."

He glanced briefly at Terran as he paused yet again. He then looked back into the horizon, back the way from which they had come.

"They roamed the wastelands and the outer boundaries of the great cities, now bathed in decay and ruin and disease. They took and took without remorse or recompense. They overcame singular resistance, killing men, women, and children. They tormented the captured women, making slaves of some. But organized resistance deterred them."

He looked back at Evan.

"But in recent years even that has changed. They have become emboldened, driven. And more organized themselves. They appear to have help from without. Contrary to their selfish, petty nature they seem to be growing into something greater than they should."

Another pause.

"And they have uncovered things. Evil things. Monsters is the only way to describe them. I had only heard tales before. But not long ago I encountered one such thing. These creatures are abominations. Evil abominations. One such was behind us, heading our way.

Terran stood at this and began searching the horizon to their rear. He held the hands of both his children as he did so.

"Are we being followed then?" He looked pleadingly at Alex.

"I don't think so." *I hope not.*

The Wanderer shook his head slowly. He did not seem quite sure enough to satisfy Terran.

"Either way we must keep moving. We need to reach the safety of the camp before nightfall." He nodded to the west.

They finished their meal in silence. Once done, they took to the unseen path. The Wanderer led the ragtag group toward their destination.

Several uneventful hours passed with only brief moments of respite in which the Wanderer stopped the small group to drink from their supply of water. Evan wondered how much longer they would be able to keep up their pace. They were all weary. He would push himself to any extreme to stay with the Wanderer, but he was not sure about the others.

Terrran was showing signs of exhaustion. He had fallen farther and farther behind the Wanderer as they traversed the patchy desert floor. Evan and Finn remained near him as they walked. Kiran had asked to walk but her father refused. He could see that she was in no shape to make the attempt. He held onto her as if nothing else mattered. Evan watched the two with keen interest as they moved deeper into the wasteland. Warmth and utter dedication flowed from father to daughter. Terran would sacrifice himself mind, body, and soul to keep her safe. The strain he placed upon himself was great, but it would not defeat his will. Evan was not sure about the strength of the body, however.

He glanced again at the wasteland around them. He had never dared to travel so far into the west. It was known to be desolate and barren. He knew little of the people still living there. His decimated village had been too near the wastelands and had been overrun by murderers. He did not know how anyone else could survive out here. At least for any considerable amount of time. Occasionally they passed within sight of small towns, long-since-abandoned farmsteads, and the occasional dilapidated settlement. The Wanderer's path did not take them near enough to notice if anyone, of either good or ill intent, was near. Evan felt eyes watching from some of these locations on a few occasions. They crossed paths with no one.

Later in the day, as the sun moved closer toward its descent, the Wanderer picked up his pace and headed toward a large outcropping of rock in the near distance. Not large enough to be considered mountainous, but considerably grander than any bumps they had heretofore encountered, the rocks signaled a slight change in their terrain. Some 200 yards away, the rocks delineated the start of a rockier, upward-sloping terrain. Farther into the distance Evan could barely make out what appeared to be forestland and the beginnings of mountains.

The Wanderer had moved well ahead of the group. Evan was first to notice the widening gap between them. He called out to Finn who was busy staring through the ground before his feet. Evan thought he saw the other boy's lips moving slightly as he counted his every step. He almost hated to interrupt him and cause him to lose count. Oh well.

"Finn. Look ahead."

Finn raised his head, turning to face Evan. A weary smile crept slowly onto his face. "I like you, Evan. You're nice. Can we be friends?" He frowned slightly and looked toward Terran. "Father doesn't allow us to meet others. He says others might hurt us and take our supplies. Our food and water. We always hide from everyone as we travel. But this time was different." He looked back into Evan's eyes, the smile returning.

"I know, Finn." Evan's face mirrored Finn's. He smiled at his new friend. "I am your friend. And so is he." He motioned ahead toward the Wanderer. "I think we may be getting close to...wherever it is he's taking us. Look ahead."

Both boys looked in the near distance as the Wanderer climbed a brief outcropping of rock jutting out of the dry desert floor. As they watched he reached the low summit and seemed to peer into the distance. For but a brief moment he was limned in luminescence as the deepening sun outlined him. Evan's heart skipped a quick beat as the vision passed. He turned to ask Finn if he had seen it, but the other boy spoke first.

"What's he doing?"

Evan turned his attention back to the Wanderer and noticed him drawing something from the large pack on his back. He put the item to his eyes and looked toward the west.

"Binoculars. He's looking through binoculars."

Finn stared blankly at Evan. "What are binoculars?"

Evan regarded his new friend, much as a big brother might look upon his younger sibling.

"Binoculars are things that help you see a long way into the distance. When we catch up to him we can take a look for ourselves." Evan and Finn continued toward the Wanderer, beginning to put a slight bit of distance between themselves and Terran. The wagon they pulled began to throw up a bit more dust from the hardpan as their pace quickened. Terran also seemed to gain a bit more energy as he took note of the Wanderer. He stepped up his own pace, though not as much as the boys. Kiran appeared to be sleeping in his arms.

The boys eventually reached the foot of the outcropped rock formation. They were both breathing hard with looks of anticipation on their faces. Evan and Finn both wore grins as they looked up toward the Wanderer.

The man stood still, facing west and staring intently through the binoculars he held to his face. He appeared to not have moved since they first saw him take position on the low summit. Several more moments passed in silence as the boys stared first at the Wanderer and then at one another.

Terran finally arrived and set Kiran lightly to the ground. She was awake and looking at the boys. She smiled broadly when her eyes met Evan's. He smiled as well and both looked away quickly. The Wanderer remained silent even as he lowered the binoculars.

"What is it? What's wrong?" Terran's query invaded the quiet without preamble. "Something's wrong, isn't it?"

Without turning to face the group, the Wanderer spoke evenly over his shoulder. "There is trouble ahead. I'm not sure what it is, but something is definitely wrong."

Evan made the brief climb to the Wanderer's position. He stared into the distance but saw nothing that caught his attention. The Wanderer gave him the binoculars. He looked in the direction the Wanderer had been staring. He noticed several clusters of trees and a sliver of road winding out of the deep west and turning to the north. Then he saw it. Smoke. It wasn't much, but it was there. A thin line far in the distance. Its source was hidden behind the trees. But it appeared to be near, if not on, the roadway. Evan returned the binoculars to the Wanderer, who looked upon him gravely.

"We don't have to keep going that way, do we?" Evan almost whispered. The Wanderer only turned and returned to the hardpan. Evan instinctively understood the dangers. The fire meant people. Most likely a certain type of people. People unafraid of starting fires in the open, near a roadway were normally not the type to cross paths with. It was almost certainly a group of marauders. Only they would be so bold. And judging by the amount of smoke it was a large fire that meant a large group of men. Evan hoped the Wanderer would be able to get them around the marauders.

Terran stood in front of the Wanderer as he stepped onto the desert floor. His eyes pleaded with the strange man as he attempted to keep the tremor out of his voice. "What is it? Is it something new to threaten us?"

The Wanderer looked back into the weary man's eyes briefly before responding. "I don't know who or what it is. There is smoke coming from the roadway more than a mile in the distance. We have to get to that roadway from this direction before dark. If we don't..." He paused as he glanced at Terran's children. "If we don't there will be danger."

Terran looked at his children. Since the death of his wife he had never felt the possibility of hope for his children until he met the Wanderer. Hope. It had turned into an almost foreign concept. But now? It infused his very essence. His soul ached with it nearly as much as his bones and sinews ached with the weariness garnered from the march through the open, harsh desert. Here was hope incarnate. Or so he wanted to believe.

The Wanderer, and what he might well represent, gave him strength to risk himself in ways he never would have before. If there were any way to save the most important remnant of his family he would give his all to achieve it.

He nodded slowly as he looked back at the Wanderer.

The Wanderer indicated a water break by sitting in the shade on the eastern side of the rock formation. The others followed suit as Evan returned to the group from the low perch on the rock. Everyone sipped slowly of their water and snacked on dried meat and nuts. After only a few minutes the Wanderer stood and shouldered his pack. It was time to move again. Kiran stood and walked over to her father.

"Papa, you must allow me to walk on my own." Before he could protest or offer any resistance, Kiran held up a hand. "I know you are worried, father. But you have suffered for some time while I have grown stronger. I can walk this last distance to our destination. And if I grow too weary and am unable to keep pace I will let you know. I will let you carry me again."

"Child--" Terran began, but he stopped. He had been prepared to make her travel in his arms again. But looking at her he could see she was indeed better. Healthier. He was definitely more tired than he wanted to admit. And every muscle in his body seemed to ache. He looked at the straight and tireless back of the Wanderer as he cinched his pack into place. He saw the boys securing a few loose items on the wagon with renewed energy following the short break they had just shared. He then took stock of his own weariness.

Looking upon his daughter again, he simply nodded and spoke softly, "Alright. Alright."

The Wanderer again took the lead as the group fell into place behind him. This time Kiran walked ahead of her father with the boys. Terran was comfortable walking behind his children and watching them interact with their new friend. The miracle boy. The one who had saved his daughter. Looking farther ahead he tried to draw strength from the immutable back of the Wanderer.

Each step took them closer to the source of the smoke that waited less than two miles distant.

Holden was jolted from a dreamless sleep. The vehicle lurched repeatedly as it slowed to a crawl. Holden looked out the window as they unceremoniously exited the roadway and struck a tree. He looked through the glass partition into the driver's area and noted the soldier slumped forward, motionless. Holden immediately opened the rear door and got out of the vehicle. A strong odor of ozone overwhelmed him. Thick white smoke was beginning to waft out of the front end of the vehicle. He opened the driver's door and checked on the soldier: alive but unconscious. Holden noticed a decent amount of blood on the upright portion of the driver's seat and saw the soldier's back was tacky with it as well. Apparently he had not escaped the previous night's firefight unscathed.

The smoke was becoming thicker and beginning to fill the inside of the vehicle as well. Holden hooked his hands under the arms of the young man and pulled him from the car, dragging him to the opposite side of the two-lane roadway. He was light-headed and nearly lost consciousness. He had not fully recovered from his own ordeal. His neck throbbed and his head ached. He felt a wave of nausea pass over him and he fought an urge vomit. He lost the battle. Retching uncontrollably for what felt an eternity he then fainted and was out for several minutes. He awoke to flames devouring the front end of the car on the opposite side of the roadway.

The soldier lay beside him, still unconscious. Holden looked around, taking note of their surroundings. They were on the fringe of a moderately large forestland. The road before them was well used but in good condition. Any supplies they might have would be in the car. The car currently beginning to burn freely. Holden stood and looked over at the burning vehicle. He noticed flames at the front end and entering the front seat area. The rear was not yet on fire. He walked across the roadway and approached the vehicle's rear door. Heat met him as he came near, and he wasn't sure he would actually make it to the car.

He reached the door and opened it. A wave of heat pushed him back. He raised his hands instinctively to shield his face. He crawled inside to retrieve as many supplies as he could. He filled his own pack that he had left in the car earlier. Grabbing as many things as he could while holding his breath he stumbled out of the vehicle and made his way back to the opposite shoulder. The young man stirred briefly, looking up into Holden's face.

"Who...who are you?" He was struggling to rise to a sitting position. Holden dropped the supplies he had rescued.

"Relax. I'm the one you rescued yesterday. You need to relax." Holden retrieved a canteen and knelt beside the soldier. He held it to the young man's lips. "Drink some water."

The young man began to drink greedily before a coughing fit overcame him. Blood filled his mouth and he spat red onto the ground. He wheezed as he attempted to catch his breath and hold onto consciousness. Holden knew the injury was bad. He had seen his fair share of deaths from gunshot wounds lately. He tried to help as best he could. He did not think the soldier would last the day without medical attention. Holden was no healer and had little experience attending such injuries. A lung had been pierced and that most surely spelled death for the young man.

He seated himself near the soldier and lifted the man's head. He gave him some more water.

"Drink, but more slowly this time."

The young man did so, sipping some water then resting briefly before drinking more. After multiple sips he pulled away from the canteen. His breathing rattled in his chest. He was fighting the urge to cough, but could not stop it. Again he hacked up more blood. Its bright red hue indicated the wound still bled freely within him.

Holden laid the man's head gently on the earth and began rummaging through some of the supplies he had gathered from the vehicle. One of the recovered items was a medical bag. He looked for several moments until he found what he needed. Using a needle and syringe he drew a fair amount of morphine from a vial and returned to the soldier. The young man looked into his eyes. He opened his mouth to speak, but Holden stopped him with an upraised hand.

"Listen carefully." He spoke slowly and surely to help relax the young man. "I am no healer, but I have seen this type of wound. Your lung is pierced. You have a lot of bleeding internally and externally." He took a deep breath to steady himself. "I need to tend the wound in your back if you're going to have any chance of surviving. I have to stop the bleeding." He said nothing about the blood in the man's lung.

They looked at each other for several moments before the young man nodded. Holden knelt beside him and carefully removed his hauberk and body armor. The soldier grunted softly when the armor was removed from him. A rifle round had indeed made its way through the armor and had entered the man's back. The wound was still seeping blood. Knowing the pain he was about to cause the young man, Holden prepared the needle for injection.

"I'm going to inject this in your thigh because...well just because. I'll do it quickly and you should feel it fairly quickly. You'll likely feel pretty loopy for a moment, then fall asleep." Hopefully it wouldn't be enough morphine to kill him. Holden didn't know how much was too much. The soldier nodded again and without further preamble Holden jabbed the needle and emptied the syringe into the young man's left thigh. The blue eyes widened and glared at Holden briefly. A sharp intake of breath was the only sound the soldier made as he gritted his teeth. He then began breathing deeply as he relaxed himself. After a few moments his body began relaxing and he smiled wanly at Holden.

Holden hoped the drugs would not kill the young man. But he'd had no choice. He needed to act quickly to mend what he could. If he did nothing the man would surely die. Even if he were successful with this quick fix the man would likely still perish out in the wilderness. He pushed aside the thoughts attempting to crowd in on him. He needed to act now. The soldier opened his mouth to speak, but only unintelligible murmuring escaped his lips. Holden nodded and smiled at the young man and watched him until he passed into a deep sleep. He then moved as quickly as his tired body would allow.

He removed the undershirt from the young soldier and turned him onto his right side. Using water from the canteen he cleaned the wound as best he could. He then opened the small packet he had found inside the medical bag. He poured the crystalline substance directly onto the wound. It was a fast-acting coagulant. He had seen it used before on a wound similar to this one, albeit much sooner. Using his finger he plunged the substance deeper into the wound. The soldier grunted slightly but did not awaken. He did, however, begin to cough reflexively spraying a new shower of red from his mouth. Holden hoped the young man had not lost too much blood. Again pushing such thoughts aside he continued working. He applied more of the coagulant to the wound once he was satisfied he had gotten it deep enough. He used the entire pack on the wound before moving on.

The pack containing the coagulant had been in a larger plastic bag. He placed the clear plastic bag over the wound, more than completely covering it. He made sure of his timing, placing it on the wound after the young man had taken in a full breath. He then secured the plastic on the wound with a wrap around the torso of the soldier. That last required him to use nearly every bit of energy he had at his disposal. He had to lift the unconscious man several times to get the wrap around him.

After he finished dressing the wound he sat back and watched the burning vehicle. Though it had been fully engulfed while he had worked on the young man it was now nearly completely consumed. He ate some dried meat from his pack and drank some water from the canteen. The soldier breathed evenly, though the fluid rattle remained. The red stain of his life's water colored his lips, drying on his cheek and being swallowed by the thirsty earth. Holden watched the smoke rise from the vehicle, marking its progress into the early evening. Night would arrive in a few hours, bringing its own perils. But Holden had no room in his wearied consciousness for such concerns. He could only watch the smoke rise and hope against hope that he could conjure some way out of this situation.

His last thought as he drifted into sleep was of the young woman who had saved him. Whatever had happened to her?

The Wanderer had slowed to a more manageable pace as the quintet exited the rocky escarpment and entered more wooded terrain. The smoke could be seen above the tree line, but its source was not yet visible. The smell, however, was in the air. They were drawing near. The Wanderer had not spoken since they had begun toward the source of the smoke. They had traversed the open area of the desert and the spottily covered uprising of land littered with rocky outcroppings with some dogged determination. There had been no conversation. No hint of concern from the Wanderer except the need to move forward.

Nearing the first few trees he had slowed somewhat. Now, as they passed through the fringes of the forest, he moved with deliberate stealth. He paused at intervals seeming to listen or scent the air. The group was no longer stretched out but was near enough to discern the change in the Wanderer's demeanor. He was bothered, but no one dared to interrupt. The tension was nearly palpable. Everyone in the group could feel it. Terran's children had taken position at either side of him, each holding a hand. Evan hung near enough to touch the Wanderer, though he dared not. He felt the man's percipience extended to its limits and feared to break his concentration. He tried to stretch his own senses but was unable to understand that which his percipience discerned.

Fear was upon them all. All except the Wanderer. Evan could feel apprehension, but not fear, emanating from the man before him. The fear he felt was his own, Terran's, Kiran's, and Finn's. They feared the unknown dangers. They feared what troubled the Wanderer.

Abruptly the Wanderer turned and faced them. The look on his face seemed to confirm their worst fears. Evan felt an itch within him though he could not place it, could not name it. The Wanderer spoke to Terran.

"No matter what transpires in the next few minutes you must keep moving west."

His words conveyed a sense of urgency and command. Terran could do nothing but acquiesce.

"Yes. Of course," he replied. His eyes were wide and searching. He looked into the Wanderer's face seeking something but apparently not finding it.

The Wanderer quickly knelt in front of Evan, grasping the boy's shoulders. Evan was shocked to find the steely eyes directly before him, probing into him. The hands on either shoulder conveyed more urgency than the words the man spoke.

"You are more important than you know, boy. You have been gifted. Be it God or some other divine providence I know not. But I do know that before this day it has been a lifetime since I have made this vow."

The Wanderer removed his right hand from Evan's shoulder and placed it upon his breast. Head bowed he spoke evenly and with an austerity that resonated with the swath of forest they occupied.

"From this day forth I, Alexander Horatio Sloane, defender of Truth and Light, Knight of the Northern Realm, do hereby swear loyalty, fealty, life and limb to this boy, Evan."

An audible gasp escaped Terran. Evan also was astonished at what was happening. What *was* happening?

"Unto my body's undoing I do make this oath, binding myself freely and willingly to be released from my oath by death alone. I do so swear to bind myself to the life of this boy, Evan, in the presence of the life of the land." The Wanderer looked up into Evan's eyes. Evan wasn't sure but he thought he saw something other than veiled pain for a mere moment. Then that passed as the Wanderer stood and looked into the eyes of Terran.

The father looked back at him and nodded briefly. Tears welled in Terran's eyes. His children looked up at him questioningly. He smiled reassuringly down to their upturned faces. Looking back at the Wanderer he mouthed a silent *Thank You*. The Wanderer nodded curtly and turned as if to walk farther into the forest. Evan's head swirled with questions. He was dumbfounded.

"Wait." His voice sounded feeble and weak to him. He did not expect the Wanderer to stop and was surprised that the man, the knight, did stop. The Wanderer turned to face him again. "I don't understand--"

"Evan." The Wanderer spoke with an air of import. "We don't have much time now. We have to move. Quickly." He looked over Evan's shoulder, in the direction from which they had come. "We have more to worry about other than any words I have spoken. More than the unknown ahead of us. Our hunters are nearly upon us."

Evan turned quickly at that, looking behind them. He had forgotten about their possible pursuers. But now he felt it. The malice at their rear. It was close. Not quite close enough to see, but it was close enough for him to feel. He turned to face the Wanderer again.

"We must keep moving, Evan." His eyes reflected the light of life and shadow of death simultaneously. He pleaded with and commanded Evan with his glance.

Evan felt himself sliding out of place as he looked into the grey orbs. His breathing became shallower. He felt light-headed. With considerable effort he turned to look at his other companions. Terran and Finn appeared ghostly and ephemeral. He seemed to be able to see through them. He tried to speak to them but his own voice seemed to shatter upon the air as if it were losing its place here as well. Panic nudged at his mind, seeking to gain a foothold.

Then he looked at Kiran. She was whole and solid. He focused on her and felt his own weight return to his body. Reality snapped upon him. She smiled shyly. His own smile felt like a grimace on his face.

He turned quickly to the Wanderer again.

"Ok. Lead on then. I'm ready." Not sure of anything at all anymore, except that he definitely was not ready for any of this, Evan spoke with what he hoped passed for a fair amount of confidence. He had waited for the time to travel from the wasted life he had been living. He had waited a long time for the Wanderer. And now he was traveling away on an incredible adventure. And he was more afraid than he could remember ever being in his young life.

The Wanderer stared into Evan's eyes for several seconds before turning and leading them deeper into the woodland. He still paused from time to time while walking as fast as he dared. He would many times stop and turn as if trying to listen ahead and behind them at the same time. They traveled in an arc as they approached the source of the smoke. Within half an hour they reached an area at which the Wanderer halted them. He removed the binoculars from his pack and peered ahead.

After only a few moments he returned the binoculars to his pack and turned to the small company.

"We will move much more quickly now." He looked at Terran. "When I give the word you must all run to the west, in the direction of the setting sun."

He looked at Evan then and his words frightened the boy more than anything he had seen or imagined before. "No matter what, you must keep going. Even if it appears that I am lost to you, you must continue west. I will find you. No matter what, you must not stop." His eyes bore into the boy, seeking and finding acquiescence.

Evan nodded, tears filling his eyes and falling from his face.

The Wanderer turned quickly and led them ahead. Terran stayed close to the children as they followed. Looking at Evan, he was prepared to keep his word to the knight. He appeared to have discovered newfound strength following the Wanderer's revelation. He strode with pride in the presence of one of the land's protectors. He had heard stories of the knights in his youth but had never seen any of them. He thought them all removed from the Southland. Only loose stories recalled their greatness outside the North. Travelers to lands near the great North spoke of passing encounters with knights, but none had ever spoken with or deigned to hope to travel with or be in their care.

Terran swelled with pride. And hope. More than he cared to admit. He pushed himself to limits he only thought he had possessed. He would get his children, and Evan, through the hazard before them. He would strive to equal the charge given by the knight. He would rise above his station in newfound service.

They moved even faster than they had before. The Wanderer seemed to walk with a distinct purpose. Abruptly, the company exited from woods onto the shoulder of the roadway. They were north of the source of the smoke. Some 100 yards south of them on the same shoulder they stood rested the remnants of a smoldering vehicle. The fire was all but extinguished. In the wan light of early sunset they saw another vehicle stopped on the roadway near the burned husk. Five men had already exited the car and were standing near the wreckage. The men looked their way just as the company noticed them.

"Now. Run!" The Wanderer's words surprised Terran and the children. But the father urged the children to move.

Evan looked over his shoulder as he crossed the roadway with the others. Shock took him, and panic stopped him. The Wanderer was moving toward the marauders. He wasn't just moving. He was running. His assault rifle was at the ready as he moved. Terran had moved with his children to the tree line on the opposite side of the roadway. He stopped and called for Evan. The boy hardly heard him.

He was appalled and mesmerized by the Wanderer. Evan watched as the knight fired a barrage of rounds in the direction of the group of marauders. The men had drawn weapons and were firing at the Wanderer. He dodged back into the tree line on the eastern side of the roadway. He disappeared from view as a hand gripped Evan's arm. Evan turned in fright and tried to pull away, but the grip was firm. It took a moment for Evan to recognize Terran. The father was pulling frantically.

"Evan, come! We must hurry! Come, now!"

Evan allowed himself to be led away into the tree line. He moved quickly, and soon he and Terran were running with Kiran and Finn. The other children moved with their father unquestioningly. They trusted him implicitly. Evan felt the devotion flowing between the family members. He was torn. He loved his new friends. But the Wanderer was more. The Wanderer embodied something for which Evan felt compelled. He was unable to explain his connection even to himself. But somehow he felt his own fate tied to that of the Wanderer.

Another barrage of gunfire brought him back to the group. He concentrated on their surroundings. The forestland was thickening on the western side of the roadway. Terran was doing his best to keep the children moving in the right direction, but Evan felt that they were getting off track.

"Wait!" Evan stopped moving and called for Terran and the children to do the same.

"Evan, we must keep moving. The Wanderer, the knight...he said... Evan, we have to go."

The boy stood still. He held up a hand, silencing Terran. He closed his eyes for a brief moment. The others looked at him then at one another. Terran had already been mesmerized by the boy's abilities on more than one occasion. He waited silently. The children did likewise.

Evan had left them briefly, searching outside himself. Gunfire in the near distance registered in his hearing but did not pierce his concentration. He could discern the plight of the Wanderer. The knight was in real danger. He was outnumbered, but his ability was great and the marauders were not as well trained as he. Terran and the children were likely to be in greater danger if they got off course. Evan searched and searched. He continued to look beyond himself, beyond the forest.

Mountains loomed in his mind's eye, and a passage opened before him. He was there. He could see it and could see where they needed to go.

Evan opened his eyes and looked at the family staring at him.

"I know where we need to go. Follow me."

Before Terran could protest, Evan began moving in a more southwesterly direction. The children moved next, and Terran brought up the rear. As more gunfire sounded in the direction of the roadway, Terran offered silent prayers for the Wanderer. They had seen five marauders. But might there have been more?

After separating from his company of travelers, the Wanderer allowed instinct to take over. Without thought he unslung the M-4 from his shoulder and fired several rounds at the marauders as he moved toward them. As expected they scattered and returned fire. He ran into the wood line to the east and continued toward them more slowly. He made an attempt to keep most of them in sight as he moved through the cover of the trees. One of the marauders had moved into the trees on his side of the roadway. The Wanderer could hear him trying to flank him deeper in the woods.

Firing a few more shots at those taking cover at their vehicle, the Wanderer maintained focus on the solo marauder in the woods to his left and front. He then moved deeper into the woods himself and set his pack on the earth at a fallen trunk. He then disappeared into the thickening woods.

The single marauder heard the shots from the solo shooter to his front and left. He continued circling deeper into the woods. After a few moments he thought he was near enough to sight in the shooter. He slowed himself and crept closer. He spotted the man hiding behind a large fallen tree. He crept a little closer and lined up a shot with his own rifle.

"Hey there, you piece of scavenging crap." The marauder called. He sighted down on his target and began to squeeze the trigger when a shot rang out. The impact tore through the marauders groin, destroying the left testicle and severing his femoral artery. He doubled over and looked down into the face of the Wanderer barely uncovered by the lush undergrowth of the forest floor. As he stumbled backward the Wanderer sat up and fired another round from the .40 caliber Glock into the face of the marauder. The body dropped lifeless onto the ground. The Wanderer moved quickly to retrieve his pack and take his next position.

The other marauders had scattered when the shooting started. Some hid behind the car on the roadway while others retreated to the other side of the road. All of them had drawn handguns or covered down on the Wanderer with long guns. They had returned fire at random, not able to clearly sight in their target. After a few moments they began to coordinate their movement toward the target. As they approached they heard two more shots sound out in the near distance. They advanced more cautiously. Two on the same side of the roadway, two on the opposite side.

The first duo of marauders on the same side of the roadway entered the wood line and fanned out. The other marauders continued to move down the other side of the roadway in an attempt to flank the stranger. Four more shots rang out after several moments. The marauders on the far side of the roadway watched the stranger exit the tree line near the vehicles. The man was quickly approaching their vehicle in the roadway.

One of the marauders quickly crossed the roadway, and then both began moving toward the Wanderer. He had moved beyond their vehicle and around a slight bend in the road. The marauder on the western side of the roadway saw him crouched near the two bodies on the shoulder. They had not had a chance earlier to check the soldier and scavenger on the side of the road. The stranger seemed to be intent on that task now. The marauder began to raise his weapon to fire when the stranger whirled and fired a handgun in his direction. Two shots hit him in his body armor and caused him to fire his own weapon wildly. He fell back as the stranger advanced on him. Two more rounds struck him in each thigh as he hit the ground. Another round struck him in the right shoulder. He yelled out in pain.

The stranger now stood above him and fired a final round into his forehead. He only had time to register the grey orbs looking into his own eyes before everything went blank.

The other marauder had made it down the other side of the roadway quickly. He heard the shots being fired as he ascended the roadway and came about the other side of the vehicles. He crossed the roadway with his rifle held at the ready. He saw his comrade lying on the ground, lifeless. He paused and checked his surroundings. There was no movement. He saw the two bodies of the soldier and scavenger on the shoulder. He looked into the tree line and thought he saw something but he was not sure. Then he felt the round hit him in the chest, just before he heard the report of the shot being fired. He rolled to his left and brought his weapon up to fire. He was struck by another round in the throat.

He fell back onto his left side and brought his weapon up and squeezed off several wild shots. The rifle fell useless before him as he tried to stem the flow of blood from his ragged throat. He placed both hands at his neck and breathed deeply. He watched as the man exited the wood line and approached him. The stranger held a rifle at the ready and walked slowly toward him. As the stranger stood above him he noted the grey eyes as the man sighted on his face. He tried to speak but no words could be formed by the ragged hole of his larynx. The shot turned out the lights and all went dark. He never heard the shot.

The Wanderer moved toward the two bodies on the shoulder. He noted the garment of the soldier of the North and the hastily dressed wound. The soldier was near death. He could not help him. He looked upon the other man. The scavenger was wounded but in far better shape; he looked tiredly up into the knight's face. The Wanderer knelt before the two and heard the men approaching behind him a moment too late. He whirled around and fired a shot into the face of the first man. A simultaneous shot echoed from behind the Wanderer. The second marauder fell over with the first.

The Wanderer had fired only one shot. Both marauders were dead. He looked over his shoulder at the scavenger. The injured man held a pistol in his right hand, aimed in the direction of the two recently dead men. Holden stared into the Wanderer's eyes.

"What took you so long?" he asked huskily. He smiled wanly at the Wanderer as he spoke. "I've been waiting a while for you."

He took a deep breath. "Please tell me you're the knight. I pray to any God still willing to listen that you're him. I don't think I have the mental capacity to make it farther."

The Wanderer was taken aback for a moment. He had never seen this man before but thought he should know him.

"How is it you have been seeking me, stranger?"

The man placed the weapon on the ground and sat up. He looked into the Wanderer's pale grey eyes and spoke to the man's heart.

"She told me to seek you. The lady. In my dreams."

The Wanderer only nodded. He helped the young man gather his belongings. When Holden stopped over the young soldier, the Wanderer only shook his head.

"He is too near death. He will not last the night. You have done him a great boon in granting him the ease of the bandage and medicine, but we cannot rescue him." He briefly thought about the boy then just as quickly pushed the thought from his mind.

"My name is Holden. I'm not sure what's happening, but it's bad. Really bad."

The Wanderer spoke more harshly than he meant. "Quiet, Holden. There may be more of those men coming. If you value your life, quiet. We leave now."

114

The Wanderer moved swiftly after gathering a few essentials from the marauders' vehicle. He removed ammunition and magazines from the bodies of the fallen marauders as he left the scene. Holden followed quietly.

The Wanderer led him through the woods to the west.

6 A Path, Divergent

Evan continued forward through the thickening woods. He moved as if possessed with the knowledge of his own doom. Each tree he passed whispered its own secretive knowledge, its own lore, of the coming destruction of the company. They flowed beyond without giving pause to the silent ravings of nature. Evan felt malevolence and pain all around him. He felt the intense fright and apprehension of his companions as they moved farther and farther west.

The terrain worsened as they traveled. The land began to slope upward and become more rocky and harsh. Several times he slipped on pine-covered, rock-littered ground. His hands and knees bled from small wounds opened by the sharp earth. He pushed himself to continue. He felt his breath come in ragged gasps as he looked over his shoulder at his companions. They, too, struggled to continue forward.

As they moved deeper into the forestland they heard the various exchanges of gunfire at their rear. It was probably a good thing that they were so harried on their way; there was no time to voice their shared fears regarding the Wanderer.

Evan led them deeper into the woodland and higher into the landscape. After a time the earth became more rock than dirt. The trees opened to the base of a range of low-lying mountainous protrusions. Without slowing Evan began to climb. Terran stopped and looked up at the heights growing before him.

"Wait!" He called up to Evan and his children, who had begun to follow the boy up the shallow incline. "Is this the way he wants us to go?"

Evan did not stop to answer. He continued up the rocky, sandy slope. Finn was near on his heels. Kiran stopped and turned to face her father.

She looked into his eyes and spoke one word before turning: "Life."

Then she was following Evan and her brother. Terran breathed deeply and began the climb. He was aware of his labored breathing as he ascended higher up the base of the lower mountain. He noticed a low plateau prior to the rise of the mountain proper. He only hoped the boy was leading them to a location on that level patch of land. Their path took them through several twists and turns up the base of the mountain. After what seemed an eternity they reached the plateau. Evan stopped and looked toward the southern side of the mountain, where it joined another set of peaks. Terran was resting briefly on the hard earth. The sun was almost completely set behind the mountain. Somehow, in all the chaos of their run for freedom, Evan had managed to maintain control of the wagon.

Terran was looking back in the direction from which they had come, down the hillside into the forestland. He heard a great commotion and saw movement in the distance. Then the entire company stood and looked into the forest as a great crash and unearthly howl erupted. Every hair on Evan's body stood on end. The beast the Wanderer had warned them about had found them.

"Follow me. We cannot stop here." Evan spoke with an unknown air of authority. He moved more southerly skirting the base of the mountain. He appeared possessed. Terran had no time to waste on watching their rear. The children had begun moving again. He followed without question. They indeed had to keep moving. Whatever followed could not be thwarted by any means they had in their possession. He hurried to keep up with the children.

118

Evan made his way through a narrow pass, pulling the wagon behind him. Ahead of him the pass opened into a shallow valley. Evan continued forward, turning more to the south. He made his way toward an opening in the mountain wall. The mouth of the cave was wide and low. He entered without pausing. Kiran and Finn followed. Terran stopped for a moment outside the cave entrance.

Another blood-curdling shriek behind and below pushed him into the darkness.

Entering the cavernous opening he noticed the electric glow of a lantern. Evan held the light out before him, searching the interior of the cave. He walked slowly about until he found a slight passage near the rear of the cave. He hurried back to the company and handed the lantern to Terran. Immediately he rummaged through the contents of the wagon. He handed small packs to the other children.

"Fill these with food. We won't be able to carry the wagon any farther." The children copied Evan. They likewise filled their bags and placed them on their backs. Terran also filled a sack and made sure to shoulder several water skins. There was still a great amount of provisions left in the wagon. Thoughts turned to the Wanderer as they beheld the full ammunition cans.

Evan removed a small flashlight from another small bag on the wagon. He checked it, and then he shouldered the small bag. Setting the electric lantern on the cave floor, Terran also looked through several other bags and placed another on his shoulder. He stood and looked at his children. Both were frightened, wearing their emotion on their faces. Eyes wide as saucers they looked at him, waiting. He looked at the boy. Evan also was frightened, but the look he wore was different. The fear was not so evident. Terran could not place it, and there was no time to try.

I can do this, Terran thought he might have spoken aloud but was not sure. The children were waiting.

"Okay. Let's move." He turned and began walking toward the interior passage. Kiran, Finn, and Evan fell in behind him.

The rocky passage twisted and turned. It seemed to lead upward for quite some time and then abruptly take a downward grade. For some time it remained wide enough for the company to walk two abreast. Kiran walked with her father when able: Finn remained with Evan. They moved with as much haste as the passage allowed.

Evan watched as the light from Terran's lamp bobbed and weaved ahead of him. Many times it disappeared as the passage turned sharply upon itself. As he struggled to keep pace and not lose sight of Terran, he fought the urge to keep the flashlight on. Whenever necessary he turned the light on only when he could not see by the light of the lamp. The floor of the passage was treacherous. Littered with craggy fissures and uneven rock, the ground seemed to reach up and trip him with each step. After only a few minutes in the passage he felt Finn's hand take his. He gladly held onto the younger boy's hand as much for himself as for Finn.

When the passage thinned so as to allow the company to travel only in single file, Evan was forced to keep the flashlight on as he brought up the rear. He had seen additional batteries in the small pack, but there were only a few. He was trying to conserve them as best he could. They had slowed quite a bit. The passage sloped downward considerably at this point.

The air had cooled and had become staler. Evan noticed plumes of vapor coming from each exhale of breath. His breathing was becoming labored. The muscles of his thighs and back burned with exertion.

The company came to a halt as they entered a larger opening. Terran's breathing was shallow. Kiran held her

120

father's hand and also seemed near exhaustion. Finn was healthier and not nearly as tired. He stood near his father and sister with concern for them both. Evan looked upon them in the electric light and felt a brief pang of pity. Things would get worse before they got any better. They had to keep moving. Ahead of them was life. Life. At their rear, coming for them, death. It would not stop. It would keep coming until it found them or until it was stopped. He was not sure of the Wanderer. He could not sense him. And there was no help outside of him. They would have to keep moving or die.

"We cannot stop here. We have to keep moving."

Terran looked incredulously at Evan. He had traveled across a desert into an unknown land at the urging of the Wanderer. And now the boy was pushing him farther. His body ached to its very core. He was beneath an unimaginable weight of mountain. Lost in a winding cavern. Running from a monster that his mind could not comprehend. And this boy continued to compel him onward.

He looked at his children. He took note of the many small cuts and bruises they had suffered. The many pains they suffered. This ought not be. His children ought not have to suffer so. His will began to falter. A shudder began to take him as the immensity of their plight fell upon him. His mind faltered in indecisiveness as a bleakness cast its pall upon his consciousness. His eyes closed as he fell into himself. Despair was upon him and he had no defense. What hope was there for them? He could not do this.

Then the boy touched him.

Evan had silently moved directly before him. The boy's hand barely touched his cheek, wiping a precious tear that had traveled from his eye. That simple act invigorated him. Hope was here with them. The boy had saved his daughter once. Terran had no understanding of the workings of the world any longer. The only thing that mattered to him was saving the lives of his children. He was not sure of anything else. But he would give all for them. God help him.

As he straightened his back and readjusted the straps on his shoulder, they all heard the echo of a howl much farther back in the direction they had just come. Their pursuers were in the tunnel. They had no way of knowing how much distance they had put between themselves and the monster.

Though startled, they were not daunted. Terran continued forward. Kiran stayed at his side holding his free hand. Finn paused a moment, smiling sadly at Evan before moving to keep pace with his father. Evan steadied himself with a deep breath before moving forward.

They delved deeper into the mountain.

Holden strove to keep pace with the Wanderer. The man moved fluidly through the thickening woods. He flowed between the trees, eyes searching before and around him at all times. Holden was amazed at his speed, considering the Wanderer carried twice as much weight in his considerable pack as did Holden. The sun had fallen behind the crest of the mountains that rose before them. In twilight they glided, making little noise on the forest floor.

Ahead of them something else traveled. The Wanderer paused briefly and listened. Holden heard and felt something much farther ahead at the base of the mountain they approached. The Wanderer began moving ahead slowly until they came across the path made by several careless travelers. The Wanderer stooped briefly and touched several nearby trees and looked intently at the ground.

The man turned and looked intensely into Holden's eyes.

"Hurry. I have companions ahead and they are hunted."

An eerie wail pierced the preternatural silence of the forest. The shriek came from farther up the mountain.

The Wanderer immediately moved at an unbelievable pace. He nearly sprinted toward the mountain. Holden gave chase, keeping the Wanderer near. As they exited the deep woodland many minutes later and began the upward climb to the mountain base, he wondered who or what would dare hunt this man's companions.

They continued onward and upward, their progress slowed by their ascent and the relentless pull of gravity. Eventually the air began to take on an unpleasant odor. Though Holden could not place it, he instinctively felt its wrongness. Upon the plateau and further toward the cave entrance the scent lingered and grew. When the duo entered the cave the odor was nearly palpable. Musk, dirt, blood, rotting flesh, malevolence. Holden tasted bile at the back of his throat and fought an urge to vomit.

It had become dark outside the cave, and inside there was nearly no visibility. Night was settling upon the land. Holden had no source of illumination. The Wanderer removed a flashlight from his pack and searched the cavern. He found the wagon near the rear wall. He approached and noticed many of the supplies removed. He gave a quick visual search of what remained and decided on a few items that he hastily shoved into his pack. He took only one ammunition can. If they survived the coming encounter he would have to find more ammo. He was thankful that most of the food and water had already been taken.

Holden, continuing to battle a gag reflex, stood nearby as the Wanderer stooped over the wagon. Unable to remain silent any longer he asked, "What is that smell?"

"It is what hunts my friends. They are known by a few names, the most common being a Stalker. It will not stop until it kills them." The Wanderer stood quickly and moved toward the interior passage opening. Holden felt fear pulling at him, urging him to turn back. The scent was so strong here. The Wanderer was reloading the magazine from his M-4.

"I must continue forward, stranger. If the lady bade you seek me, then your path lies with mine. But it is your choice." At that the Wanderer turned and began through the smaller passage.

Holden only paused briefly, thinking how much his life had changed in the past two days. He then hurried after the Wanderer into the passageway. He caught up with the gunfighter quickly and they moved side-by-side for a time until they were unable to do so. When the passage narrowed Holden fell in behind the strange man, attempting to keep up with him. Falling several times to his hands and knees, Holden scrambled to keep pace. He suffered innumerable scrapes and abrasions. Ignoring them he fought to keep down a growing apprehension that he might be approaching his own death deep within the mountain.

The odor of sweat, decay, and putrefaction grew stronger as they moved. They descended for a time until they entered a larger chamber. The Wanderer stopped briefly and seemed to gather himself. Holden stood with hands upon his knees as he gasped for air. The Wanderer panned the light around the small chamber, finding the continuation of the passage. He began moving forward.

"Wait." Holden panted. He looked pleadingly at the Wanderer. Then he vomited what little he had in his stomach onto the floor. He panted sickly for only a moment. He looked up at the Wanderer and smiled as best he could.

"Okay, now I'm ready."

The Wanderer might have smiled or grimaced; Holden could not tell in the indirect light of the flashlight. Then the man turned and started moving again. Holden followed again, concentrating on keeping pace. At odd intervals the light began to reveal his breath coming in wispy, vaporous exhalations. Holden barely noticed the slight chill in the stale air; his body's exertions kept him warm.

The Wanderer pushed himself physically, but his mind remained calm throughout. His thoughts turned to the impossibilities come to light by the boy. The Wanderer had told the company to continue west. But how in all the earth had they managed to find this entrance to this pass? This, the pass he had intended on taking. Even as they scrambled through narrow passages, he noticed that they had managed to continue on the correct path as the passage split at different locations. How could the boy know? He hoped that he was not too far behind. He knew where the pass led and had only one chance to help the company of travelers ahead of him. One chance to save the boy.

He veered right at a sudden split in the passage. The air became considerably more tolerable. The stench of the Stalker immediately dissipated, and the air became cooler as well. The passage maintained a steadily rising incline. After what seemed an intolerable amount of time he and Holden exited onto a brief promontory within an immense chasm. The passage continued on to their right. The Wanderer immediately looked down and across the expanse. He was searching with his flashlight, slowly panning the beam of light across the chasm.

An almost imperceptible rumble in the bedrock of the mountain reverberated through his boots. He stepped away from the edge of the chasm.

Impossible.

"What's impossible?" Holden asked between panting breaths as he stood on the natural platform (though much nearer the wall of rock at the passage's opening).

The Wanderer was not aware that he had spoken aloud.

Another rumble, this one loosing rock millennia old, shook them without question. Holden fell to the floor, cursing. After stepping from the edge of the precipice and regaining his footing, the Wanderer approached the edge and peered into the gloom. He was not using his flashlight. After a moment he peered across the chasm again. He then removed his binoculars and searched again. Scanning the lower side of the great span he muttered his own curse and unslung the covered rifle with the high-powered scope. He knelt and began sighting in and firing shots across the chasm. After four shots he was forced to stop. The earth began to shake again with even more force.

Pieces of rock began to fall nearby, some striking their path to the right.

The Wanderer took time to look down the chasm again and quickly shouldered his rifle. Flashlight in hand, he turned and began running up the slope to the right. His gruff, "Hurry!" was unnecessary as Holden was quick on his heels.

Holden noticed as they ran that the air was no longer cold. It wasn't even cool. He was sweating profusely. And he could see his surroundings in an ever-increasing red haze. After nearly a minute of running the two reached another landing. The Wanderer turned and watched just as an incredible red explosion of magma erupted into the lower portion of the chasm below them.

Holden watched in disbelief as the molten rock violently began to fill the massive cavern. The opposite side of the massive vault appeared more than 300 yards distant and was more difficult to discern through the searing haze rising from the fiery flow beneath them. He was able to barely make out what appeared to be a figure within the magma splashing about wildly. It was then that the shrieks began to reach them. The creature that had been hunting the Wanderer's companions was struggling madly in the fiery flow. For a brief moment Holden thought he could actually see the creature's red-rimmed eyes across the distance. It appeared to have stopped struggling and after a few more moments it finally was consumed in the molten rock.

Neither the Wanderer nor Holden could discern any other person or living thing in the distance.

Several moments passed as the Wanderer watched the flow creep higher. It began to flow into the passage on the opposite side of the cavern. It was the passage to which the left turn in the split would have taken him. It was the passage he hoped his small company had reached before the partial eruption. He had little time to contemplate as the magma continued to rise in the chamber. The passage on the other side was 30 yards below their own perch. They had to hurry into their own passage.

He turned and led Holden farther up through the passage. Holden was happy to follow. The heat was becoming intolerable. More than that he needed the simple act of movement and base survival instincts to return his mind from the horror of the burning creature in the chasm. Even with the heat of the great furnace pushing at his back, he shivered as the image replayed itself over and over in his mind.

Dear God! he thought. *What...in...God's...name?* He had just looked upon evil. An evil that had gazed across the span of the rising lake of magma. An evil that through burning eyes had seen him and looked into him. And smiled. He could feel, more than hear, a deranged laughter. Insane cackling filled his thoughts, his mind, his ears. He covered his ears and closed his eyes. He tried to scream before realizing the laughter was coming from him.

The Wanderer slapped him so hard he fell to the ground. Holden looked up at the man who was now reaching out to help him to his feet.

"I am sorry, friend. I was not aware you had locked eyes with the Stalker. It's glare--." He paused briefly. "It places a glamour upon those whose gaze it meets."

Holden grasped the Wanderer's hand and was pulled roughly to his feet.

"We have to keep moving. The flow has slowed, but it continues and will likely make it through these passages and to the surface. We need to get out of the passage and onto the mountainside soon."

The Wanderer motioned Holden to the lead. Holden shook his head quickly and began moving forward unsteadily. After only a few steps he began to regain himself and his pace quickened as they moved up the passage. He asked over his shoulder, "How far behind had I fallen before you realized I was no longer following?"

"I was more than 30 paces ahead when your laughter began." The Wanderer paused briefly. "Again, I apologize for needing to strike you so. It should not have been."

Holden thought he heard a touch of self-reproach in the Wanderer's voice. He did not push the matter. He had failed others and himself on more occasions than he cared to remember. He continued forward in silence for some time.

After several hours the passage leveled and straightened more or less. It widened, and the two men walked abreast. Their pace quickened even more. The Wanderer took long, even strides and Holden fought to keep up with him. Less than an hour later they exited onto a high ledge overlooking the northern night sky. The Wanderer continued onto the western side of the ledge, making his way farther away from the cave opening, before beginning a modest descent toward the west.

Holden was content to breathe the cool, open air. He followed silently, nursing his injured psyche. The eyes of the Stalker still burned within him. Slight beads of sweat crowded his brow. He wiped at them absently and concentrated on the straight back of the Wanderer. Each step was a struggle, but he refused to give up. His muscles quivered as he walked. His mind was a jumbled mix of troubling images: the monster in the magma, escape from Northern Alley, the princess, the lady of his dream, his own unlikely victorious gunfight. Thoughts of the princess steadied him. He focused on her slight frame, her kind eyes, her concern for a stranger such as he. He focused on that indefinable quality which consumed her and which he had felt reach out to him. Her concern. Her love.

Holden focused on her and maintained the strength to keep moving. He also maintained his sanity in the process. The Wanderer continually glanced about as he moved, the flashlight dancing in his grasp. He watched the path at their feet and farther ahead. He also kept a continual eye upon Holden. He knew of few men could withstand the gaze of a Stalker and survive. Of those, most eventually went utterly insane. He personally knew of only two men had looked full upon the Stalker's gaze and survived with no ill effects. He, himself, was one such. The other was someone for whom he had sought for many years.

The two men reached the base of the mountain just before midnight.

Evan easily stayed within view of Terran and his children as they ran through the tunnel ahead of him. He could feel the exertion flowing from their bodies in waves. They were nearly exhausted from the forced run through the darkness. They had been in the dark tunnels for nearly an hour. Their path led them down as it grew narrower. Eventually the passage opened onto a broad ledge. The company trudged out onto the expanse as Terran attempted to gaze forward into the dark abyss before him. He held out the lamp and peered ahead incredulously. He could not see the far wall or the bottom.

Evan stood at the rear of the company and peered into the passage behind them. He extended his percipience farther into the coil of tunnels to their rear. His eyes closed as he went farther and farther away from his friends and sought out his pursuers. They were there, just beyond his reach. He could get close, but something repelled him. He began to feel a crawling sensation on his skin. Ants, beetles, flies, wasps, cicadas; they were all landing upon him in ever-increasing numbers. Their buzzing filled his ears. Dark, dank earth consumed his nostrils. The scent held hints of decaying plant and animal life. Evan began to shake as his body tried to revolt against the intrusion of the creature. The steadily coming creature. They had managed to gain some distance as they traveled through the more narrow passages, but once the monster reached the abysmal cavern it would move with great speed as it had in the open desert and forest.

Evan began to return to himself when he felt the monster reach out with its own percipience. It seemed to sense his spirit nearby. It stopped moving briefly and laughed. The sound caused the squirming insects on Evan's skin to rush to cover all his body. For the briefest moment Evan was caught and held by the guttural guffaws he heard in his head. Then he was able to break free and rush back into himself. When he opened his eyes Kiran stared into them. Her concern was unmistakable.

"I'm all right." Evan offered her a quick smile as he gave her hand a brief squeeze. She immediately smiled in return before looking into the passage at their rear. She faced him again, the question known before she asked.

"Are they close?"

"Yes. We have to hurry." He began to pull her toward the ledge to the left of their current perch. The ledge was not more than five feet in width and traveled at a slight ascent. The light of Terran's lantern pierced far enough ahead for them to run at a good pace. Terran did not hesitate to move at Evan's urging. He led them forward again. Evan kept his flashlight on as he brought up the rear. He trotted easily behind his friends, knowing that they would not reach the next passage, the one they needed to reach to continue their journey. Even if they reached it in time the creature would catch them in the next set of catacombs. They were too exhausted to keep their hurried pace.

Terran did not know how near the threat was behind them. He only knew to keep moving, to keep pushing himself, to keep his children safe. He was armed with his crossbow, but the weapon hung on his back useless. He believed the Wanderer in his description of the unnatural beast that pursued them. They needed to escape. Without the protection of the Wanderer they had no other recourse. They must run until there was no place left to flee. His only thought was to keep moving, moving, moving; when the crash of the beast entering the chasm reached his ears he almost did not register it. Instinctively he looked back and saw that Evan had stopped and turned to face their rear as well. Evan had stopped several moments before Terran. He was more than 20 running strides behind them.

"Ev-!"

His voice caught in his throat. He was about to call out to the boy but was unable to do so. He realized that the only reason he was able to see the boy was that he was outlined in glowing luminescence. The light from his lantern did not reach back that far. A soft amber glow emanated from around Evan as he faced backward, down the slope. His arms were extended out before him and rising slowly. The ground beneath Terran trembled and he was left without his wits. He struggled within himself for but a moment before giving the lantern to his daughter and sending her and Finn onward up the rise. He watched for a brief second as they continued running. Then he turned and quickly began walking toward the boy.

Evan had been running at the rear of the company. He had not known what was going to happen. He knew that they were doomed if they could not stop the beast behind them. They would not be able to outrun it. He felt the creature's impossible energy moments before it burst through the passage opening. Evan had stopped and turned to face it. They had made it more than three-fourths of the way up the rise to the next passage, but that was not enough to escape. The thing would get them before they even took ten paces in the passage, if they could even reach the passage in time. Evan knew that he had to try something.

He had felt a growing strength within him as he made it out of the desert and into the forestland. That presence within him seemed to become even stronger after entering the caves and traveling deeper into the mountain. There was great power here and it called to him. It whispered to him in catches, as he touched bare rock and soil. As his desperation mounted, as he turned to face the beast a few hundred paces to his rear, he tapped into that power.

And he called it to his service.

The creature seemed to explode onto the landing they had moments before occupied. Rock, dust, debris cascaded down the chasm. Evan's eyes were closed, but he could see the beast clearly. It vaguely resembled a man in that it had two legs, an upright torso, two arms, and a head on top. There the resemblance ended. The creature was an utter abomination. Whatever devilry, sorcery, or aberration of science had created the beast had made a mockery of the beauty of creation. It was filthy and covered in open sores. Its skin was more hide than anything else. The hide was a sickly pale grey color, with mottled patches or tufts of black fur at odd intervals throughout. Its legs were massive trunks of muscle. And the arms were almost a foot longer than any man's. They too were ripe with musculature. Evan realized the length of the arms allowed the thing to run on all fours.

Eyes closed, he allowed himself to be exposed to the full extent of the creature's virulence. He was too overcome by the power opening itself to him to be concerned about any ill effects. He had to save his friends and himself. The monster poured out its malice toward Evan. He heard the slow cackle from the mouth of the beast. With his percipience he looked into the gaping maw as the thing laughed and slowly began to move onto the ledge. The face of the beast was centered about a large, gaping mouth filled with rows of multitudinous sharp teeth. There were nothing more than imperceptible slits where a nose should have been. And it had large obsidian eyes limned in glowing red. It stared right at Evan, sucking at his will, drawing upon its vast reserves of hatred and its stark need to feed to fell him.

Evan was too full of his own newfound power to heed the call of the beast. It was there. He felt it. But he was not compelled. Raw earthen energy filled him to near bursting. All fear was burned away. It was replaced by a bubbling ecstasy. He smiled at the creature. The beast hissed and began to move quickly up the slope.

Several loud cracks echoed within the massive chamber as the creature dropped to all fours and began to run up the slope. Somewhere nearby a rifle was being fired. Three of four rounds struck the beast in his upper torso but did nothing to slow its charge. Its thick hide and iron-like musculature absorbed the rounds like natural body armor.

Terran reached the boy just as Evan's arms jerked up above his head and the bottom of the chasm erupted in red flame. The ground shook beneath their feet. Terran instinctively reached out to protect the child, but Evan stood solidly as if the shivering earth had no effect on him. His arms were still raised above his head. A fiery red glow filled the entire chamber and heat rose from the burning abyss.

Terran watched as Evan emphatically dropped his arms back out in front of him and clapped his hands. Evan began to slump to the floor of the ledge just as Terran enveloped the boy into his arms. As he rose fully to his feet he saw the creature coming up the rise toward him. Outlined in the fire-red glow of the flaming magma rising in the cavern, the beast was a demon from hell. Charging on all fours it came with such blazing speed that Terran could do nothing but watch as it closed the distance between them. He did the only thing he could at that moment; he placed the boy behind him and began to unsling his crossbow, knowing he would not get it drawn in time.

Fifteen yards away from the man and boy on the ledge, the Stalker scented the man and boy. He felt the man's fear. The boy was strong, but not strong enough. He would taste even better than the man. As he stretched out his long, lean body in preparation for his final leap and pounce he was struck by a massive chunk of stone. The rocky mineral formation had fallen a great distance, gaining velocity and power in its descent. It took the Stalker and a ten-foot section of the ledge down to the magma below.

Terran watched in disbelief. He stood, shaking, for several moments looking ahead at the new gap in the ledge. He did not realize he was holding his breath until his lungs began to ache. He let out the held breath and fell to his knees. The rising heat brought him back to his straits. He scooped up the boy and ran faster than he would have thought possible. He reached the mouth of the passage quickly. His children waited just inside the opening.

Relief on their faces, shock on his, they continued through the passage. Kiran led the way with the lantern. Finn followed, and Terran maintained the rear while

134

clasping the boy to his breast. The boy had saved his family again. Somehow.

Nothing was to be the same. Nothing.

They traveled through the night. Through twists and turns (though no branching divisions from which to choose) they traveled an upward slope. Terran lost all concept of the passage of time. After a time the heat and light from the magma at their rear receded and did not return. They traveled by the light of the lantern. After an eternity they exited the cave and stood on a large shelf of rock. Night stars greeted them silently in a cloudless canopy. Terran looked up into the night sky and breathed deeply. He looked at his children and stifled an urge to weep. They had endured so much. They were beset by bumps, bruises, abrasions, lacerations; dust, dirt, grime; and pain, loss, the constant threat of death.

Then he looked into the face of the boy he held in his arms. He too was covered by the same injuries, the same filth, the same shadow of looming demise. But he continued and persevered. And he had saved them. He was hope. Terran heard the pledge given by the Wanderer as it played in his mind. He tried to remember all the words. He felt the import of the boy and understood the reason the knight had revealed himself. The oath was irretrievable, unswayable, immutable. The knight's pledge was itself a promise of hope; the boy was hope's embodiment.

Terran could not recall the exact words, but he felt the import and the meaning of the sentiment. Exhausted and physically failing, Terran looked upon the sleeping boy's face.

"I, too, pledge myself to you, Evan. I take you as my son and promise to do all I can as a father to protect and serve you."

Tears welled in his eyes as he spoke. He thought of the Wanderer, the knight. He hoped the man had escaped the marauders and would be able to find them. He was none too sure exactly where they were to go. Except west.

His children had seated themselves on the shelf of rock and were beginning to doze.

"Kiran. Finn." They both looked up at him, exhaustion painted plainly on their faces. "We cannot rest yet. We need to get away from this cave and make it off the mountain before dawn."

Both children rose to their feet. Terran retrieved the lantern from Kiran and, still carrying Evan, led the children down the mountainside. The trek was difficult and painful, but they made it to the base of the mountain an hour before dawn. Using a collection of large rocks as a natural set of blinds, Terran set up a hasty camp. Aside from the welfare of the three children in his care, his last thought before he drifted off to a dream-filled sleep was regarding the crossbow he had lost in the great cavern.

It was no great matter, he thought. It hadn't proven very useful when danger had presented itself in the caves. It likely would not be of much use hereafter.

Darkness closed about Evan. A depthless cold filled his senses. And the earth seemed to be swallowing him whole. His eyes saw nothing after his final awakening of the mountain. He had called for help and had felt the mountain heed him. He had lost consciousness before the beast had been taken into the chasm. His ears heard nothing. The crash of the rock all around never reached him. Instead he had traveled. He had transcended himself and the present. He had left himself and gone away. And it had not been his doing.

He had been drawn.

He felt a dank, tacky stickiness on his hands and exposed arms, on his back and neck. A fetid odor filled his nostrils. He opened his eyes and saw the dark canopy of the night sky. The innumerable pinpricks of stars lit the clear

136

sky above him. He realized he was lying on his back. Turning his head left and right Evan noticed he was in a muddy ravine. He sat up quickly and looked around more carefully.

He was alone.

The beast was gone. But so too were Evan's friends. He hoped they had all survived the chasm. He tried to imagine their faces and found he was unable. He tried stretching himself toward them. He again was blocked. Something was very wrong. Evan looked down at himself and saw that he was covered in the muck of the ravine. The ground was slick with it. Some putrid runoff seemed to mark its passage in the earth beneath him.

A light mist was creeping into the hollow. As it rapidly filled the slight ravine the stench of decay grew stronger. It seemed to coalesce around him in swirls of malevolence. Evan felt its wrongness and jumped to his feet. He ran to the top of the ravine and stood alone upon a dirt roadway. The road stretched out into the darkness in either direction. The darkness did naught to conceal the desert surrounding him. Evan turned and turned in growing trepidation as he realized his predicament. He was alone in the dark night of the desert. His breathing came more quickly as he fought against himself, seeking control. After a brief moment he noticed the mist again. Though lighter in this more elevated position, it still flowed toward him. Looking in the direction from which the mist seemed to flow, Evan noticed a pale auburn glow in the distance.

Instinctively he stepped backward. The glow was miles distant but far too bright. His percipience did not fail him in this: he looked into the red distance and was pulled into it. His feet continued to propel him backward, but his mind was pulled into the desecration looming in the distance. He felt himself burning within. Fire began to consume him. His flesh ignited. His bones flashed to burning fagots within and his mind wailed. An argent flame escaped his open mouth as a silent rending escaped him.

He tripped and fell over something in the dirt road. First his tailbone, then the back of his head, smacked against the hard earth. Grayness filled his vision as he began to lose consciousness. The swirling mist tugged at him, calling for him to lie still, leeching at his will. Then he heard a faint, soothing whisper in the night. Eyes fluttering he sat up, careful to aver his vision from the east. The glow from the east continued to burn into him. Slowly he stood. The mist clung to him, pulling at him, demanding his surrender. It now covered his feet completely.

The voice spoke softly to him again. It called from the west. Beginning with ginger steps, he started walking toward it. The mist pulled at his feet with each step. He fought against it. But he was so tired. And he hurt all over. Each step into the swirling whiteness drew more energy from him. Numbness spread up from his feet into his legs and throughout his entire being. His heart labored within him. He could feel its slow beat laboring with each step. The lub-dup thrummed in his ears.

The voice called again, urgently. Evan realized he had slowed to a shuffle, his feet not even rising out of the mist to take each step. He was looking down as he moved. The voice jerked his head up, brought his vision to the clear sky in the west. His steps quickened as he kept his head up and his vision forward. He began to trot lightly. His heartbeat quickened to normal in response to his renewed pace.

A howl in the distance behind him pricked his spine. And spurred him forward even more desperately. He moved until the mist dissipated. The night remained, so too the desert.

He had traveled. He was here and not here. He was lost and not lost. He was alive and not alive. He was afraid and not afraid. He had traveled before, but it had never been like this before. This was too intense.

Evan stopped moving and looked around. He chanced a glance behind and noticed the virulent radiance was gone. All was silent. No creatures stirred. He moved forward again and eventually noticed a faint glow before him. Unlike the desecration that sought him from the east, this glow was soft, pleasant, inviting. Instead of drawing forth his percipience and pulling him in, it only invited him forward. Any compulsion to move was his own.

The boy moved at an even pace toward the source of the glow. Time and distance lost meaning when he traveled. One hundred feet or 100 miles, the distance could have been covered in the same time. Briefly, Evan stood before a branch in the roadway. A well-worn path diverged from the roadway to the right: northwest. The light seemed to have moved onto this path. He paused only slightly before taking the split. As he moved the desert transmuted to forest. The forest to low hills. The hills to mountains.

Finally he stood within a deep valley, near a great mountain. The light of dawn was creeping into the sky above the mountain's peak.

"Your path lies here."

Evan turned, startled, and looked into the eyes of the woman behind him. The stark emerald green of those orbs enveloped him. His heart stopped for a moment as he became lost in them. Her long, flowing blond hair fell to her shoulders. Her fair complexion was in stark contrast to the small, yet full, pink lips situated below her small, straight nose. The rosy cheeks were situated on high prominent cheekbones. Her white gown fell full to the ground at her feet. A white glow limned her entirely. Evan could only stare.

"For now, anyway. Your road has been hard, but I fear it will grow harder." She looked beyond Evan. "For all of you." She began to walk toward Evan and for a moment he stiffened at the prospect she might touch him. She walked past him and motioned for him to follow. Evan took a deep breath and regained himself. Then he fell in step with her, though he hung back slightly, afraid to look directly into her eyes again.

"Who are you?" Evan asked shyly.

"A friend, Evan. I have known you for a time, although we have not truly met. I…" She hesitated as they passed a large group of toppled stone and rock. "Evan, you must stay with them. They need you." She looked around a large boulder as she moved away from him. He stared unbelievingly at her. Her speech and demeanor held implications of fathomless portents.

"I don't understand. What's happening to me? Why me?" Evan pleaded with her. The look she returned was one of sadness mingled with gladness.

"I don't know, Evan. I don't have such answers to give." Again she looked away, down toward the ground in the distance. Evan moved to get a better look at what had drawn her gaze. As he turned the corner and looked upon the three sleeping bodies lying on the ground she said, "But I know that no matter what transpires, you must trust yourself and your friends. They are precious. As are you."

Evan looked upon his new friends, his family. As he gazed upon each of their faces in turn he felt tears grow in his eyes. His vision blurred as he blinked, and hot tears rolled down his face. He did not know why he was crying. The multitude of emotions coming out left him confused. Sobs unceremoniously began to rack him. He fell to his knees as the emotion poured out of him.

A hand softly caressed his head.

"All is well, child. All is well. Stay with them and remember to be true. Be true to them: and, more importantly, be true to yourself."

The hand was removed and Evan remained kneeling for a time. He suddenly stood and turned. "What about the Wanderer? What has become of him?"

"Fear not for him. He seeks you even now. He will find you yet again." The voice came to him from a distance. "Sleep now with your friends. And be true. We shall meet again. Soon."

Evan was then lying on bedding between Terran and the children. He closed his eyes and slept.

The first light of dawn lit the tops of the mountains. A light mist covered the floor upon which Evan and the others lay. He slowly sat up and looked at his companions as they slept. Kiran and Finn lay close together to his right. Terran, close to his left. Their exhaustion emanated from them in almost visible hues. Evan looked around and noticed his surroundings. They remained as they were in his dream. Their hasty encampment lay in the midst of several loosed boulders and large stones. The floor upon which they rested showed signs of having recently been covered in loose shale and grit from the mountain's brief awakening.

Looking again at his companions he saw they were covered in numerous cuts, abrasions, contusions, dirt, and grime. They indeed had had a hard road. And it would only grow harder.

He quietly gained his feet and took stock of himself. He too was covered in uncounted wounds. But he was shocked to note that dried muck clung to his clothing, arms, and legs. He touched the back of his head and felt the dried mud there.

The dream came to him with astounding suddenness. The cold, wet earth; the mist; the conflagration in the east; the lady limned in luminescence. It all came to him with such stark clarity that he stumbled forward. His breath caught in his chest as he gasped a sharp intake of breath.

He had confronted a monster, the monster described by the Wanderer. Then he had gone away from himself, away from his companions. He had traveled in the night. The fact he had traveled was not entirely new to him. He had done so before but only on a few occasions. He had seen things and people in those incidents. He had remembered important details at opportune moments that had helped keep him safe. But all those times before had been as a dream. Thoughts whispered in brief remembrances. This time was much different.

This time he had actually been gone from this place while still being in this place. He had left himself in ways he could not explain. And he remembered everything with startling clarity. No detail was lost to him. The sickening touch of the mist and the malice in the glow from the east. He felt the pull on him even now.

And he remembered the lady. She was a vision he would ever hold within. He was drawn to her in ways he could not comprehend. Her soft, yet severe, countenance held sway over his thoughts. He wanted to see her yet again, to revel in her soft glow. She was a beacon in his mind's eye.

A stirring from his companions drew his attention from his brief reverie. He turned and looked into the perplexed visage of Kiran. She looked upon him with nothing short of unadulterated love in her eyes. Evan felt a sharp sting of guilt within and looked away quickly. Kiran was real, and he had shared himself within her when he had healed her. And he had unwittingly shown himself to her in the process. They had become connected in ways no one would ever comprehend. He could not yet comprehend them. And so he felt shame as he looked into her beautiful, round eyes.

His obvious discomfort was not lost on her, but her concern for his well-being overshadowed any other thoughts she might have. Looking quickly at her father and brother to make sure they had not been roused, Kiran stood silently and took tentative steps to Evan who had moved several steps away from the sleeping company. She stopped within reach of the boy and waited for him to look at her and speak

Evan's gaze had remained averred as she stood and approached. After only a few moments that seemed an eternity he looked into her eyes and spoke softly. "We cannot stay here much longer. We have to keep moving."

Kiran seemed to be searching for something within his visage as she looked into his eyes. She nodded almost imperceptibly then looked down. A frown creased her brow and she took a deep breath as something seemed to pass from her. Evan felt a sadness settle upon her: a resignation. She had come to some realization. He was uncertain of what he should say. He wanted to comfort her but was not sure how. His heart ached within him. His consternation must have been easily recognizable. Lost within his own ineffectiveness he did not notice Kiran once again looking at him.

"Since the first time I looked upon you, I knew you to be different." Kiran spoke softly, evenly. Her voice was thick with emotion. "You saved me, Evan, and I will forever be..." She paused in uncertainty. "I will forever be thankful. When I awoke from that sleep, when you returned me to my family, I looked upon you. And I felt a thing I had not felt before."

Evan looked into her eyes then and saw the tears forming. His heart pounded in his chest. He became lost in her then. He felt an unbridled desire for rightness resound within him. He felt the promise of beauty and flourishing verdure. Swaths of sounds melodic as waterfalls, the soft soughing rustle of wind over fields of summer blossoms, susurrant waves on smooth crystalline beaches; scents of flowers in bloom, patches of tall grasses growing wildly, crisp and cool airy rightness: all these images and sensations rushed into him and took hold.

Instinctively he stepped forward and took her into his arms. Kiran stiffened only briefly in surprise then she urgently held onto him. Her arms locked around his neck, her face buried into his chest.

No words needed to be spoken. Each felt what the other felt. Evan looked beyond Kiran at the forms of Terran and Finn. He pretended not to notice the boy peeking from one eye. All the same he found it hard not to return the unconcealed smile on Finn's face.

The Wanderer sat at the edge of the rim of light from the small fire he had built. He had recovered enough fuel from the woodlands around the base of the mountain to keep the blaze going through the night and into the morning. He had surveyed their surroundings in the dark as best he could while keeping a wary eye on his new companion. He could discern no immediate threat, and he and Holden desperately needed to rest. The young man was resilient, but he was fading. Their trek down the mountain had not been easy. The Wanderer was tired from his own journey, but he felt the desperate burdens of the sleeping form on the other side of the flames flow over him in waves of exhaustion and consummate struggle.

He had noticed the bandages on the man's neck. The man was weak and recovering from some earlier ordeal. And now he was forced to battle the wicked emanation from the Stalker. The Wanderer could only watch in silence as Holden lay huddled in his blanket, brows knitted fiercely, his mind locked in its own private battle. Normally, he would have left the man alone to his

144

own fate. He would have continued on his own journey. He would have made his way forward to continue after the boy, his charge. But Holden had named the lady. *Damn her!* he thought with a brief snort. Fate had linked them.

The Wanderer looked away from Holden and let his mind wander to thoughts of his company. He hoped they had made it down the western face of the mountain whole and unharmed. He closed his eyes, slowed and evened his breathing; he entered what might have appeared to be a trance-like state. To the unknowing eye he appeared just another sleeping form near the fire. But he had entered a state of hyper-awareness. Shutting his autonomic response to external stimuli he allowed his every sense to be amplified. His sense of perception increased until he could hear the rustle of leaves on nearby trees, smell the scents of nearby nocturnal animals, and feel each step said creature took upon the earth which still thrummed with the receding rumble of the mountain's earlier awakening. All these sensations were translated from his subconscious to his conscious mind in a steady stream of subtle intimations.

In that way he rested.

Holden's slumber was fraught with a very different mental landscape. Though his body rested in what would best be described as unconsciousness, his mind was swept into a whirlwind of sensation. Only the constant wrinkling of his brow belied any internal struggle. His breathing was deep and slow. He lay still, curled in a light blanket.

And his mind battled for its very existence.

A sea of dark virulence engulfed him. Holden could sense nothing but pain. His every nerve was alight with a burning conflagration. In his mind's eye he sensed his dilemma as an internal struggle, but was not consciously aware of its true meaning. It was all too real. It was hell. Every sense was rife with it. Sulfur clogged his nostrils, gagging him with every breath. His skin was alive with the stinging of unseen wasps. Every sinew burned as if alit from within. And yet he persisted. He continued to live. He opened his mouth to scream and his tongue was immediately overcome with flame.

He smelled his flesh as it roasted and then began to char. The sickly sweet scent of meat cooking on an open flame mingled with sulfur on the air. He felt his mind becoming lost in the pain, the unending hell of being burned alive. A fire without end, ceaseless flame. With every nerve maintaining its ability to send signals to his brain. No one could survive such torture. His mind raced with the impossibility of his situation. And he understood.

He was not really here, wherever here was. His mind was lost in some prison. He was not here.

But the pain! It was so real. It consumed him. It demanded his every attention. It was so real.

But it was not. It was only in his mind.

He opened his eyes and looked upon his surroundings. He stood in the midst of a sprawling landscape of ash and soot. He immediately looked himself over and saw that he was still whole. His flesh remained unmarred by the burning flame that had previously ravaged his mind.

The pain, which before had consumed him, evaporated with that realization, and he was startled at its departure. He looked around slowly and noticed the barren wasteland, heat weighing heavily in the air. The odor of sulfur remained. Multitudinous motes of ash and tiny debris floated in the air. Each breath he took was a labor unto itself.

He quickly began to regain himself. This was not real. But in a way it was.

Slowly, Holden turned around and scanned the horizon in each direction. Every vista was the same. The rising haze limited the distance he could effectively see, but he was certain that there was not much to see beyond what his vision could discern. He seemingly stood in the middle of a vast wasteland. But unlike the desert to which he was accustomed, this wasteland was void of all life. The very earth was a smoldering remnant of itself. Ash covered everything.

He took several steps forward and noticed the unnatural warmth at his feet. Looking more closely at the nearby ground he could make out crevices in the earth. From within he saw a red glow emanating with a faint yellowish fume accompanying it. It was then he realized that there was no sunlight. Everything existed in a dull orange haze and the sun was not present above. He slowly scanned the sky overhead and was ultimately at a loss for words to describe the dread that accompanied the sight. A low-lying canopy of murkiness covered the land as far as he could see. There was no sign of daylight, no seeping of sunlight through the deepening coils of gaseous muck hanging above. The sky appeared as charred as the ground upon which he stood.

"Where the hell am I?" Holden whispered to himself. Looking around again, he thought, *And how do I get out of here?*

Absent any recourse other than staying in his current location, he began to walk. He was unsure of any true direction, but he was loath to remain in the middle of such desolation. He moved slowly at first, careful not to step on any of the smaller crevices and charting paths to avoid the larger ones altogether. After a time he began to move more swiftly as he tried to focus on getting to imaginary points in the distance.

Though his path altered as he moved toward his imaginary goals, the landscape remained. Eventually, he slowed his pace and then finally came to a stop when the realization came that there likely was no way to walk out of this place.

"This is not real. I am not really here." He spoke slowly and evenly to himself. "And if this is not real, if it is only in my mind, then I should be able to think my way out." He was struggling to breathe and his lungs hurt. He wiped sweat from his brow as he stood contemplating his situation.

"You are lost, pleasant one."

Holden turned at her voice. It had seemed just over his shoulder, but as he looked all around he saw no one. His heart hammered in his chest with excitement. The mere prospect of the Lady was enough to gladden his heart. Actually hearing her voice engaged more hope and peace than he remembered.

"Be still and remember yourself. This place is not for you. Not now. Not ever."

No matter which way he turned the voice came to him from behind. He turned around fervently, seeking for her as she spoke each word. But she was not to be found. There was gladness in the hearing of her voice, but sadness in the absence of her being.

"Where are you?" Holden pleaded. *Please help me?*

Silence.

She was gone almost as quickly as she had arrived. Her departure nearly left him bereft of hope. How could he find his way out of here? He was indeed lost. He was in hell. He had no idea how long he had been here, but it felt like an eternity already.

It was then that he felt a rumble beneath his feet. It began ever so slightly, almost imperceptibly. But Holden felt it as it grew stronger. The rumble quickly increased to a full quake. Holden felt the ground beneath his feet lurch. He fell to his knees as huge sections of earth rose at varying angles in the near distance. Several of the crevices opened into fiery chasms as flames sprang out, greedily lapping at the air. Fear gripped him as the very ground beneath Holden began to rise and settle. He fell flat to the ground as it rose. Flames erupted all around and a wave of heat enveloped him.

A searing hand gripped his shoulder and spun him about quickly. The molten heat baked into his flesh as he stared into the face of a roaring inferno. The heat burned into his flesh, lighting afire every nerve in his body. His mouth open in a perpetual scream while no sound escaped. He looked into the deep dark abyss where eyes should have been, upon a fleshless skull wreathed in flame, into a flame emanating outward in an ever-expanding arc. Deep, dark pits of hell, orbs of black called out to him silently sucking in his soul. He stared into this and thought to himself so this is death, death come for me.

Holden awoke abruptly, rising to a sitting position. He stared wide-eyed into the glaring eyes of the Wanderer who stood above him. The two locked eyes for what seemed far too long before a wave of nausea overcame him. Holden turned away to empty the meager contents of his stomach. Once the retching ceased Holden gained his feet unsteadily and turned to face the Wanderer again.

"What...what happened?"

The Wanderer had moved from his position near Holden to a small campfire. A small pot simmered over the fire. Holden could smell a stew cooking. He realized he hadn't eaten in quite some time. He was nearly famished. The Wanderer returned with a small bowl.

"Sit friend. You need some rest." The Wanderer handed the bowl to Holden as Holden clumsily seated himself back upon his bed. He immediately began to slurp up the hot stew, feeling its warmth and energy flow into his body. As he finished the bowl he looked sheepishly at the Wanderer.

"Sorry. I guess it's been a while since I had something to eat. Can I have a little bit more please?"

Without a word the Wanderer refilled Holden's bowl. As Holden started on the second bowl of stew (hare stew!) the Wanderer returned to his own bed. He sat down and for a long moment looked off into the distance. Holden became lost in the aroma and flavor of the stew. His strange new companion must have trapped a hare or hunted one down at some point during the night. Actual wild hare!

"I did not think you would survive. The beast you looked upon and that looked upon you is a terrible creature. More times than not its gaze instantly kills, and for those unlucky few who survive the first look it drives them utterly insane as they live out the next hour or so in excruciating pain before mercifully passing away."

Holden had stopped eating while the Wanderer spoke. He now dove back into his bowl finishing the stew with much less fervor than he had the first. The Wanderer had risen silently to his feet and moved to retrieve the bowl from Holden. As he took it he held Holden's gaze.

"You are one of only three men I know of to have looked upon such a creature and survive."

Holden squirmed a bit uneasily until the Wanderer looked away. When the man had returned to his own bed and seated himself Holden asked, "Who were the other two?"

The Wanderer remained silent for some time, and Holden began to think that he would not answer. He felt waves of drowsiness began to overcome him as he lay back upon his bed. His eyelids became quite heavy. He felt them closing. Again the Wanderer surprised him when he spoke.

"One is a man for whom I have searched for some time yet have been unable to find. A great friend that I lost some time ago and to whom I owe some debt."

Holden's eyes were closed at this point but he thought he could hear a hint of acidity in the strange man's tone. Again a brief silence from the Wanderer. When he spoke again Holden knew the man was staring intently at him.

"I am the other."

Holden drifted off to sleep, a real sleep. Although thoroughly confused by the last few days' events he rested peacefully this time, dreaming of expansive fields of flowers and their heavenly aroma.

7 The North Road

Holden opened his eyes to a bright morning. He was covered in stiff bedding as he lay on the even stiffer earth. He looked around the small campsite and discovered himself alone. The stranger was not within the circle. As he sat up Holden felt pain flash through his body. He ached and hurt in muscles he never knew he had. His entire body felt as if it had been through hell and back. A wave of nausea came and went rather quickly. He was thirsty.

A full canteen rested near his bedding. He hurriedly opened it and began drinking. The cool water was heavenly.

"Careful not to drink too quickly lest you sicken yourself and spew it back up."

The Wanderer had come up behind Holden so very quietly. Holden was startled and inhaled some of the precious liquid. He immediately began coughing, and water came out his mouth and nose. The Wanderer walked past and into the center of their encampment. He seemed to ignore Holden's coughing fit as he went about the business of packing their scant items into his large backpack.

Holden had to seat himself back on his bedding as his head began to swim from his brief coughing fit. As he sat and watched, everything before him began to blur into a chiaroscuro of color. Swirling light and dark mingled with the colors of the day. Sounds muted into a swelling ocean storm: rain, wind, and waves. And he was lost to it all. The stormsound swelled to a deafening crescendo as all vision bled into one darkness. As the sound reached its loudest and the darkness grew to an all-encompassing view, Holden felt himself becoming lost. Then sight and sound crashed.

All was silent. And Holden was nearly blinded by the absence of color. He was lying on whiteness in a field of whiteness covered by a sky of whiteness. He was unable to discern where the ground began or ended. As he lay still he began to hear sounds in the distance. The sounds grew slowly but surely and he sat up. He could see in the unending distance a wavering motion in what would likely have been the horizon. The sounds grew to become more noticeable as voices. He strained to see who was coming, but he was unable to make out any distinct forms. The wavering in the distance came closer but remained unidentifiable. It was almost as if he were seeing ripples on the atmosphere from rising heat. The voices continued to grow as the ripples came closer. There were many different voices though they somehow managed to converge as one even when mingled together. All very melodic, but some carried tones of anger, while others traveled on tones of hope.

The voices stopped in the near distance and the ripples stopped as well. Holden looked in their direction as he sat upon the white nothingness. He thought the ripples, the entities, somehow were looking at him.

"They wonder if you might take up the challenge." The soft voice of the lady startled Holden. He turned to look up into her softly smiling face. "They discuss amongst themselves your ability to perform. They don't always see as I do."

Holden thought he heard some resignation in her voice and noticed a brief sadness pass over her visage. It hurt him to see any sadness afflict her so. He began struggling to his feet before she put a hand on his shoulder.

"Nay, pleasant one. Stay as you are." She was smiling down at him. He was lost in the warmth of her presence. He immediately relaxed back to his seat. "Since you found me I have sought to discern the meaning of your coming. I have embraced it." She looked back into the distance at the ripples. "The others are still debating."

Holden tore his eyes from her face and looked back toward the entities in the near distance. "What are they debating?" he asked. He sensed several juxtapositions within the mass of ripples in the distance: power and weakness, resolve and uncertainty, resistance and acquiescence, life and death. Hope and despair. All that and more emanated from the vague forms. As each moment passed he could feel each opposing emotion flow into and through him. He began to hear little snippets of conversation between the ripples. An unknown language in a multitude of voices began as whispers. Anger battled joy. Empathy fought disdain. Love resisted hatred. Hope fended off despair.

"They debate you, pleasant one." Her voice was just above a whisper. As Holden turned to look up and over his shoulder into her eyes, he felt a conflagration of emotion swell within him. All that was within the entities as separate emotive responses, all that they debated, was all within her. She felt it all. He saw the tears at the corners of her eyes. She continued to look at the others in the distance.

"They fear all you might be, all you might do. The future has become so very unclear, even unto them. They are unaccustomed. You represent so many things, either good or ill, and that frightens them. Yet..." She looked down at him, smiling, as tears fell from her clear eyes. "Yet, even among them there is hope." She took a deep breath at that and began to walk forward, toward the entities in the distance.

Holden realized he had been holding his breath as he looked upon the lady. Her appearance was a shock in and of itself. He knew her even though he had not seen her on previous occasions, yet he was not so overcome by that alone. The enormity of all that had befallen him since walking out of that forsaken town crashed upon him. How could any of this be happening to him? He was at a loss for words. He watched, dumbfounded, as she walked past him and took silent step after silent step toward the others. He inhaled deeply as if to yell out to her, but before he could do so she stopped and turned quickly, glaring at him. She was no more than fifteen paces from him, and he could see her face plainly before him.

A fierceness burned in her eyes. His voice froze useless in his throat.

"Be true, pleasant one. Much depends on you. Even he will, in the end. Despair seeks him at every turn, and in the end you will have a say. Make your words true to your soul."

She glared at him several seconds longer before turning to continue on her way. Holden watched entranced as he labored to regain his breath again. She began to fade as she got closer to the others, and all he saw began to bleed into white. The raging stormsound quickened and boiled over as darkness greedily enveloped him.

Holden opened his eyes and found a pair of grey orbs looking intently into his. The Wanderer knelt beside him with the water skin.

Terran watched his children as they sat with the boy. As he gathered their meager supplies to prepare to move, he wondered how they would make it to wherever they were to go. The Wanderer had been taking them west, and he meant to continue that way. But he did not know where their ultimate destination lay. And he was not prepared to protect them as he might need to be. He was too far from any place he was familiar with. This land was foreign to him and so too its dangers. He was lost and needed to regain himself.

Looking upon the three children he noted the grime upon them. They were all dirty and ragged. Their trek through the mountain had made wretches of them. He had seen beggars and vagabonds who had looked better than they. He called to his son, "Finn."

His boy came eagerly to him. "Yes, dad?"

"Finish packing our supplies, son. I will be back in a few moments." Terran stood, looking down at his son as he spoke. Finn beamed proudly up into his father's face, listening. Terran paused for a moment before leaving, taking the time to rustle his son's dirty head of hair. Finn's toothy grin nearly undid him. He returned the smile then turned to leave their camp. As he walked, various thoughts entered his head. He remembered small details he had not thought of in many years. He vividly saw the smile on his son's face as an infant. Finn always had been a happy child, so quick to smile and laugh openly at the small things others took for granted.

He reminisced about the times he had been able to spend with his family while his wife was still alive. She always managed to keep a positive outlook on everything. It was her strength that kept him going even after she was taken from them. Even as she lay dying she urged him to be strong for the children. She had made him promise not to weep in front of them. They would need his strength, she had said. He could not afford to wallow in pity. The world had become too hard a place. There was no place for pity. No one would show pity; no one would come to their aid. They would need him to be strong and care for them.

She had smiled at him and spoken lovingly as she admonished him. There had never been any malice in her. Her love had been absolute. Her love for him, for her children, for their little family. He so very much had wished to trade places with her. She had not deserved to waste away and die. Of the few people he had been able to get to know in his lifetime, she was the one person who deserved life. He had made pleas and deals with the God above to trade places with her, to take her pain and death as his own. But she had heard one such plea before the end and had scolded him.

"No, Terran. You are the stronger of us. You will save our children. You will find them a home. You are the better of us to do this. If either of us had to get sick and die, better it should be me. You will save them, our children. And in the end I will wait for you. Through the veil, my love. But save our children first, before you seek me out."

He had shed a tear then. Hard though he was, he was still human. And he loved, mightily. He had promised her he would save them. He would save them and keep them safe long before he sought her out.

She had fallen into a fever-laden sleep a day later and died two days after that. Less than a year had passed since. More times than not he had thought his strength failing, but he had continued on. Now he was in the midst of something preposterously greater than himself, greater than anything he had ever imagined. Incredible dangers lurked in the dark places of the world, those same places he had avoided his whole life. And great evil roamed the land, searching out innocence. He was in the midst of it all. And though he was frightened beyond belief, he was proud to be a part of it too. He was proving his love correct in her belief in him. She had told him again and again, before and up to the end, that he was the stronger of them. He had no intention of letting her down.

He stood before a creek. Its slow, steady rill flowed effortlessly through his imaginings. His mind slowly returned to the present. He found himself smiling slightly at the memory of his beloved. He knelt at the water's edge and looked upon his wavering visage in the flowing water. Even the rippling flow could do little to disguise the grime. He frowned at himself before scooping up a double handful of cool water and splashing it upon his face. He scrubbed the filth from his face then dunked his head beneath the surface, letting the cold water clear his mind.

It was colder and cleaner than any water he had felt before. He scrubbed his head vigorously as he held his breath underwater. After several moments he brought his head up, gasping for air. The water felt wonderful and refreshing. He stripped off his dirty, ragged shirt and began scooping double handfuls of water onto his torso. The cold water pleasantly stung his exposed flesh, and he closed his eyes as he scrubbed himself with scoop after scoop of clean water. After a time he realized he was standing in the center of the creek, the water flowing just below his knees. A distinct and almost forgotten sense of pleasure flowed through him. He opened his eyes, not even aware that he'd had them closed. Everything looked so much clearer than it had before. He knew what to do. No matter what, he would continue on with his children. All three of them. He smiled as he envisioned his beautiful wife's approval. She would approve. She would demand it, if she were with him now. Evan was his charge now, and until the knight returned (*if* the knight returned) he would protect the boy as one of his own. His beloved would've had it no other way.

He splashed another double handful of water on his face and stood straight and tall, his head tilted back and his eyes closed. He smiled and relished the cool sensation as it flowed all over his exposed flesh. Water soaked his filthy pants as well, but he did not care. A cool breeze flowed between the trees and sent a welcome shiver through his entire being. He could feel his beloved in the air. She would forever be with him.

His eyes flashed open as his head snapped forward. Had that been a stifled scream in the distance? Terran stood still, listening. He heard nothing at all in the near distance. He rushed out of the water, retrieving his few belongings as he hurried back to the camp. His mind panicked as he began to run the short distance back to his children. Horrible images played in his mind's eye, and he stumbled several times before bursting into the small clearing.

He found his children quietly seated cross-legged with their supplies before them. The three sets of eyes looked upon him in unison as he made his way into the campsite. Four armed men stood behind the young ones. His children's eyes pleaded with him. Fear emanated from Kiran and Finn and shone forth in their open-eyed stare. But the boy, Evan, looked upon Terran with a calm smile upon his face. There was no fear. A slight nod of his head and an aside glance intimated that there was no danger. Terran was unarmed and not much of a fighter anyway. The soldiers would have taken him without much effort. The four standing behind the children wore pistols on their hips, and one had a rifle slung on his shoulder.

It was the one with the rifle who spoke.

160

"Speak honest, man, and give us your name." His tone was direct and full of danger. Terran read the situation as dire. He glanced again at the boy. Evan smiled openly at him now.

"I am Terran, father and protector to Kiran, Finn, and Evan, the three children you stand above now." Terran spoke as he looked into the calming eyes of Evan. As he finished he looked into the eyes of the soldier. He noticed the man glance aside. It was then he realized he had been flanked by an additional two soldiers at his rear. Evan looked at Kiran and Finn and seemed to speak softly to them. Terran could not hear Evan's words.

The soldier looked squarely at Terran and appeared to relax. He took a deep breath, and Terran noted that his right hand moved away from his holstered sidearm.

"Come, join your children, stranger. We will not harm you." The soldier motioned for Terran to come forward. Evan was still speaking quietly to Finn and Kiran. Terran looked at his children. The fear he had first seen was gone. A calm seemed to have settled upon them. He remembered the sensation. The boy. Evan. Terran stepped forward, never taking his eyes off the children as he moved. Evan looked up into his eyes and smiled lightly. Terran could feel the positive energy flowing from the boy in steady and caressing waves.

He knelt down with the children and checked with them each in turn. He hugged his girl, his boy, and only slightly hesitated as he took Evan into his arms. His breath caught for a moment in his throat and his mind went far away for but an instant as the jolt of peace reverberated within him. It was a peace he had not felt since his first encounter with the boy. But this was almost too much for his mind and body to keep in. He withdrew from Evan in what felt too brusque a manner. He looked around at the soldiers, but they all seemed to have relaxed considerably. Their captain had walked away from the children to sit upon a small boulder near the rear of the encampment. He was looking intently at Terran and the children. He appeared perplexed yet relaxed. He looked at his hands out before him and shook his head. He stared at his palms for a time, and then he turned his hands over still staring at them. He dropped his hands into his lap and looked up again.

The boy was smiling at him and he was compelled to smile in return. His men had travelled far to reach this place. They were farther south than he had ever led a patrol. They had been attacked by a large band of marauders. Larger than any he had heard of before. Their training had taken over and they had prevailed, but not before losing more than half his men.

Strange happenings.

He decided that they would rest for a brief time, replenish what water they could from the stream the father of the children had found, and then they would leave. They could not tarry. He was sure of it. They had to hurry home.

And the small family they had happened upon would accompany them. There was something about them that called for him to keep them near. The one child was different. Very different.

Evan looked away from the soldier. He looked into the eyes of each member of his new family. Sure that he had their attention, he spoke: "We will be safe for a time." Glancing in the direction of the soldier, then looking back to his new family he smiled reassuringly. "We will be in their company. We will see the North. We will be safe. For a time." He then stood abruptly, motioning for Kiran and Finn to join him. The children looked hesitantly at their father. He only shrugged and looked up into the calm face of Evan. Evan acknowledged him with a nod then looked at the children again.

"We need to go bathe before we begin our trek. I'm certain we look a mess."

Finn and Kiran stood and walked away with Evan. Two soldiers followed at a casual distance. Terran watched them leave the camp and head toward the creek. After a time he stood and began packing the remainder of their belongings, few though they were.

The Wanderer and Holden had secured the last of their gear and had walked away from their campsite before sunrise. Another day had come and gone before then. Holden had required such time to recover enough to continue. The Wanderer had waited as patiently as he could, feeding and caring for the other man. Once he felt Holden well enough to travel, he had prepared them for their journey. As they walked from their campsite, he set a modest pace. His companion was strong and had recovered quickly, but the residual effects of the Stalker would linger for a while longer. They would need to pause for several breaks along their way.

He led the way through the forest and Holden followed. They had a long way to travel around the mountain and had lost two days' time. He was sure the company had made it out the cavern and down the mountain safely. He hoped that they were still safe though. There were a great many dangers aside from the monster that had hounded them into the mountain. Terran and his children were hardy, but he did not know if they were capable of making it much farther without his aid. The boy was his charge. He needed to get back to him.

But the Lady had brought his current companion to him. So he found himself delayed. He also found himself in old familiar straits. He did not like being in this predicament any more than he had in the past. Self-reliance had suited him for a long time. Companions muddied the water and made for difficult decisions. He had gone from being responsible for no one other than himself to caring for a boy, then a family of travelers, and now another stranger. All in the space of a few days.

He stopped with Holden again. They were near a small footpath not far from running water. The Wanderer halted Holden so that they were out of view of the creek ahead of them, but so that he could hear it in the near distance. Holden had been walking for the last several minutes with his head down. He managed to keep the Wanderer's steady pace, but it was wearing on him. Although he followed behind Alex, his increasingly labored breathing hinted at his weariness.

As Holden took a seat and rested against an old fir, he wondered how the man he was following always seemed to know exactly when he needed to stop. They had begun in the pre-dawn darkness and had traveled what seemed an eternity, though the sun was not yet in its midday position. He had traveled for over an hour in the early darkness, the Wanderer wearing a glow-stick at the rear of his waist as they walked. Holden kept close to the strange man as they walked in silence. Their first stop had been just as the sun rose into the trees. The two men enjoyed some cool water and a light breakfast of cold oatmeal before they had continued on. They had stopped at regular intervals since then, always eating a small amount of jerky and drinking a little cool water. Holden drank some of his water now. His canteen was very low.

"Finish the last of it."

Holden looked up at the Wanderer who stood near but looked toward the sound of the water.

"Drink the last of your water, friend. I will go ahead and fill our canteens. The water ahead is clean. You can rest for a while longer while I scout ahead just a bit."

Holden finished drinking the last of the water in the canteen. He handed the empty vessel to the outstretched

164

hand of the Wanderer. The man took a few steps away then stopped.

"Be sure to remain seated where you are while I am gone. The footpath ahead, although very lightly used, is still a viable route. If any travel this way they will likely come by that small road. You will be hidden from view for a time and will be able to hear any approach."

The Wanderer turned and looked Holden in the eyes.

"Trust your ears and heart more than your eyes. There are certain things released to the world that can cast a glamour upon men. Beware, and take them not lightly should any come in my absence."

At that the Wanderer turned and walked away. Holden stared into the woods where the man seemed to have disappeared. He'd seen true warning in the eyes of the Wanderer. He took a deep breath and repositioned himself on the patch of earth at the foot of the tree. He did not know how long the Wanderer would be gone, but he got comfortable enough and in a good enough position to react to any threat which might make itself known in the meantime. He removed the handgun from its holster and placed it in his lap. He then steeled himself to keep vigil until his companion returned.

Three minutes later he was fast asleep.

The Wanderer filled the canteens quickly then crossed the rocky stream. They were close enough to the mountain to continue getting clean, fast-flowing water. Their chosen path was taking them ever westward. They had skirted the mountain rather closely during the dark hours of morning but had moved into the woodland prior to daybreak. The mountain had moved farther to the southeast as they traveled. Soon they would be approaching a very traveled road. The North Road cut the land in half: east and west. To the south a great many people lived spread out through the more temperate climate. Small communities. Some in towns, enclaves, fortified holds. There were many such groups. And some verged on becoming true cities.

But to the north there was but one city. Grand in scale, it was the only city of its kind. The inhabitants of the southlands called it the Northern Kingdom. It was mythical to many. Traveling from south to north was almost unheard of. But there had been recent travel north to south. And times were changing rapidly. There could just as likely be the unseemly travel out of the wastelands into the realm of man. So he scouted ahead to check the road and be sure of safety in crossing it. He had no intention of traveling on that road. Especially not north.

Alex made his way to an area near the edge of the wood line near the maintained road. It was empty and quiet. He noticed a multitude of tracks on the roadway. More than there should have been. There had been movement on the road this day. And there would likely be more. Much was happening in the land recently that spoke to great change. Whether that change would be for good or ill was yet to be seen. But Alex felt things speeding up. Too much was happening too soon.

He waited and watched for a while.

The road was quiet for quite some time. For more than an hour he remained silent and still. Then he saw them. A group of men traveling from the south. He watched through his binoculars as they came nearer and the size became clearer. They were nearly a dozen men. They wore the garb of soldiers of the North. They came even closer and Alex saw that they were hale and spoke heartily to one another. They were headed home. Their captain lingered near the rear of the group. With him traveled a man and three children. As Alex looked through his binoculars at the individuals in the group he found the face of the boy. Evan was looking directly at him, though Alex was hidden deep in the woods off the roadway. He watched as the boy smiled then mouthed one single word.

Alex immediately began to return to his companion. He traipsed through the woods back to the place he had left Holden to rest. As he hurried he felt a nagging in the pit of his heart. Things were moving far too rapidly. He had thought himself prepared for this, but he knew that no matter how well he thought he had prepared he would never be truly ready for any given moment until he actually faced it. His mind was still wandering a bit as he neared the tree he'd left Holden to rest.

His companion was gone. And his pistol was lying on the ground where he had been seated.

The Wanderer grunted his disapproval before picking up the pistol and then picking up the trail left behind by Holden as he had left his resting place. He walked briskly and carefully as he followed the trail. Holden had traveled due south from the location, and his trek through the woods had been fairly reckless. And there were no other tracks.

A haunt.

Alex had come across them before. He picked up his pace, beginning to run quickly through the woods. He would have to hurry if he wanted to save his companion. Unless... He wondered about his new friend's capabilities. Holden had encountered the lady. He had survived the Stalker's stare. Could he possibly overcome the call of a haunt?

As he expected, after a time he came to a small, secluded body of water. It was hidden by overgrown clumps of shrubbery and well away from any traveled path. A small clearing was all that encircled it. Holden stood at its edge. He faced the small pond and remained still as Alex entered the clearing. Alex remained silent and began moving around the edge of the clearing. He continued moving until a shriek filled his head.

The haunt had given voice to its disapproval of his arrival. Alex and his brethren were known to them and theirs. Alex smiled. He looked at the center of the water. He waited with the wry grin on his face. He made no other moves and spoke no words. He simply waited.

Why do you come here, empty vessel? We have not called you. The voice of the haunt flowed melodically on the air. In almost all men, the sound compelled them. It was soothing and commanding. It projected peace and beauty, hope and prosperity, love and eternity. It was a call that could not go unanswered. The weak-willed fell to it. The strong-willed did as well. A select few were known to be able to resist them. The haunts referred to those men as soulless. Empty vessels. They fed upon the energy of men. They craved the strongest, boldest, and bravest of men. But fools who wandered too near were just as easily devoured.

The haunts could not take their prey by force. They were without physical form. The men they consumed had to give themselves up to the water that housed the spirit of the haunt. Most men simply walked straight into the water and drowned without a fight. Some of the stronger men of character fought at the very end, when life was leaving their drowning forms. But an even smaller number fought at the edge of the water. It was for most a brief struggle before the final plunge into the cold abyss. But for some it was a monumental struggle. For some it was a brave and valiant battle. For some, the strength of character shone as a small but brilliant star in the night. And on occasion some men won.

Holden stood still at the water's edge. His body seemed relaxed and unmoving. There was no sway. He breathed deep and rhythmically, keeping a steady pace. But his heart hammered in his chest. His face was rigid with struggle, his eyes wide and staring over the water, his teeth clenched behind pinched lips.

Alex could see the right side of Holden's face. His battle was easily beheld. Holden was at war with the call of the haunt. Sweat covered Holden's brow and began to bead as it rolled down his face. Several minutes passed.

Alex still watched silently. He could have stepped in physically and removed Holden from this place, but he did not believe it was what was needed. This was a test. Holden needed to make it through this on his own. Alex decided not to interfere. Instead he did something not even the haunt expected. He briskly turned and walked out of the clearing.

Holden was trapped in a chiaroscuro of sight and sound. Soft, melodic whisperings filled his senses. A calm flowed through his entire being. He had been sleeping beneath a tree one moment, and the next he was here, before the serene pond. The still water silently called to him. A melodic voice bade him forward, ever forward. All would be forever peaceful, forever right if he would just move forward. All he desired waited for him. All he wanted was here. Come forward. Come forward. The compulsion was so strong. All he saw was beauty. At every turn, beauty. But something deep within him gave him pause. Something inside wanted so desperately to scream, *No!*

The battle was entirely within him. He realized his eyes had been open for far too long. He thought to close them, but the fear of losing the beauty before him entered his mind sharply. *What if you close your eyes to blink and it all goes away?* It was not his thought. It did not come from him. He had to close his eyes. He had to heed his heart. His heart. What did his heart tell him? Damn it. He could not heed his heart because he could not hear it. The visions before his eyes drowned out the voice of his heart. But he sensed its call. And so he fought.

Alex waited as patiently as he could on the other side of the thick bramble of overgrowth. He sat quietly on a large, flat rock. He was drawing pictures of some scene in the dusty earth and appeared lost in his own world when Holden stepped quietly into view. Alex only looked up and grunted in what might have been an approving manner. Holden wasn't sure. It could just as easily have been a grunt of resentment.

Alex handed Holden a canteen without speaking. Holden dumbly looked at the container in his hand before the realization that he was parched came to him. He turned the canteen up to drink greedily before thinking better of it. He only took a few sips before snapping his head toward the Wanderer.

"You were here? The entire time?"

The Wanderer only nodded as he looked off into the distance.

"But why didn't you come..." Holden's voice trailed off as a realization came upon him. This man before him was so very different from other men. As different as he. They were not alike, per se. But their very differences seemed to make them similar. Neither of them fit into a category of types of men. This encounter was another example of that. The Wanderer had known he was in danger, mortal danger, and yet he had not come to his aid. Why? Because some part of the strange man had known Holden was capable of surviving this encounter. While in the midst of battle some part of Holden had known it as well.

Holden drank a little more water. He continued to sip slowly. His gaze wandered off into the distance as he drank. His thoughts also were wandering as he contemplated his current situation and situations past.

The Wanderer casually glanced at his companion as his own thoughts returned to him. He took a deep, audible breath. Holden looked him in the eye with an immediate

170

question forming in his raised eyebrows. *What now?* He continued to sip water from the canteen.

"Now we go north. Our path has become quite plain." Alex thought about Evan. The boy walked easily on the road in his mind's eye. Flanked by his new family, he seemed at ease. To the casual eye he might even seem peaceful. But Alex had seen the fear hidden beneath the surface. The boy was afraid of something. And the silent plea made to him was unmistakable. It epitomized the fear he had seen in those eyes. He saw the boy's lips form the words and imagined he could hear them as well.

He took the time to tell his new companion as much as he could about Terran and the children. He skipped over much of the boy's uniqueness. He concluded with his finding of the family on the road. Holden kept quiet during the brief telling. There were many questions he wanted to ask, but he knew the time was not right. He could wait. Something nagged at the back of his mind. Something was wrong with the man before him. He wasn't sure of what, but he figured the Wanderer probably felt the same when looking at him.

The Wanderer looked away after finishing his brief tale. But he did not turn to leave. Holden waited an eternity before asking, "What are we waiting for?"

Alex turned to face Holden. This time there was no mistaking the fire behind those eyes. Holden felt a fear grip his insides, twisting them into knots. But that sensation only lasted a moment before turning into a not too unpleasant sensation. There was death in that glare. And it was unwavering in its intensity. And in its call. A sense of desire washed over Holden. It left him almost as quickly as it came. But it was not unnoticeable. Holden almost felt ashamed at it.

"There is no rush, Holden. We travel north to the North. Our destination is known. Our road is not. We will arrive there in due time." There was an undeniable tone of disdain in the Wanderer's voice when he spoke of the North. Holden was certain of it. Fear and excitement confounded him again, and he was forced to look away.

Alex again turned away, this time seating himself on the flat rock again. He saw the boy's face as the word was mouthed to him. One word with so many implications. He felt the past pulling at him, tugging fiercely in an attempt to bring him back to a life he had left so long ago. The word sat heavily in his mind. The boy's lips mouthing it over and over slowly in his eyes. *Angela.*

He abruptly stood and brusquely handed the pistol to Holden. As he turned and began to walk back toward the earlier resting spot beneath the fir, the Wanderer seemed uncharacteristically out of sorts.

Holden wisely followed without speaking.

In the earliest days following the Great Fall, many men fought against one another for the simplest things. Small enclaves rose and fell. Pettiness filled the hearts of most as men scraped the earth for the simplest of treasures. Small fiefdoms grew and declined. The strongest of the weakest took power when they could but were always undone by the weakness of their character.

But a boy in the north grew strong as his family struggled. He was raised in one of several small towns that thrived near the largest body of clean water. He learned from all the men and women in his family and in his clan. He grew to manhood early and united his town into a strong fiefdom under his rule. As he grew into manhood he grew in ambition. He saw into the future and there was a need to improve, to better his fellow man. But he saw that it would not happen soon enough. He saw a storm swelling in the distance, beyond his time. But it was great in scope and ferocity. It would consume everything if none stood to face it.

He used every ounce of his will to unite the nearby villages, the nearby towns, the nearby fiefdoms. His power of persuasion was keen. Through guile, cunning, or absolute might he brought the north under his rule and created what he hoped to be a lasting symbol of the greatness of man. He passed on his vision to his sons and so the light of the North grew legendary.

He took the name Arthur early during his rule. He surrounded himself with men he chose personally as the hands of his rule. These men he named his knights. He trained them in every art of war and diplomacy. They became his confidants and with them he shared his vision of the future. The vision his rule sought to bring and the vision of the storm. Each of the men in his camp saw it. They were consumed by the vision as was their lord. Each of them swore an oath to defend against it. All save one. One knight held darkness in his heart. He spoke the words as did his fellows, but his true desire he kept hidden.

The king did not see it. The other knights did not see it. He hid it well until he could hide it no longer. But there was one who saw it.

Not a knight, the woman who saw the treachery in the one knight's heart kept it to herself for a time. She held it close and tried to rid her mind of the thought. It was foreign and without merit. The knights loved their king, loved the kingdom, and loved the land. Surely not one of them could hold such darkness in his heart.

Sarah, wife of Arthur, held her tongue for so very long. There came a time when the vision of betrayal became too much to conceal. She devised a plan to test all the knights' commitment. A game of skill was called in her name. The games lasted a full week and the bravest men from every corner of the king's rule attended.

Holden sat up in his bed. He and the Wanderer had stopped earlier in the evening to camp for the night. The Wanderer had stated that they would not need to travel any farther after only a few miles. Apparently they were traveling faster than the group they were following. Holden looked now at the Wanderer in the waning light filtering through the light spattering of trees. They had moved into a rough area lightly dotted with evergreens. They were a few hundred yards from the road. Alex had kept their course parallel to the road without getting too near the others.

"What happened at the games?" Holden asked after a time. Alex was looking away from the small campsite. Holden waited for some time then lay his head back down. He had come to the realization that it was not necessary to repeat himself when speaking to the Wanderer. Alex heard everything and was gathering himself before continuing. Holden closed his eyes and waited.

"Her plan worked. She drew out the traitor, at least to her own satisfaction. But in so doing she nearly split the kingdom." Alex settled himself in his own bed and continued. "She called out the darkness in his heart, but he denied it and made a compelling counteraccusation. Men began to choose sides. Knights began to choose sides." Again he paused.

"The king was forced to make a judgment. Whom should he believe? Whom should he embrace? His wife, the strong and devoted woman who had given birth to his boys? Or his man? One he had chosen based on his belief in that man's strength of character. He was torn and unable to decide.

"Two sides formed as the king held judgment for the day. Knights and men rallied to the queen, while others chose the maligned knight. The king took notice and gave his judgment early the next day. The knight was to journey on a quest into the west. He was to return with a talisman known only to him and the king."

Holden waited as the Wanderer paused again.

"Then, and only then, would a final judgment be delivered."

Holden tried waiting it out but the Wanderer only sat quietly looking into the distance. Several minutes passed in silence. Holden could stand it no longer.

"So what happened?"

The Wanderer solemnly looked at Holden in the deepening shadows. His mien appeared grim and almost forlorn as he spoke.

"The knight took up the quest and trekked into the west. He took with him three trusted brother-knights who had heartily stepped to his side as the queen spoke ill of his intent. They left with the blessings of the king, but the queen would not see them on their way. As they left the kingdom, none of them looked back."

Another pause, then: "And it was many years before they made it back."

Holden took in the story eagerly. He had heard of the knights as a boy. They were men in tales told by old women and old men of various villages. Some of the elderly claimed to have met one or to have seen a knight earlier in their lives. All the stories were tales of great strength, valor, and compassion. The knights were men of legend. But he had not ever heard this tale or any variation of it. It was compelling and grand. He wanted to ask if it were true. Or at least ask if the Wanderer believed it. He thought better and instead closed his eyes and imagined the great city in the north. They were headed that way and would hopefully be there soon.

Alex remained seated on his bed, looking at his tired companion for a time. He then looked away and let his mind wander. It had been so long. He had wandered for so long that he had thought he could forget the city and all its greatness. He had thought himself capable of forgetting the radiant jewel in the crown of the land. He had thought he would not ever see it again. And now he feared his return. So many thoughts flooded his mind, and to his chagrin so too did so many emotions.

Alex looked out into the distance alone with his thoughts for a very long time before he lay his head down within his bedding.

8 Border

A great bridge before them, the company continued walking forward. None of them had seen anything quite so grand. The bridge spanned a wide, rushing river flowing in a southeasterly direction. It was a bold construction in an old style, ornate in design. Terran, Evan, and the children had each seen bridges in their lives. Small, newly constructed things and old collapsing monstrosities covered the southland. But none of them had ever believed a bridge could be a thing of beauty until this day. It was made entirely of marble. Though it was wide enough for several columns of men to walk abreast, it was still of a streamline design. Towers stood as sentinels at the near side of the bridge as they approached. They loomed high above the arcing midpoint of the bridge, allowing any occupant to see well into the distance to notice any advancing travelers, friends or foe.

The soldiers who accompanied them had split into two elements four days before as they traveled the road. Six walked ahead and six to the rear. The captain had stayed near during their trek and had shown a great interest in Evan. On several occasions he and Evan had separated from the others and walked ahead near the front of the column. Terran had kept a vigilant eye on the two during those times although he knew he would have been unable to intervene if the captain had had any malicious designs. But he watched anyway.

Evan seemed to be at ease with the armed man, always walking eagerly with him. As Terran watched them he noticed that Evan spoke very little, but the captain spoke at length as they walked. The soldiers also noticed and seemed to feed off their captain's relaxed attitude. They felt that things were improving and would be even better once they made it home. Their pace was a good one as they traveled the road. And once the bridge came into view it appeared that the pace quickened even more so. Terran was tired after four days of travel. They had made adequate stops along the way but he was beginning to grow weary. His feet were sore and exhaustion was creeping into his bones. He did not believe he would be able to make it much farther.

Terran and his children had stopped walking for only a brief moment as Evan pointed out the bridge to them upon it first coming into view. They all looked in wonder at the towers pointing into the sky. In the early evening light it shone with a soft radiance that called them forward. As one of the soldiers spoke into his ear to please hurry, Terran could hear the gladness in the man's tone. The company continued forward with renewed vigor.

As they drew nearer the bridge Terran noted a contingent of men coming forward to meet them. Half a dozen men met them a few hundred yards from the bridge. With them were two riderless horses. Once the men finished exchanging hearty greetings with one another the leader of the six asked of the captain regarding his few numbers.

"We were attacked by a large number of marauders. I have never seen so many of them together, and acting in concert. We rallied, but this was all that remained." The captain gave a brief telling of the finding of the family they now accompanied. He made no mention of his affinity for the boy.

"Our eyes in the towers spotted you traveling the road as you approached and we sent for horses for your companions. They looked far too tired to keep up with the likes of such warriors as you." The sergeant was smiling broadly as he spoke. "Or perhaps some of your men would have a rest as you continue on your way." It was a jest, a game of words, and the captain could only smile as his men laughed gruffly at the jab.

"Thank you, sergeant. My men have traveled long and far, but they have no need for such luxuries as these steeds. We are foot soldiers and as such we will maintain our march and return on foot to our home to report to our lord. But these travelers are indeed sore of foot and will put your fine steeds to good use." The captain played along with the jest of the bridge guard. Both men looked upon one another for a moment longer before each laughed aloud and embraced.

Within a few moments Terran was being assisted onto the back of one of the horses. Evan was placed at his rear on the animal. Kiran and Finn were raised onto the back of the other beast. The company began moving again, the horses each being led by a soldier. The company continued to the bridge and across its great span. The clopping of the hooves echoed in the quiet day. No one spoke, aside from the whispered chatter of some of the men of the foot patrol as they spoke briefly to the men of the bridge guard. Once the party made it across the bridge they were left alone again. The bridge guard had returned to their posts, with a hearty farewell to the soldiers who continued on.

Terran found himself drifting to sleep on the steed's back. He startled himself awake a few times before the voice of the captain playfully admonished him.

"Careful, friend, lest you fall from this beast's back. You could injure yourself from such a height."

Terran looked severely into the captain's eyes and noticed the light mood there. He relaxed. He took a deep breath and smiled into the sincere face of the soldier. He was learning to trust, but it was a hard lesson. For so long he had had to rely on only himself to care for his family. It was very difficult to go against what had become instinct. But he sensed no harm in this man. What he did sense was something he was unaccustomed to. He could not name it. If he'd had the words to do so, he would have called it honor.

He smiled wanly at the captain. "Indeed, sir. I suppose I am tottering on the brink of destruction."

The two shared a brief smile at that. "Fear not, weary traveler. This horse you ride upon is a wily beast to be sure. But all our horses are trained for long travel. He will not let you fall or fail. Rest yourself. You have earned it."

Terran smiled appreciatively and closed his weary eyes. He drifted off to a very light sleep, his mind still a step away from consciousness. Tired as he was he still was not able to relax completely in his current predicament. His children remained in need of his care.

The Wanderer paused at the edge of the wood line. The North Road was before him. Holden stood nearby at his rear, waiting. The road was empty. None stood before them. Evan and the rest of the company had passed this way a few hours prior and had already entered the Realm. The North called to him, yet the Wanderer hesitated. He had missed something, but it escaped him. Something was so terribly amiss. He could not see it. Exhaustion clouded his vision. The bridge was near. Not long after they stepped onto the road and continued north they would be spotted. He knew this. Time had grown short. His path remained before him.

He stepped the few paces to the road and turned his face to the north. Holden wasn't sure, but he thought he saw the makings of a smile for a brief moment. But it was a passing thing; it left as soon as it appeared. The wanderer turned to his companion.

"Come, friend. Let us see what the rest of this day has in store for us."

The Wanderer began forward at a much less hurried pace than Holden had expected. It was almost leisurely. The two walked for only a few minutes, the Wanderer seemingly without a care in the world. Holden kept waiting for something from his companion, but the Wanderer was silent. His head forward and shoulders drawn back, he walked with an air of grandeur. Holden thought to speak a few times, but was compelled to silence by a sense of foreboding.

After far too brief a time, the Wander halted. Holden stopped to his left and a step to his rear. The Wanderer was looking ahead as he raised his hands in surrender. Holden looked puzzled at the warrior beside him.

"Do not resist, friend." The Wanderer spoke evenly. He was calm and reassuring. "We are approached by guards of the Kingdom. They only do their duty to protect the entrance to the realm."

The Wanderer looked intently into Holden's eyes: "Do not resist. These are my kinsmen."

Holden only nodded and followed the Wanderer's lead. He held his hands up in surrender. A moment later a contingent of half a dozen armed and armored men approached them in the roadway. Five held rifles in a low ready position. A sixth walked at the front of the group. His rifle was slung and his hands were empty. As they neared to within a dozen or so paces the leader of the soldiers held up a hand and his contingent stopped. He continued to within less than half a dozen paces before stopping himself.

"Name yourselves, travelers." He spoke steadily, evenly. Holden noted the surety in his voice, his command presence. His men were ready, prepared for a fight, though not relishing it. They were soldiers. They had seen battle. They had been victorious, and had yet lost so much, so many brethren.

The Wanderer saw all the same and more. He took a slow breath and marked the visage of each soldier before him. His eye settled at last on the sergeant. He looked him in the eye and steeled himself.

"I am Alexander Horatio Sloane, citizen of the Northern Realm, Captain of His Guard, Knight of The Realm…and exiled of her heart."

Holden could almost feel the breath escape the sergeant. The words had come from his companion with the sting of royalty. The sergeant was taken aback for a moment. He stepped forward, staring intently into the eyes of the Wanderer.

"Sergeant!" One of his men called to him. He stopped, still looking intently into the eyes of the Wanderer. Alex only glared into the eyes of the young man. He made no movements and spoke nothing further.

The sergeant stood less than an arm's length from the Wanderer. His breath came in ever-increasing ragged inhalations and exhalations. He stared into the steel-gray orbs and Holden was amazed to see the beginnings of tears form at the rims of the sergeant's eyes. For some time the two men only looked into one another's eyes. Holden was unsure what to do or say. The soldiers also seemed to be lost. They glanced at one another nervously, awaiting some decision from their sergeant.

The Wanderer stood watching, waiting. He stared intently into the eyes and soul of the sergeant. He saw honor and loyalty there. He saw steadfastness. He saw his kinsman. He saw what might have been in a distant past a fellow knight. The man was true to the North, true to the land. Alex smiled the briefest of smiles. The sergeant had seen him too.

The sergeant slowly knelt before the Wanderer. It was something his men had not seen before. Only royals were knelt before. And royals had not crossed the southern borders in an age. They looked hurriedly at one another again. Then they looked questioningly at Holden. He could offer only a shrug of the shoulders.

"Stand, brother. I am no royal. Only a brother in arms." Alex spoke directly to the sergeant. The sergeant stood and openly wept as he gazed into the eyes of the Wanderer. Alex stepped directly before the sergeant.

They embraced one another before the soldiers or Holden had time to react. A somber sob escaped the sergeant as the two embraced. Alex held the man in his arms for an extended time as he looked at the bridge in the distance.

Perhaps coming home would not be such a bad thing.

9 Court

Thirteen years had passed since the maligned knight had left on his quest. The men and women of the North had continued living a good life. Tradesmen flourished under the rule of the king. Goods were manufactured, sold, traded, and communities near and far prospered. The royal household resumed a sense of normalcy almost immediately. At least it appeared so to the casual observer. There was an unspoken yet palpable anxiety between the king and queen. They were both in their own way heartbroken. The queen's accusation and king's judgment weighed heavily upon them, and a rift began between their hearts.

The king grew old and embittered within this time. He doubted more and more his commitment to his woman, his wife, his queen. They had separated to different bedchambers not long after the judgment. He took advantage of this and began to take mistresses of the court. Three illegitimate children were born of these trysts: two girls and one boy. The children were known to the queen. She was not a fool. She had her sons. Three boys, princes of the Realm. They would rule one day. The king and his bastards be damned.

For thirteen years poison festered in the heart of the king. Until the day his knight returned. The knight errant came home to his king. He had retuned thirteen years to the day at nearly the exact hour of his departure. He returned and made straightway to his king. The knight and his three loyal compatriots returned and met with the king and his sons. It was a grand occasion in the mind of the king. He entered the private meeting chamber, the room of the knights. Some of the other knights had assembled. He and his sons seated themselves at the table, and the knights all followed suit. All but the knight-errant and his three. They remained standing.

The king looked into the face of his knight. The man wore his full battle regalia: sidearm, sword, hauberk, and armor. His three knights were likewise geared. The king and his sons were in their robes. The four other knights who had made it to the chamber thus far were likewise attired. The king studied the face of the man on the other side of his round table. And he wondered how it was he looked exactly the same as the day he had departed thirteen years past. He wondered at that and feared the answer.

"My king, I have traveled far and wide to seek *your* talisman. To prove myself worthy." Was that a sneer? The king was unsure. The knight began to move ever so slowly, making his way around the table.

"I have found the thing you desire." Still moving, the knight spoke directly to the king. He skirted around his seated fellow knights. His three brothers in arms remained standing, though not moving. The king thought he saw a slight burst of argent escape the hauberk as his man approached. Could it be?

The knight reached inside his clothing and removed a silver chain necklace. Suspended within a pendant of white gold shone an argent light emanating from a dull, rough-hewn ruby. It was the diameter of a man's thumbnail. The knight held the chain up as the stone hung suspended before the eyes of the king, his sons, and seated knights.

The king slowly rose to his feet as the knight continued moving toward him. His eyes were fixed on the stone. It seemed to pulse lightly as he stared into it. His breathing and heart rate increased as the talisman drew nearer. His sons also stood with their father. They, too, were held by the stone.

"Yes. Yes, it is as I saw it in my dreams. I never doubted you. I knew you would find it and bring it before me. Its power is...is..." He took a deep breath.

"Incredible. Yes, I know." The knight stood near the eldest of the king's sons as he spoke. "It holds the key to a great power, my king. Immeasurable, actually. But you will never know its touch nor feel its greatness."

The king heard the words but had trouble comprehending. He was trapped in the hold of the stone. He could not tear his eyes from it. But he could hear quite well. The sound of swords being drawn across the table was unmistakable. And he could discern the slight snick of a dagger being drawn near him. Nearer his eldest.

"No. Please, no." He could only whisper the words. The stone held sway over him. He could not resist it. His muscles were held tightly, and he could not move. His will was sapped and overcome by the stone. "Not my sons. Please."

"It is too late, my king. It has started." Then his knight cut three throats, in order from eldest to youngest, all while holding the talisman before the unwavering eyes of the king. The assembled knights were struck down, some without a fight as the stone held them, others as they attempted to break free of its hold. They were without armor or weapon and no match for their former brethren. After only a minute the king stood alone with the returned knights. Tears flowed from his eyes as they beheld, unblinking, the ruby. Soft moans escaped him.

"War is upon you, old man. We will await you upon Farrow's Field in the morning. Bring what men you have left to defend your land." The knight threw the bloodied blade upon the table. "I will meet you upon the field and there make myself a king."

The king's eyes glazed over at that and he slumped back into his chair. His body still was not his own to command for a brief time. When he regained himself and called for aid the traitors were gone from the city. He remained seated at the table for a time. His sons' bodies and the bodies of the majority of his knights remained with him. He would allow none to remove them. He stared into the distance and beheld sights unseen to others. The stone had held him prisoner, but it had also shown him much. He had seen war. He could still see it. War was indeed upon him. It lay like a burden on his heart. He was filled with it. Crimson clouded his visage. His blood boiled within him and his heart pounded in his chest. The anguish grew to overflowing. Hatred took hold and compelled him to action. He drew a deep breath and let loose a wail unheard before or since in the chambers of the king.

The doors to the chamber flew open and he exited swiftly into the hallway. His aides and staff were startled by the cry and his sudden departure. They followed quickly on his heels. He gave orders for the removal of the bodies and the room to be cleaned and sealed. He then gave orders for the remainder of his knights to be assembled in his private chambers. He went about the business of preparing for war.

But his wife, the queen, had no such diversion. She watched as her husband exited the room. He took no notice of her standing in the hallway. She entered the room as he barked orders to the courtiers.

She looked upon her sons.

"No no no no nooooooo." She moaned as she swept them up into her bosom. All they had been rushed into her. All their promise. All their purpose. Her world had been in them. She had lost her husband slowly over the last thirteen years. That had darkened her heart. But this was too much. She held her boys close to her as she continued to weep. They had been her only purpose in life. For a long time she sat on the floor of the chamber, holding her boys close.

She looked into the faces of her boys, each two years apart: 14, 16, and 18. Their heads lolled about at odd angles. The knife had cut deep into the flesh, severing blood vessels, exposing the innards of the larynx, rending muscle and sinew. Her children were dead. The royal bloodline was gone from her. For several hours she sat there, lost to her sorrow. Her pain was so raw, so incredible that her ladies knew not how to respond. They attempted to enter the chamber to comfort her, but she refused to hear them. She glared at them when they tried to get her away from the carnage. Eventually they waited out in the hallway.

As she stared into the face of her youngest, the queen saw the faces of three other children. Three children though not of her body, yet still of royal lineage. Those faces became seared into her mind until they were a reminder of the pain and heartache lying in her lap and upon her bosom.

Her mind snapped.

She quietly stood, picked up the knife from the table, and exited the chamber. Her ladies followed, confused. She gave instructions in passing for the preparation of her sons for burial. As she made her way to her chambers, a thought crept into her conscious. It was a devious and evil thought, but it seated itself and seeded itself. Once at her chamber door it was no longer a thought. She had decided.

She called for the three illegitimate children to be brought before her in the morning. One at a time. Starting with the girls.

The wanderer sat across from Holden and stared off into the distance. Holden kept quiet, waiting for the man to continue. The two were seated at a table in one of the barracks inside the city. Fresh food and drink had been brought to them and they had been left to themselves. They were in a small room with two beds and other essentials necessary for a fighting man to rest. Holden wasn't sure the story would continue just now. It seemed to drain the Wanderer in some way, the telling of this tale. He was not sure how, but it held some deep meaning for the man before him.

"Well I guess we shoul-"

"You wish to know what happened next?" The Wanderer interrupted Holden with his question. Of course he wanted to know! But he kept quiet. It seemed the Wanderer was only steeling himself for whatever was next in this tale.

"The king rode out to meet his one-time knight in battle. It was a great and terrible battle. The king had taken all his remaining knights and soldiers to meet his former knight on the field. The former knight had mustered a formidable host of his own. Many men died. In the end the former knight was routed, but only just. He fled with but one of his knights in tow. The king had been wounded by a stray round in his thigh, but he refused medical attention on the field. He returned to the gates of his city where he fell unconscious off his horse. He died two days later."

The Wanderer stood and walked to a nearby corner of the room. He was facing away from Holden as he spoke again.

"The queen murdered the girls in her bedchamber. One at a time as they were brought to her. She used the same knife which had cut her sons' throats." He took a deep breath and turned to face Holden before continuing. "Before the boy, just shy of his thirteenth birthday, was brought to her she learned of her husband's wounds. The king lay dying from his battle wounds. When the boy was brought to her she did not kill him. Instead she had a servant prepare him a room. She never visited her dying

190

husband, and when the king died she turned her attention to his bastard son. She kept him and adored him, much as a mother adores her own son. But it was not so. She was grooming him."

The Wanderer walked to the other side of the room before continuing.

"Three weeks later, on his thirteenth birthday, she gave a big party for him. He was very happy. At the end of the night she sent for him to come to her. She was in the king's bed chambers. The boy entered and found her there." Again, the wanderer paused and looked at Holden.

"She took him in the king's bed that night and every night for the next three weeks. When she was sure she had conceived..." Another pause. "She killed him in his sleep. The same way she had killed his half-sisters."

Holden sat slack-jawed. He had heard none of this before. Could this all be true? He felt the truth in the man's words, but he was dumbfounded by the scope of the tale. Even here, in this shining city of hope and prosperity, could there be such evil? Apparently so.

"There is more to this tale, my friend. But alas, I grow weary of the telling. Mayhap we shall finish it later. I need to rest." The Wanderer looked appreciatively at his new companion, his new friend, and smiled crookedly. "By the looks of you, we both need to rest."

Holden smiled back at the man standing before him. Yes, he did need rest. He wasn't sure he would be able to sleep with the tale so fresh upon his ears. But of course as soon as he laid his head upon the pillows, he was taken by exhaustion. The Wanderer rested as well, as best he could. He was back home after a very long time. But he knew he was not truly safe. He had, after all, been exiled.

Terran awoke to a soft white light showing through an eastern window. Soft bed linens held him and fluffy pillows cradled his head. He glanced about him and noticed his children asleep in the bed with him. Kiran and Finn breathed steadily and softly on either side of him in the big, soft bed. And it was a real bed: off the floor, with posts and everything. He breathed deeply as he looked up at the ceiling. He was in someone's home. In someone's bed. The soldier, the captain, had brought them to his home in the city. He had told Terran to rest with the children. He had fed them, found a change of clothes for them all, and then given his bed to them. He had then left them. That had been the evening before. Another day had come.

He slowly sat up and looked around the room. There were a great many books on a nearby bookshelf. A simple desk with more books sat across the room. A mirror hung from a closet door. A chest on the floor at the end of the bed. All was quiet. He listened and heard only the breathing of his two children. They slept so peacefully. He looked upon them and smiled. For the first time in a very long while he felt a modicum of peace and hope for them.

Then he remembered the boy. Where was Evan?

His heart hammered in his chest as he began to climb over Finn to get out of the bed. His son began to awaken as he exited the bed. He looked at his boy and whispered for him to return to sleep. He did not want to alarm them. He looked at his daughter. Kiran slept on, smiling slightly. Finn closed his eyes too and returned to his slumber. Terran quickly made his way out the room and into the modest home. As he searched the few other places the boy might have been he began to panic. He became more and more frantic as he looked. Eventually he burst out the door into a small garden at the rear of the home. There he found the boy.

Evan stood in the soft light of morning, surrounded by a brief multitude of verdure. The captain had a bit of a green thumb, it appeared. The boy was lost to the flora. Terran looked on as Evan smelled flowers and gently caressed the leaves of so many growing plants. There was an air of serenity filling the atmosphere. Terran was immediately overcome by it and thereby calmed. He could feel it all, the sheer wonder the child was feeling. There was a promise in this garden that might have been lost on many. But the boy felt it, and through him Terran felt it. It was beautiful.

"Have you ever seen anything like it?" Evan asked as he faced the man before him. Terran could but shake his head slightly. "Neither have I." Evan smiled broadly. He looked around slowly at the greenery as he began to walk toward Terran. He stopped before the man, looking eagerly into his face. Terran had to tear his own eyes away from the garden to look into the boy's face. There he saw a sad smile and tears forming at the rims of the boy's eyes.

"What is wrong, Evan?" Terran immediately thought of his children, but the boy shook his head.

"We are safe. Finn and Kiran are safe. I...I just am overcome. It's so much. All of this." Evan lifted his arms as he looked around him. Terran remembered the boy's arms rising and falling in the cave and briefly shivered. There was power here, in the boy. Great and terrible. Healing and destruction. But the child had saved his family. More than once he had saved them. And the knight! It was too much.

"If it's not too much to ask, will you stay with me a while longer?" Evan was looking away into the distance. He did not seem to be looking at anything in particular. Terran had an eerie feeling the boy was seeing something he could not see.

"Of course, Evan. I'll stay as long as you like." To his own surprise he took Evan's hand in his own. The boy shocked him by tightly grasping the offered hand. They walked around the garden hand in hand for a while longer. The boy quickly returned to his earlier happy state as they examined the flowers and plants. It almost seemed to Terran the plants responded to the boy's touch. He certainly did. He had never experienced such a beautiful morning as this. It seemed a shame it could not last.

The boy stole a few glances at the man. He pushed the sad thoughts away as best he could. He did his best to give Terran peace and beauty this morning. The children were safe, but he had no vision of Terran after this day. That is, in his percipience he did not discern a future for Terran beyond the day. At some point today, Terran would die.

Later in the morning, shortly before noon, the captain returned. He was not alone. With him were three soldiers. They were all four of them armed and armored. The captain entered his home slowly while the soldiers posted outside. Terran and the three children were seated at a small table, eating a modest meal put together from the foodstuffs in the captain's pantry and a few of the many fresh herbs and vegetables growing in his garden. Terran thought the man appeared the slightest bit out of sorts as he slipped into the small dining area.

"I hope you don't mind. We were a little hungry and I took the liberty of preparing a mid-day meal a little early." Terran spoke apologetically, mistaking the somber look on the captain's face as that of disapproval for the meal he had prepared.

"It is quite all right, friend. My home has been opened to you fully. I have no issue with you using it as I would and do." There was something else though. The captain appeared to be gathering himself to speak further.

194

"You are troubled, warrior." The words came not from Evan, but from Kiran. She was looking intently at the man standing before them. As he looked at her she continued, "There is something wrong, and you are troubled by it. It involves us, doesn't it?"

The soldier took a deep breath and exhaled slowly before speaking.

"You are to appear before the court of His and Her Majesty...immediately." The concern on his face was unmistakable. Something was terribly wrong.

Questions began to fly from Terran to his host. What's the matter? Have we done something wrong? Is there a problem with us being here? Are we suspected of something? Is it a good or bad thing to appear before the court?

Evan heard the concern in Terran's voice. He could feel it emanating from the man. But he was fixed on the captain. He stared at and into the man standing before them and saw danger. He could feel the danger inherent in their appearance before the majesties. The court was treacherous. Life and death hung in the balance. The captain feared for them.

"It will be all right, father." Evan spoke the words as he touched Terran's arm slightly. Terran stopped speaking almost immediately and turned to look into the face of his newly adopted son. More than a wave, it seemed a flood of peace overtook him. He smiled gratefully into the face of the boy smiling at him. Terrible power or no, Evan was the key to a great deal of good for so many. Terran felt himself fill to bursting with nothing but love for this boy. He looked slowly into each of his children's eyes as well and smiled at them in turn. They smiled in return.

"Alright then. So be it." Terran stood from the table and stood straight before the captain. "We are in your care, captain. We follow you to court."

The captain looked Terran in the eye and smiled as best he could.

"You are a brave man, Terran. Your children are very lucky to have you as their father. I know not the outcome of your appearance today. But whatever it be, know that I am a friend. And I hold you in high regard."

Evan watched the captain intently as he spoke those words to Terran. He felt the words' honesty. The captain eventually looked in Evan's direction. The two held each other's gaze for a brief moment. Evan gave a slight nod before the captain looked back at Terran.

"I will wait for you outside." At that the captain turned and walked out the front door.

Terran again looked at his children and smiled.

By all appearances the court of the majesties was a grand and cordial affair. Only the direst of cases were heard by the young king and the Queen Mother. The boy made final judgment in these cases with the assistance of mother of course. But the cases were mainly other royals and their petty crises as they dealt with one another. On very few occasions did true crimes make it to this court. But of late more and more cases from commoners were being requested. And some cases were being brought before the court as a matter of due course. The queen was calling for a great many commoners be brought before her and her son. Especially those from outside the known borders of the Realm.

The captain had led Terran, Kiran, Finn, and Evan from his home to the castle proper at the heart of the city. The three soldiers had fallen in behind the travelers. They passed through neighborhoods of modest homes much like the captain's before entering what most likely was a great commercial district. They passed markets and storefronts.

A few people seemed to mark their passage with more than the occasional glance, but most hardly gave them a second look. The closer they got to the castle, the less people seemed to take note of them.

Once they passed through the gates of the castle and into the main courtyard, everything and everyone took on an altogether different appearance. The division between the courtiers and commoners was quite noticeable. Any commoners working or with any business within the castle made sure to make eye contact with Terran at least, and some even said hello and smiled at the children. Not one of the courtiers spoke to them, and only a very few seemed to visually take note of them.

The main courtyard of the castle was vast in size and within many people hurried to and fro. There were vendors within the walls of the castle. The vendors were commoners who brought their wares within the castle walls to sell to the courtiers and hopefully some royals. Evan and the children watched several exchanges between these different people as best they could as they walked through the spaces teeming with throngs of people. Although there were many people within the courtyard, the crowds seemed to part as the captain and his charges made their way through.

They exited the courtyard and made their way down a grand corridor. Obsidian-clad guards were posted at varying intervals throughout the corridor. There were adjoining corridors and doors along the way, but the party continued until the captain stopped before an incredibly large and ornate set of doors. He then turned and faced his charges.

"Be careful any words you speak in here. Truth is discerned from lie in the ears of some in attendance. There is a charm on this place, I think. None have ever entered these halls and been able to deceive the crown." He looked at Terran as he spoke.

He then turned and motioned at the guards at the door. The doors were opened and he led them into the chamber. A wave of nausea passed over Evan as he entered the large room. It was gone almost as soon as it came, but its potency was such that it left a mark upon him.

"Are you all right?" The concern in Kiran's whispered voice was itself soothing. Evan nodded and smiled at her in return. They walked just behind Terran and Finn who followed behind the captain. The party walked upon an aisle marked by massive white columns of alabaster upon either side of them. There were crowds of people in the great hall too. Upon the massive wall to their left were large stained glass windows, each depicting a heroic act performed by a former knight of the realm. To their far right there was a gallery of seats that seemed to be quickly filling.

The captain led the company down some brief steps to a slightly depressed area. There the company halted. In front of them was a raised dais upon which rested two thrones. The dais and chairs were of the purest alabaster. The thrones were ornate of design and manufacture. And the pillows were of such deep and dark red that Evan became lost in them. He felt himself being drawn outward, into the shadow world of his daydreams. He was brought back to himself when he felt the squeeze of his hand as Kiran held him.

Evan looked into her eyes and saw the fear there. What had happened? He was breathing hard, and he felt extremely nervous. He tried to calm himself by looking outwardly into Kiran. He focused on her eyes and her concern for him as he let his own inner strength flow out. His breathing slowed, and he relaxed with each subsequent intake of air. He could feel as much as see the same effect upon Kiran. As he began to relax and draw his strength back into himself he felt an inexplicable push of power.

Someone or something very powerful had entered the chamber. Evan felt the tiny pinpricks of fear begin to work upon his psyche. He closed his eyes and tried to focus. He thought about his new family, his old friends, the Wanderer, but nothing was working. Fear was working its way into him. He opened his eyes again but Kiran was not looking at him to help this time. She, along with everyone else in the chamber, was looking at the king and Queen Mother as they made their entrance.

All were quiet as the two approached the dais from their own chamber entrance. Evan watched as the pair made their way to their thrones. The young king was but a boy, seemingly Evan's age. He walked with his mother, escorting her to the thrones. As she was seated in her seat Evan took the time to look at her closely. He could not see her. Not in the way he was able to see others. Something was wrong. He looked at the king and tried to look into him.

Again he was met with failure. He could not see into him either. He was breathing too hard. Sweat began to form on every part of his body. Something was so very wrong. The air suddenly became thick and hard to breathe. Kiran was squeezing his hand so hard, but he could not regain himself. He felt himself sinking into oblivion. His vision began to blur. He realized his eyes were filling with tears. A well of emotion seemed to empty into him. He could not take it. It was too much.

Then she came to him. He closed his eyes and thought of her, the lady. The one who had led him back to his friends when he had been lost before. He thought of her and he saw her. Her comforting smile brought him back to himself. She was there with him and brought him back. And she spoke to him, of course.

"Beware your heart, lest it betray you. Especially in this place. Be true and honest, yet make no promise."
Then she was gone.

Evan opened his eyes slowly and noticed the Queen Mother looking intently at him. There was no emotion in the glare. She seemed to simply be boring a hole through him with her eyes. Then she looked away as she mutely surveyed the room.

Evan was able to keep himself in the now as he stood with his new family. Kiran held the hands of both boys, Evan on her right and Finn on her left. The younger boy was lost in wonder as he tried to take in all the exquisite finery in the court: the pageantry, the courtiers, the royals. All these things held him in awe. He looked about as one thunderstruck. He was mute with wonder, and it was so very evident on his face.

The family stood before the king and Queen Mother for quite some time as a great many cases were heard. The depressed area upon which they stood was large enough for two separate tables. At one table was the prosecutor who along with several lackeys held a great many stacks of paperwork on his table. He was dressed in a fine suit of dark blue. As the family listened, several cases were presented to the king for judgment. Those on trial were escorted to the additional table before the family. All who went before them were at least of high standing in the community and were represented by some form of legal counsel. Judgments were discussed briefly after some questions and answers. The king and Queen Mother would speak so very softly to one another before the Queen Mother spoke directly to the prosecutor. The prosecutor would then hand down the verdict to the accused.

Almost all the cases that preceded them involved the payment of some fines to the treasury and possibly to some other affected party. There was one severe judgment handed down just before the family was to be presented to court for judgment. An outlander was brought before the court. The prosecutor read a laundry list of charges against the man, but it was the last two that brought a subdued hush over the entire assemblage: espionage and conspiracy against the crown.

The man had no representation, formal or informal. He was alone as he stood before the crown. The case was presented against him. No objections were made. The man was given his own chance to speak in his defense. His fear was nearly palpable as he tried to speak before the court. His unpolished speech sounded all the more unpalatable as he nervously stammered over his words. After a few minutes of almost unintelligible stammering, the man simply stood there silently.

The enthroned royals barely looked at one another before the Queen Mother briefly nodded at the prosecutor. The prosecutor retrieved a document from his table and held it before him as he faced the accused man. He read out loud for all to hear.

"It is the ruling of the crown that you are guilty of all charges leveled against you. As such you are sentenced to death. Upon completion of today's proceedings you shall be hanged until dead, and your body shall be placed in a conspicuous location upon the West Road just outside the western border of the Realm to serve as a deterrent to those others who would seek to do harm to his and her majesty and the Realm of Avalon."

The man looked around at the many people assembled. His eyes finally found Evan's and stopped. They looked at one another for only a brief moment, but Evan could see the need for understanding in those eyes. Unbelievably the man smiled briefly as he looked at Evan. He then turned back to face the prosecutor and the crown. The man was carried away, sobbing silently, to await the end of the day's court proceeding and his impending death.

"And now, your majesties, the intruders from the south." As the prosecutor spoke Terran and his family were urged forward by firm hands. Court guards, wearing the darkest black garb and armor Terran had ever seen, had come around behind the family and began to urge them forward. The family was now at the table opposite the prosecutor's. There were no documents upon the table. It was an obsidian slab void of any markings or blemishes. Evan looked at the table and felt himself being drawn into its emptiness. He reached forward with his free hand to steady himself. As his hand touched the smooth stone table he felt a surge of power course through him. His percipience exploded outward. And the intermingling of images and emotions overtook his perceptions. He reeled at the jolt, but Kiran was there to support him. Her concern and love was great and noticeable even in the face of all the other static in the room.

He did not remove his hand from the table. The power, though great and difficult to comprehend, was a welcome divergence from the loss of percipience he had experienced while in this great chamber. He was now grounded. He allowed himself to become lost to the power and so began his search. He began looking for the source of the energy he had felt earlier, that which had reduced his percipience to nothing in an instant. And so he was lost to the proceedings.

The prosecutor read the charges against Terran, Kiran, Finn, and Evan. Espionage and conspiracy against the crown. The case against them was nearly identical to that presented against the earlier man: almost word for word. Terran listened intently to the flourishing language of the prosecutor. He was determined to mount some sort of defense. He was afraid, but he was also committed to protecting his children: the three of them.

The prosecutor finished his presentation. He then turned toward Terran and the children. "Are there any who would step forward to speak on behalf of these suspected enemies of the crown?" He paused long and hard as he smiled at Terran. He looked at each of the children in turn as he walked slowly between the accused and the dais. He stopped on the other side of the accused table and looked at Terran. "Very well then. If none will speak on your behalf perhaps you would like to speak to the assembled and the crown in response to the charges before you."

Terran's voice betrayed him as a squeak escaped his open mouth when he attempted to speak in the affirmative. He cleared his throat and opened his mouth again but was cut short by the voice of another.

"Wait." The captain stepped into the open from the group of guards behind the family. He stood near Terran as he continued. "I will speak on behalf of this man and his children."

The room was filled with an almost simultaneous gasp from the assembled crowd. Hushed conversations began soon afterward as the captain stood stolidly before the prosecutor. A furrowed brow on the young king's face and a slightly raised brow on that of the Queen Mother were the only indication of surprise from the thrones. The prosecutor seemed quite flustered however. He looked to the crown for a moment before he seemed to recall the proper protocols of the court.

"Very well then." He motioned to the open floor as he returned to his lackeys at his busy table.

The captain looked at Terran and spoke quietly. "No matter what, keep quiet. I will do what I can to save you." Terran simply nodded. It was apparent from the chatter all around the chamber that this was not a normal occurrence.

The captain, clad in his armor and hauberk, stepped forward to address the court. He spoke far more eloquently than was likely expected. His voice carried with it the authority of command, yet he spoke in such a tone as to convey deference to the court and crown. His words were of his initial meeting of Terran and the children. He spoke in great detail regarding that moment near the South Road and all that had transpired since.

Evan heard the voice of the captain. He even heard the words to some extent, but he was lost to their meaning. He was lost to almost everything that was happening around him. His right hand remained firmly attached to the table, and his mind methodically searched the large chamber. He was looking for the other, the one similar to him. There was someone here who had power. It was very difficult for him to search for the source of that power. He scanned the room as he perceived each face, each soul, each heart. He looked from one to the next, his percipience stretching and moving about the chamber. Then he found it.

He opened his eyes and looked at the two royals seated on the dais before him. He could see them with his eyes, but they remained shrouded from his inner vision. A shimmering emptiness enveloped them instead. A stark darkness seemed to fill the space behind them. There was someone else in the chamber with them, someone invisible to him and everyone else.

Evan closed his eyes and pushed against the barrier. It repelled him. He pushed harder and felt it begin to give way slightly. He pushed again and began to slide into it. The power returned to him by the obsidian stone upon which his hand rested seemed to encourage him. He was emboldened and perhaps overly confident as he pressed forward into the barrier.

The barrier was not a wall, but more the psychic consistency of gelatin. As Evan pushed through it in his attempt to reach the king and Queen Mother he felt the push against him begin to grow in its strength. He felt himself getting closer and closer until he reached a point in which his progress was halted.

A pair of eyes and the soft features of a face appeared behind the two royals. Evan pushed even harder and the face solidified and a small frame came into being as Evan was flung back into himself. He opened his eyes as his head snapped back from its downward position. He was looking at the space behind the thrones on the dais. There was nothing there, yet there was someone there. The space appeared empty, but it held a great secret.

Evan looked over at Kiran, but she was lost in the words of the captain, who continued in his historic defense of Terran and his family. Evan looked back in the direction of the royals and was met by the gaze of the Queen Mother. She was looking at him intently now. Evan tried to look away but was held by the intensity in her gaze. After a brief time she smiled at him. A severe chill went down Evan's spine at that. Though he had no percipience to guide him, he felt the danger in that smile.

She held him thusly for a brief moment longer before looking back in the direction of the captain. He was finishing his defense at any rate, and there would need to be some final decision made as to the disposition of the case. Evan was more than relieved that she had stopped looking in his direction. He wiped his brow with his free hand, the hand that had been on the table at which they stood. His left hand still held that of Kiran's right.

"Therefore, I submit to the court, His and Her Majesty, that this family would not be here in our fair city were it not for my own judgment. Their appearance near the South Road was fortuitous for them. We had already engaged with a great number of marauders the day before. This family was lucky enough to be near our return trek home after our patrol." The captain continued to speak with an air of surety and confidence.

Evan snuck a glance at the Queen Mother. She was looking at the captain and seemed not to notice Evan at all. He wasn't convinced that was so. He still looked back at the area behind the seated royals. He placed his hand on the table again and observed the barrier still in place. It enveloped the dais and seated royals completely and seemingly with more substance. He noticed a brief flash of emerald orbs from the near distance behind the royal thrones. There but for a moment as the barrier pulsed outward in an obvious show of force.

Whoever was there was displaying some power (and perhaps a warning). Evan took heed and removed his hand from the stone slab. He was breathing somewhat heavily. He took a while longer to regain himself and return his thoughts to the events of the trial. He took a deep breath and looked at Kiran.

Her brown eyes stared worriedly into his. He tried to smile and found it somewhat difficult. He was at a loss without use of his extra senses. He felt inadequate to her at that moment. She looked for a while longer then turned her attention back to the captain, who was finishing his defense of their family.

"And so, Your Majesties, these accused were not intent on travel to our city. They sought not entry across our border. They were not even upon our road. There was not an intent to come here, let alone an intent to commit any crime within this great and fair city." The captain paused for a moment as he looked back at the family for whom he had risked so much. He smiled as he made eye contact with each of them. He then turned back to face the king and Queen Mother.

"I ask that the charges leveled against them be dismissed and they be allowed to go free. Or if the majesties be not pleased with allowing them access to our beloved realm, then grant them passage and escort to the south gate where they may leave us as they came."

The two seated royals looked at one another as they had before. Their silent exchange seemed longer than before. The Queen Mother then turned back toward the prosecutor but this time she stood quickly and looked directly at Terran.

"Tell me, father to these children, if you had to choose to give the life of one of your children in order to save the remainder of your family, which one would it be?"

206

She was glaring at him with such virulence. Terran reeled as if he had been slapped. He took a small step back and instinctively looked at his children: Kiran and Finn. They were both staring back at him wide-eyed. He then looked at Evan, but the boy was staring at the tall, elegant woman atop the dais. And she was staring back at him, a smirk growing on her face.

"Choose one, or shall you all die here today?" She glanced back into the dismayed face of Terran. He looked back and forth from her to his beloved children. He was dumbfounded. Her smirk continued to grow until her teeth were exposed in a full, relentless smile. The captain stepped forward to speak but was stopped short by the Queen Mother.

"Be silent, captain. Lest you lose your head today as well. You will not unbidden speak another word here today." She glared briefly at him as she spoke then turned her attention back to Terran. Terran was lost in despair. He looked deeply into the eyes of his daughter and his son. He could not fail them. Not now. But he knew not how to save them. And the boy.

Evan had silently taken a step around the table. He had released Kiran's hand and was about to take another step when he felt a resounding *NO* course through his body. He did not actually hear it, but he was almost certain he felt it. He continued on. He walked as if in a dream. He was on the other side of the table. The terribly beautiful woman towered above and before him, her smile cold enough to freeze him in his tracks. He stopped and looked into her cold, icy blue eyes.

"I will give my life for them." Evan spoke the words without flinching, without looking away from her, without thought for himself.

"So be it." She was nodding to the guards to take possession of the boy.

Terran saw what was happening. It could not be. The boy was precious. The boy was his responsibility. And the knight had pledged himself! He ran forward to protect the boy, his charge, his son. Before he could reach Evan he felt an incredible pain pierce his back. The shaft of an arrow protruded from his back, just left of center and below the shoulder blades. It had missed his heart but entered his left lung.

Terran stumbled and fell to his knees. Evan looked upon him, helpless. The boy moved forward to embrace the man who had stepped forward to protect him, and the man began to stand to reach for the boy again. A guard grabbed Evan roughly by the arm. Another feathered missile pierced Terran through the neck.

He fell immediately to the cold floor. A pool of blood began to spread around his face and head as he lay there trying to live. Mercifully, his spine had been severed by the second arrow. Though he could feel himself dying, he felt no pain. His final thoughts were of his family. His beautiful Kiran and Finn. And his beloved wife, Sofia. He hoped she would be waiting for him now. He was so very afraid. And so very cold.

Evan was being pulled away as he witnessed the second arrow pierce Terran. He watched in horror as his new friend fell to the floor. His mind began to cloud as he watched the captain run to take Kiran and Finn in his arms, to restrain them from running to their father who lie dying upon the cold, stone floor. The screams filled his ears as the guards continued to pull him away. He tried to make it back to his family, but the hands that held him were strong and rough. He was unsteady on his feet, unsteady in his mind, and the screams filled his ears and made him even more lost. Confusion overtook him and an imposed weariness filled his mind. It was a little while before he realized the screams that filled his ears were coming from his own raw throat.

208

Darkness overtook him as he passed from consciousness into an empty, induced sleep.

10 Meetings

Holden awoke from a troubled sleep. His dreams had been dark, abysmal things he mercifully could not remember. A light sweat covered his body and his head was consumed with a dull pain reminiscent of a previous night's overindulgence in drink. He wished he'd had too much to drink the night before instead of a night full of dark and terrible visions. Death consumed his mind and he tried to shake the feeling overcoming him.

He did not have to look about the room to know the Wanderer was not with him. He had felt alone upon first waking. The man did not seem to sleep anyway. Holden thought briefly about the strange man and the tale he had been telling. Absurdity seemed to have found its way into the life he now was living. Holden could but chuckle at the thought of anything about his life ever having been ordinary. But recent events made all he had previously experienced seem almost trivial.

Holden stepped out into the cool, pre-dawn air. Standing within the barracks' courtyard he looked about and noticed he was alone save one person. The Wanderer sat upon a bench nearby, his back to Holden. The bench faced a small, brick-enclosed pool. Within the center of the pool was an ornate fountain with a continual trill of water flowing about it. Several fish swam lazily about the cool waters of the pool as the Wanderer seemed to study the flow of water from fountain to pool. Holden only stood and watched from his vantage point of some thirty feet away. He found himself pondering the puzzling instrument of destruction who sat quietly before him.

He walked over to the bench and sat beside his new friend. He looked into the pool and observed several large fish swimming in the lightly rippling waters. The fish swam lazily about seemingly without a care in the world. Holden wondered what his strange new friend was pondering as he stared solemnly into the waters. He found himself becoming lost within his own thoughts as he sat quietly. Questions formed in his mind, but he thought it best to remain quiet for now. He wasn't sure of the stranger's capacity for intrusion, especially when he seemed so at peace.

Holden risked a look into the face of the stranger.

The Wanderer, though lost in his thoughts, was aware of his new friend, his new ally, as Holden approached and sat beside him. He was pondering a great many things as he sat in the courtyard. The waters of the fountain soothed his psyche as he thought about the boy. Evan was a constant in his mind's eye. He knew the boy was in danger but had a feeling the boy was safe for the most part. At least he had not gotten any indications otherwise from the intruding Lady who lately seemed to feel the need to regularly interject herself into his life.

Alex wondered more and more about the Lady's intentions. He could not fathom the power that exhibited itself through her, but he was bound to it and otherwise complicit in its use of him. Whatever its source, it was beneficial to him and his ultimate desire. He felt himself somewhat a monster, an outsider. Even so, he was determined to make amends for all he had allowed to transpire in his past. Darkness was at the core of his enmity. For as dark as his heart was, he was determined to fight for light.

The two men sat in silence for a long time, each lost to his own thoughts. Their thoughts were many and varied, and some of their thoughts were at times similar in nature. The Lady interwove herself into the workings of their minds, silently insinuating herself. They each took notice and let it be. What else could they do? Each man knew of her importance and her power, though they were at different levels of exposure to her. Each man had his own past to draw upon and seek forgiveness or at least desire to give recompense.

They sat in silence and in thought until the first distinct rays of light crept over the eastern foothills and illuminated the new day. Holden found himself lost within his thoughts. He slipped into a shadow of himself as he stared mutely into the soothing pool. His vision strayed and he slid even farther into an indistinct darkness within his psyche. This descent began slowly as he fell into himself, but abruptly he felt a sensation much like that of falling freely as his mind was taken elsewhere.

She had come for him.

Holden felt the first stirrings of giddiness enter his mind and heart. She was a creature of pure beauty and love. He longed to see her, to be in her presence. To bask in her light. A smile covered his face as he sat looking into the pool, though he no longer could see the waters. He was far away from the pool, the courtyard, the great city in the north. He was in her presence.

He stood upon the meadow. A myriad of colorful wildflowers bloomed unchecked all about him. Butterflies flitted to and fro in the warm air. The air itself was a boon to his weathered soul. He breathed deeply and reveled in the warmth of sun, the beauty of flora, the replenishment of love. As he closed his eyes and continued to breathe deeply and take in all the emotions coming to him, she spoke softly in his ear.

"Welcome, weary traveler." Her words caressed his ears and his soul at the same time. He thought to turn and look into her face, but when he did she was not there, though she was everywhere. She filled his heart and soul with effervescence, and he was lost to it.

"Why can't I see you? Why won't you show yourself to me?" He turned this way and that, feeling her presence, but his eyes could not find her.

"You know me no matter my form. In time you will know me better. But for now, you do see me, you simply do not realize it." The words were melodic, hanging upon the air. He could almost see the meaning in them. His soul and mind were filled with them and the possibility of greatness and love. He smiled dumbly much like an idiot he would think later, though it was a smile of pure joy, a child's smile. He was happy in this place, in her presence, in her light, in her love.

"He will need you more than he can know, more than you can know. You must do all you can to stay with him. There will, however, come a time when the two of you will part. At that point you need to be strong. You must become more than you know of yourself, but all I know you must be."

Holden was dumbfounded by these statements. How could he be more than *that* man? The Wanderer was strength embodied in physical form.

"I don't understand. How can I be more? I don't get it."

She eased his mind with the blowing of the wind. He felt it upon his exposed flesh and it calmed him. It rushed through him, a calming effect like none he had ever felt before.

"Be still, be quiet, be calm. You are more than you know, as is he. Know this, though you are very different, the two of you are nearly the same. There will come a day when you become the rock upon which he leans. Be ready for it."

The field, the flora, the butterflies flitting, all of it began to fade. Holden felt himself coming back into his physical body. A sadness began to creep into his heart because he was leaving beauty behind for a time. Yet a part of him knew he would see the lady again, or at least be in her presence once more. She was not done with him. Holden blinked rapidly as his eyes came back into focus.

He took a deep breath, let out an audible sigh, and stared quietly at the fish in the pool before him. He glanced at the Wanderer and noted the steely gray eyes looking intently upon him.

"So, she has spoken to you again."

Holden was a bit embarrassed by this. He squirmed on the bench.

"Well...she...I...I guess, yeah, she spoke to me again."

"Good. She hasn't spoken to me in some time. At least she's talking to one of us." The Wanderer continued to look intently at Holden as he spoke.

"She said-"

"I don't want to hear what she told you, unless she gave you something specific to pass to me. Her words are generally specific for the hearer." The Wanderer then took a deep breath himself as he continued to look intently into the face of his companion.

"Be wary of her words and understand that if she put you on a task, it will not be easy." The Wanderer spoke these few words almost introspectively.

Holden thought to himself, *No kidding especially as my task is to be with you.*

It almost appeared as if the Wanderer read Holden's mind and heard the words. Holden looked away from the glare of the strange man. The Wanderer looked upon him for several moments longer before abruptly standing.

"We must ready ourselves. I do believe we are bound to meet some very important people this day."

Holden wasn't sure if that was a good or bad thing. He stood as well. The two men made their way back to their room and began to ready themselves for the day's coming events. Holden asked no questions, and the Wanderer offered no further explanations.

Soft white linens enveloped Evan as he awoke to the early morning rays coming through an open window. Birds chirped lightly outside as he heard a slight bit of conversation outside his door. Snippets of conversation, words without meaning, and then the voices passed down what appeared to be a hallway outside. The soft white linens, pillows, and a huge cushioned bed enveloped him. Evan began to take note of the room as he looked about. He could see tapestries upon the wall, a large writing desk with pen and ink on it, papers nearby, and walls with several full bookshelves as well. A massive wardrobe covered nearly half a wall on its own. He sat up in the bed slowly, trying to regain his bearings as he recalled the previous day's events. He knew he had slept for a while. He'd had horrible dreams.

The lady had not come to him at all during his sleep. Some of the visions were lost to him, yet others remained. Snippets in his mind's eye. He wondered at the fate of Kiran and Finn, his new brother and sister. He began to choke up at the thought of Terran, a man who had died in an attempt to protect him. He felt somewhat to blame for Terran's death. Farther into his mind's recesses he knew this was not the case, but the feelings of guilt gnawed at him nonetheless. As he swung his legs over the edge of the bed a wave of nausea consumed him, this one of course the natural variety not brought on by any supernatural power. He had not eaten for some time and the sleep had been induced though he knew not its cause. His bearings balanced and he placed his feet upon the floor and stood up.

A table sat beneath the window with two chairs. He gingerly walked to the table and took a seat. Fresh fruit, juice, and honey milk were awaiting him. He ate some fruit and noticed his appetite had not been affected by the previous bout of nausea. He finished the fruit and juice very quickly and was savoring the sweetness of the honey milk when a soft knock on the door interrupted him. He did not answer the knock.

After a brief moment the door opened and into the bedchamber slipped a slight figure. A girl, approximately Evan's age, clothed in a dark brown cloak with the hood pulled back to reveal flowing red hair. She was tall but her facial features intimated her youthfulness. She spoke softly to Evan.

"I hope everything is to your liking. I am sorry for your friend."

She looked at him with the deepest of green eyes. Evan could but stare at her. He knew not how to respond other than to say: "Yes, the room is fine. Although I do wish to know how my friends are faring."

The girl took several steps toward him, somewhat excited as she spoke. "Your friends are fine, the girl and boy you came with. Your brother and sister?"

She raised one eyebrow ever so slightly as she asked, as if perhaps she knew the familial relationship were not as purported. Evan did not respond.

She took several steps closer. "Well, your brother and sister are fine. They too are in rooms and being cared for. They have not been harmed. The man you were with, your father, well he has been taken from the city."

Evan felt a surge of anger at that, as his brows knitted. The girl took a hesitant step backward. "I am sorry about your friend. About the man, your father. I am sorry that he died. I am sorry for everything that has happened since you have been here." She paused for a brief time and waited until Evan looked into her eyes before continuing.

"I don't know what is going on. But I know that he was not your father, that those two others are not your brother and sister. Soon everyone here will know it. You cannot stay here." She spoke in hushed tones and with an air of conspiracy.

Evan looked even more closely at the girl. Paying more attention to her eyes. He had seen them. He had seen those eyes. Now he realized he could not see into the girl. He understood that she had been in the chamber with them. She had held his power at bay. She had been with the king and Queen Mother. She had made his power almost into nothing. He could not see anything but her eyes. She smiled, a brief and innocent smile. There was no malice in it.

"Yes, I am the one that you felt, the one that you saw. I am the other one. I am like you. But you are very different. Your power is different than any I have ever come across. And I have seen many people come into the city and not make it out alive. If they find out who you are, if they find out what you are, they will kill you. You have to leave, you have to be away from this place."

She abruptly turned and headed towards the door. Before opening to leave she turned back to him and said, "I shall return briefly. Please do not leave your room. There are guards posted outside." She slipped quietly outside the door before Evan could respond.

He sat back down at the table and drank more of the honey milk. His thoughts were many, and they were varied. They went from anger to sadness to hope. For a time he thought on the Wanderer and pondered his fate, and he wondered if the hero would ever find his way to this place to save them.

Kiran and Finn awakened that morning in a room similar to Evan's, though it had two separate beds and was a bit smaller. There was some evidence the room had

218

belonged to some children in the recent past. There were some toys neatly stored in a chest in a far corner of the room. Finn had awakened early and had found the toys (he was playing with a wooden sword when Kiran awakened from her troubled sleep). Both children had been awake when a servant had brought them a tray of fresh fruit, breads, and a jug of milk. The old woman had delivered the food on a table and had not been able to look upon the children for longer than a second without shaking her head and stifling an urge to cry. Kiran had thought to ask the servant a question, but when she saw the pained look on the woman's face she thought better of it. Best not to put the woman in such a situation.

The siblings had nearly finished their morning meal when the soft knock stopped them in mid-chew. Kiran immediately stood and walked to the door. "Yes. Who's there?" She was fearful they had come for them, come to take them to be killed like father. Her own voice sounded tinny to her, barely more than a whisper.

Another knock on the door, this one a bit stronger and urgent. Kiran gathered herself and responded more forcefully than she meant: "Who's there?"

"May I enter, please?" A soft voice spoke from the other side. A girl's voice. Kiran was but a step from the door. She moved ahead and slowly opened the door. The red-haired, fair-skinned, green-eyed girl stood in the hallway. A lone, black-garbed guard stood sentry across the hallway. "Please?" the girl asked again. Kiran stepped aside, and the girl entered. The girl turned and closed the door quickly and quietly.

Kiran immediately noted the plain but silken attire the girl wore. She also could smell a soft flowery fragrance emanating from the girls person. The girl turned back to face Kiran and frowned a bit. "Please do not be frightened. I mean you no harm. I am, or I hope to be, a friend. Please, may we sit and talk for a while."

Finn had stopped eating and had stood when Kiran had opened the door. He was now walking toward his sister and the strange girl with an almost blank look upon his face. He almost appeared to be in a trance. Kiran did not notice, but the girl looked at him and began to step back from him, an almost frightened look upon her own face. Kiran turned and faced her brother. She protectively stepped in his path and grasped him, more roughly than she intended.

"Finn!"

He stopped in his tracks, but he seemed not to actually see her for a few more moments. He began to blink rapidly and eventually looked in his sister's eyes. "Kiran?" He took a small step back from her. "What happened? Where are we?" He looked around confusedly. "Where is father?" He took another step back, and his breathing began to increase. "Father...he is..." His words were softly spoken, and Kiran could feel her heart breaking in her chest. She nodded at her brother; the tears were stinging her eyes now. Finn stepped forward and embraced her as he wept loudly into her shoulder. They both crumpled to the floor in each other's arms.

The strange girl stood close by, an amber hue emanating from her. Her eyes were closed, and two silent tears traveled down her face as she felt every ounce of the sadness flowing from the siblings. She provided them peace and comfort as best she could. But some grief must be endured in order to be overcome.

After several minutes Kiran pulled away from her brother. She helped him to his feet and walked him to a comfortable chair in a far corner of the room. He sat quietly, trusting in his older sibling to care for him. She retrieved a blanket from the bed and covered him as he curled up in the chair. She lovingly kissed his forehead as he began to fall into a quiet sleep.

220

Kiran noted the girl had not moved from her position just inside the door during the entire exchange between her and Finn. She also saw the tears on the girl's face. She even thought she could feel something other but was not sure. Once Finn was dozing peacefully she walked purposefully toward the girl.

"Who are you?"

The girl had been watching Kiran with a downturned countenance. Before responding to the query she lifted her head and looked directly into Kiran's eyes. Kiran felt the slightest bit intimidated at the change in composure.

"I am Kat, and I wish to be your friend. I would help you if you would let me. You and your brothers are not yet safe. Especially the other one. Once they find out what he is, what he can do, they will likely kill you all."

Kiran was nearly speechless. "Is Evan all right? Where is he? What has happened to him?" Kat's quick finger to her own lips and her glance toward the door silenced the burst of questions from Kiran. Kat slowly shook her head as she spoke ever so softly.

"You will have to trust me and keep as quiet as you can. If anyone asks you about him you must continue to claim him as your brother. I know he is not, and I fear she may suspect it as well. But she is not sure yet. If she does discern it, she will kill him. And you as well." The girl, Kat, looked over at Finn now quietly asleep. She smiled as she spoke. "I wish I knew of familial love, the love of a father, the love of a brother or sister. I have felt it in others, but I have never known it myself." She looked back into Kiran's eyes with tears welling up in her own. Kiran felt a slight bit of sadness for this strange girl, though she knew not why. It was gone in an instant as the girl smiled and gingerly stepped to the door.

"Wait." Kiran stepped forward and took the girl's arm. A not so unfamiliar sensation coursed through her at that touch. She stepped back as she looked anew at her new friend. Kat only turned and looked knowingly at Kiran. She smiled slightly and nodded. Kiran smiled as best she could, though she was again unsure of the world and all its strange happenings. Kat then opened the door and slipped out of the room and back into the workings of the castle.

Kat walked briskly yet quietly down the old halls. She passed a few unsuspecting faces. Most of the servants and dutiful workers paid her little heed. She was not known as a royal or a trusted member of any council. She was thought of as an orphan child brought into the care of the royal family due to the courtesy and goodwill of the queen. She did not know of any other than the queen (and likely the boy king) who knew of her abilities. And she had been careful to not show the full extent of her powers. Lucky for the boy, Evan, she had not shown that yet. The queen would likely have had her kill the boy, or at least try. Kat was not sure she could actually do it. The boy was much more powerful than any she had come upon in the past.

Her thoughts held onto him for a long while as she purposefully walked the halls. She ascended several large staircases until she reached a large set of heavy, ornate oaken doors. The guards stationed outside immediately opened the door and guided her inside. Once she was announced, the guards left her before the Queen Mother. Several ladies were assisting Her Majesty with a number of deep, dark fabrics. Reds, purples, blacks: these colors were displayed from a number of large spools. After a short time and several choices were made by Her Majesty, the ladies and their servants left the room with the cloths and their notes from the Queen Mother.

Kat stood silently, awaiting some instruction. She had been before the Queen Mother on many occasions.

She understood the calm appearance before her now could easily be but a façade masking a storm of angry virulence beneath. It was always best to wait it out and let the Queen Mother speak first with no interruption and especially no assumption. After several more moments, Her Majesty walked over to Kat and stood before her.

"Well hello there, child. How are you?"

Kat looked up into the smiling face before her. The Queen Mother was a beautiful woman by her own rights. Slight lines marked the corners of her mouth as she seemed to constantly smile. Kat thought the smile more forced than genuine. That smile had been worn at many an execution. And it had no real mirth in it. It was benign at best and malicious at worst.

A chill passed down Kat's spine and she fought back a shiver. The Queen Mother seemed to not notice as she raised an eyebrow awaiting a response.

"I am quite well, Your Majesty."

"Excellent!" The Queen Mother turned and walked away toward the window. "Child, can you tell me of the world beyond the lands we control? Do you know what lies out there in the great wilderness of the world?"

Kat was a little mystified at these questions. Normally the Queen Mother only asked specific questions about happenings in the castle or within the households of other royals, especially any visiting the castle proper. She had not ever heard mention of the outside world except when court was being conducted and sentences being handed down. Kat's only view of the outside world came at the hands of a great many men and women being put to death by the vicious woman before her.

"No, Your Majesty, I cannot tell you of the world outside. I know nothing of it."

"That is right child; you have been spared the wretchedness that is out there. I have spared you. And I have let you live here in my home. I have cared for you, and I have done so with little to nothing expected in return." The Queen Mother turned and faced Kat at this. Her smile was still upon her face, but Kat noticed a distinct gleam in her eyes. The Queen Mother was genuinely happy at whatever thoughts were in her head.

"Child, the time is coming when you shall help me to bring an everlasting peace to everyone in the failing world beyond our borders. The peace of this House shall cover all the lands." She was walking towards Kat now. Kat was held by the Queen Mother's power. She wanted to look away from the eyes, the smile. But she could not. The Queen Mother had some power herself.

"You will help me, child. Yes?"

"Yes, Your Majesty." Kat was nodding numbly as she spoke the words.

"I have seen the great peace I propose." The Queen Mother slowly turned and walked toward a full-length mirror on a far wall. The mirror was nearly seven feet tall and almost four feet wide. The Queen Mother stopped before it and began to whisper almost inaudibly. Kat strained to hear the words. She could not make out all of them. She heard the words *cleansing* and *fire*. And in the mirror's reflection she could see the small smile on the Queen Mother's face grow to a full, toothy grin as the whispered words were spoken.

The Queen Mother took a deep breath and walked back over to the young Kat. Her smile had returned to its normal and previously demented state. Kat waited patiently, not sure of where the conversation was now going. Never before had she entertained anything of this nature when meeting with the Queen Mother. A new sensation coursed through her and settled in her bones: fear. She had felt brief moments of fear before, especially several years before when she had first met the woman standing before her. But she had learned over the years that the woman was easily understood. The Queen Mother craved power, but had not ever had any real designs on acquiring more than she possessed. But now that seemed to have changed. Her statements regarding the outside world and her words at the mirror, those intimations stirred up real fear again in Kat's heart.

"Is something wrong, dear child? You look a little ill."

Kat realized she was breathing a bit too heavily. Her heart was also pounding a bit too hard in her chest. She also had lost focus for a moment as she was lost to these new feelings of fear and uncertainty.

"I am sorry, Your Majesty. I have not been feeling quite well today. Please forgive me."

"Oh, dear child, there is nothing to forgive." The austere woman touched Kat's cheek with such tender care it would have been seen as that of a loving mother's touch to the unsuspecting eye. A burst of power surged within Kat at the initial touch. There was something other than the Queen Mother's royalty at work here. There was indeed real power present, and it had not been so evident before the very recent past.

The Queen Mother removed her hand and let it drop back to her side. She looked for a few moments longer at her charge, the child she had saved for her own purposes. She smiled a bit longer, remembering the day she had collected this current chess piece. An orphaned child of six, the girl was nearly lost to the streets of the city. And even in the city of Avalon bad things could still happen and did happen to the unwise and unprotected. The Queen Mother had found the child and had taken possession of her. And since that day the girl had proven most useful. And now the day was approaching when she would prove even more so.

"Child, there will come a time very soon when we shall make of the world a great place. I will do this great thing along with my son, the King." The Queen Mother had begun to walk away toward several remnants of cloth left hanging for her inspection. She walked slowly and deliberately. She stopped suddenly and spun on her heels to face Kat.

"And you will help us, help me. Won't you child?" The fire was back in her eyes, and an underlying air of power rose up in her voice. She was on the verge of transforming into something other than the woman she had been. She was very nearly that something new at the very moment she spoke to Kat. Kat was still somewhat mystified at the subject of the conversation, but she managed to maintain her sense of self and her wits.

"Yes, Your Majesty. I owe you the greatest debt and your House all the honor I might bestow upon it by whatever means I have at my disposal." She thought a second longer before adding, "And I shall evermore be in the crown's debt and shall do all in my power to protect and serve the crown."

The Queen Mother looked upon the girl for a while longer, her smile never faltering in the least. She took another deep breath then walked briskly to Kat with her arms outstretched. She embraced Kat quickly and firmly. Kat responded to the embrace by putting her own arms around the waist of the Queen Mother lightly but fully. The woman held her for what was far too long a time. Fear coursed through Kat though she valiantly kept it buried deep within.

Holden walked silently beside the Wanderer as they followed the sergeant through the streets of the city proper. They were outside the barracks and moving through what appeared to be several different neighborhoods. Children played games outside the doorsteps of some of the nicer residences, and every so often conversations were halted and movement seemed to pause as eyes marked their passage. For the most part, however, their brief trek went unnoticed and without much ado.

After a few twists and turns, the three men arrived at a modest home. The sergeant stepped up to the door and immediately turned the knob and entered. Alex and Holden entered directly behind him. They stood in a humble foyer that opened into a larger living area. Though modest by the standards of the wealthy and royal persons in the city, the home was luxurious by any standards of the wastelands and small towns to which Holden had become accustomed. Even so, the home appeared ever so comfortable and homey rather than ostentatious. Everything in the home appeared to serve some purpose rather than simply be for the sake of being.

A large fireplace almost filled the central wall of the living room. Above it was a portrait of a man dressed for battle. He was adorned in a hauberk and cape. He wore black garb similar to that Holden had seen on a couple of men similarly clad as he and Alex followed the sergeant through the city to this home. Holden noted the angular features on the face of the man in the portrait and the stern look upon the face when he realized Alex was also studying the portrait. He saw in the Wanderer something he had not seen before. He couldn't swear to it, but he thought he saw the beginnings of a smile. He definitely saw what looked like recognition on the other man's face.

"Please, sirs." The sergeant stood at a separate doorway, bidding the two men to follow. "This way."

The Wanderer looked appreciatively at the portrait again before following the sergeant. Holden followed the two into a separate room. It appeared to be a study. There were a few seemingly comfortable chairs placed about a small oval table. On three of the four walls were bookshelves with a great many books. Holden had never seen a larger collection of tomes in his life. He found himself spellbound as soon as he entered the room. He looked about the room in wonder, lost to the sheer number of ideas held in the pages on the walls before him. For a time he was lost even unto himself. He did not even hear the sergeant speak before leaving the room.

After a time he observed Alex remove a large leather-bound book from one of the larger shelves. Alex then seated himself at a small reading desk and slowly began to leaf through the volume. Holden continued to look about the room. He moved from shelf to shelf noticing a great many titles as he did so. He had never heard of most of the books. Many were histories of different regions. Most had to do with historical figures from the north or histories of the north. He also noticed a great many stories of fantastical tales from ages hence.

Quite some time passed as Holden drifted from volume to volume, removing some of the titles from the shelves to look briefly through them before moving on to the next. Alex continued to leaf through the title he had taken to the desk. After a time he came to a section in the book which he read more intently. He seemed to be studying it with some great care. He began to read with a bit more urgency as the time stretched from minutes into hours. It was nearing midday when the Wanderer closed the book and abruptly stood.

Holden had seated himself in a very comfortable chair near the one window in the room. He was deeply inured in a tale of chivalry, dragons, and other fairy creatures. He did not notice the Wanderer pacing about the room for several moments. Eventually he looked up from the book in his hands and took note of the dark figure walking about the room. Alex seemed lost to his own thoughts and totally out of character. He seemed worried.

"What is it?" Holden closed the book as he spoke. He began to stand as well. The Wanderer stopped pacing and faced him. The look upon his face was grave and bore resemblance to the face he had worn when the two had first met along the road to the North. "What is the matter?"

The Wanderer looked upon his friend as his mind began to formulate some sort of plan. He was lost to newfound information. So much had happened in the recent past to which he had not been privileged. So many things had changed, and yet so much had not. The danger inherent in his return to the North had not diminished. Indeed, it seemed that it may well have grown. How could this be? How cold it have remained, even after so long a time?

"We need to find my friends. Very quickly." The Wanderer was looking directly into Holden's eyes. Holden could see a fire burning behind those orbs. An intense heat which would sear the flesh of any enemy. The man's calm exterior belied the deadly passion which raged in his heart. Alex was more than a man. He was indeed a dealer of death. And a focused one at that. God have mercy on whoever became the focus of his ire.

"And we need to get away from this place as soon as we can." Alex was very calm as he spoke. Holden, however, could sense the urgency. Something was so very wrong.

The two men turned simultaneously and drew their pistols as their host entered the doorway. The man stood with his hands raised, palms outward, just at his shoulders. He was clad in the armor of the soldiers of the city, but his raiment was subtly more austere. He had upon his lapel a pin of white gold in the shape of a single star. Upon his right hip was a pistol, and his left held a scabbard with a sword. The hilt protruding from said scabbard was onyx limned with white gold. It was unlike anything Holden had seen before. Holden noted the resemblance the man bore to

the portrait in the living room. He and Alex lowered their
weapons slowly and simultaneously.

Power and peace, love and fear, the rule of might
and a conquered world. She looked into the mirror and saw
it all. The Queen Mother, clad in a gold-laced red gown,
stood before her mirror. She saw so much in the mirror as
she looked upon her reflection. Visions passed slowly,
swimmingly, assuredly before her. Promises and
assurances had been made, and the doubters and slow to
accede would suffer as they deserved. There would be
none but the weakest left to oppose once the war began.
The victory would be swift and judgment harsh and
crushing. Any remaining would be cleansed by fire.

The fire, burning brightly and urgently in the
distance, called to her. Its insistence remained a constant in
her mind. It burned for her. For her! She was for it and it
for her. It yearned for her and she for it. Much as a distant
and forlorn lover, it was calling to her, waiting for her, lost
within her. She was its muse and it was her champion.
The fire would cleanse the land and make all her subjects.
Everyone would bow to her or burn in its cleansing.

She smiled briefly as she turned away from the
mirror and its promise. The smiled remained for a while
longer as she breathed deeply and thought on her current
guests. One or more of them might prove useful to her.
The girl, Kat, had come to her in such a way (though at a
much younger age). There were pockets of power
springing up in the land, they need only be contained and

controlled. If they could not be so, then they had to be eliminated. None could be left to stand in her way. None.

The fire had told her, had warned her: The power of the earth will be borne of its children. Convert them to her use if possible, or destroy them if not.

She breathed deeply and her smile lessened a bit. She was wondering about her new guests in earnest. What exactly was it she had felt in them? She was unsure and intrigued. And a tinny voice spoke softly in her ear, intimating the slightest bit of fear.

Her brow creased severely, and she walked briskly out the door.

11 Into The Den

The Wanderer and Holden sat in the room with their host. The men looked upon each other for a while, each with a mug of ale. Speaking slowly and deliberately Lockland asked. "So how is it you two have come to be at my home?"

The Wanderer asked, "Are you familiar with the great tales of the City of the North?" Lockland, obviously a commander of the city of the north, a commander of men, and with his great library of the history of the north, was well aware of the history of the city and the people as well.

"Of course. I am very well versed in the history of the great city of the north. My father, his father, and his father before him all served the crown. We have all been soldiers, we have all lived and died in the service of the north."

The Wanderer smiled at this. He was well aware from his observations that his host, Gregory Lockland, was a servant of the North. Perhaps not of the current regime, but he had to be certain. Lockland could see that his guest was testing him, feeling him out, but he had questions of his own.

"So tell me, friend. How is it you have come to be my guest? Did you not travel the North Road and enter our city? Are you not a possible hostile?"

The Wanderer smiled crookedly. "I am no stranger to this place, friend. You seem to be an honorable man. I know your men have given you my name, and I see you recognized me as who I say I am. This place at one time had been my home. I have been gone for a long time, but I am of the North. I do not know if I am friend to the throne, for I know not who now sits upon it. I have heard tales, different versions of the royalty that is there now. But I ask of you, what is being done here in the North to disrupt what is growing in the east?"

Lockland seemed perplexed at the question. "We are aware of nothing transpiring in the east. Our dealings have been with the south. And now it seems we have something troubling occurring there."

The Wanderer was perplexed. "What do you mean?"

Lockland took a great breath. He looked upon his two guests. He noticed a look upon Holden's face. The Wanderer's companion seemed to be gripping the arm of his chair ever so tightly. His jaw was clenched and eyes widened.

"It would appear your friend has some knowledge of this, more than I might."

Indeed he did have information regarding that of which Lockland was speaking. He looked upon the faces of the two men before him and took a very deep breath as he nodded slowly. "Yes, I know of some things in the south. I know what the captain speaks of, and it is very troubling indeed."

Holden very deliberately told the two men of all he knew regarding the events at Northern Alley. He tried to relay every detail. He did not get into much detail related to his dispatching the men sent to kill him at the crossroads. He thought he noticed a strange look from the Wanderer but dismissed the thought as his conscience nagging him for leaving out some details.

The two men listened intently as he spoke. It appeared the captain did not have as much information as he thought. Lockland's brow remained furrowed throughout Holden's tale. Holden finished at his meeting with the Wanderer. Neither he nor the Wanderer spoke to the man of their venture into the mountain and encounter with the beast in the chasm.

Lockland had seated himself in his chair while Holden spoke. His guests had followed suit and seated themselves as well. When Holden's brief tale was done, the captain looked down at the floor and shook his head slowly. He looked back into the faces of the two men opposite him. He took several deep breaths before he spoke.

"Things are definitely worse than I had imagined, worse than any of us had imagined." He looked away and shook his head slightly before looking back into the face of the Wanderer. "The Queen Mother sent her daughter south to broker a deal with a growing city, this Northern Alley, due to its trade route with the south. It has been widely known among many in the north that the south has been growing and prospering again. A great many people have been seeking to re-establish connections with those in the southlands. The Queen Mother had been in contact with the mayor of that small city through messengers."

Holden and the Wanderer looked at each other briefly. A question seemed to form in their minds at the same time. Lockland ignored it if he noticed it all. He seemed to be piecing together his own tapestry of this tale as he spoke his own part.

"Many of us were quite wary of the princess making the journey. But the throne had made the decision. She took with her a modest contingent to protect her. Girard is a very respected member of the Household Guard. He and I were friends as infantrymen and fought alongside one another in many skirmishes with the northern outlanders when we were much younger." He paused for a brief moment as he seemed to recollect some fond memory regarding his friend.

The Wanderer waited for a time before asking: "Have you received any word regarding the princess or her contingent?"

"None." Lockland looked long and hard at Holden, seeming to attempt to read into the mind of the man before him. Holden stared back at their host and opened his mind to the man. After a brief time Lockland slowly nodded.

"I've no reason to take your words as less than true. Some of the men seem to believe you are of the old realm, a knight reborn." He was looking at Alex now, his eyes again boring into the target before him. The Wanderer simply looked back at their host, nonplussed. He remained closed to any who sought to see into his heart. But he hid no malice in him and his demeanor remained open to their host.

"We are not your enemy, captain. We have our own quest, and it must be kept. It is of the utmost importance that it be so." The Wanderer looked deeply into the eyes of their host and held him in silence for a moment.

"A family of four arrived in the city a short time before we did. A man and three children. We must get to them, and we need to do so soon. Their safety is my first concern now."

Both the Wanderer and Holden took their feet as they looked upon the troubled visage before them. Lockland looked up into the face of the Wanderer as he took a very deep breath. He very slowly rose to his feet before speaking.

"I am sorry, friend. But the family of which you speak was brought before the throne early this day. A judgment was passed by the crown." The look on his face was pained as he spoke. He swallowed visibly.

"Speak, man!" The Wanderer commanded and Holden could feel the air grow thicker in the room. The commander was taken aback at the authority in the Wanderer's words. His eyes widened as he felt a thing growing before him, a source of power and might. The Wanderer was more than even he or the soldiers who had brought him here could fathom. He felt it but could not name it or decipher its meaning. Before him stood something beyond his understanding.

"The father of the children was...he was...he was struck down in the court chamber."

"And the children? What of the children?" The Wanderer spoke as evenly as he could through clenched teeth.

Holden was not sure, but it felt as if the room had grown smaller and the temperature had gone up. He sensed the fire burning in the Wanderer, his new ally. It seemed the commander sensed it as well. The man was slightly bowing his head as he spoke.

"The children are still safe though they are in the care of the crown within the castle proper." He looked back and forth between the men, seemingly lost to himself. He shook his head visibly before regaining some of his previous composure.

"Who are you, really?" Lockland locked eyes with the Wanderer. The men stood facing one another and staring into each other. The Wanderer seemed to compose himself and let go of some smoldering thing that seemed to always wish to escape its bonds and take control of him.

Holden stood watching the two men. Both great men, though arguably for different reasons. The Wanderer was a true enigma. He was not easily categorized. He was a killer, though not a wanton murderer. He was a savior, though not explicitly good. He was a fighter, though his cause was not necessarily that of any other. Holden looked upon him and saw death. And he liked what he saw. Some people needed death. The men who had taken Northern Alley deserved nothing less.

"I am descended of men in this book." The Wanderer glanced at the tome on the table beside his chair before looking back into the eyes of his host. Neither spoke for a brief time. Lockland looked at the book.

Holden noticed the man's eyes grow in apparent surprise. Lockland stepped forward and began to turn the pages of the large tome. He poured through the pages for several moments before looking into the face of the Wanderer in earnest again.

"Is this truth you speak? Are you truly descended of any of these men?"

The Wanderer nodded rather curtly.

"I speak truly, friend. And I must know of your intent. How is it you serve? Whom do you serve?" Holden noticed a change again come over his companion. Tension just beneath the surface. Death seeking to be let loose. Did their host sense it as well? Holden could not tell. The man was nearly as stoic as the Wanderer. Lockland's chest swelled and he looked directly into the face of the Wanderer as he stood erect and began to speak.

"My house, from my ancestors to me and unto my descendants, has ever served and always will serve the House of Arthur and the Kingdom of the North. I serve Avalon, friend. And be you descended of any named in this book, I now serve you."

Holden was again taken aback at the respect and deference given his companion. Just exactly who was this man? He watched in astonishment as Lockland bowed his head and slowly dropped to one knee before the Wanderer. The Wanderer's reaction was one of relief. He breathed deeply and spoke softly to their host.

"Rise, friend. I make no claim to lead or rule. I have no such designs. My young friends are in need, and therefore I am in need of your help."

Lockland stood and looked anew at the Wanderer. Holden thought he saw something very different in their host's eyes. He saw love there. He saw hope. He saw a renewed energy. It was similar to what he had seen in the eyes of the soldiers at the bridge. But it was amplified here. Lockland knew much more than the others. He seemed to have some more intimate knowledge of who the Wanderer truly might be. Who were the men in that book, anyway?

"I will help in any way I can. There is another you should meet, friend. Another who remembers the greatness that had been Avalon. I think with his help we may possibly be able to get your young friends to safety."

The three men walked briskly through the city proper. Lockland led as Holden walked abreast of the Wanderer. They could at various breaks between structures see the castle growing closer as they continued on their way. Lockland was leading them to someone he called Gatekeeper. This man was supposedly a historian of the city. Lockland had told them of how he had acquired many of the books in his personal library. Though many of the tomes had been handed down through inheritance, the Gatekeeper had been the source of many of his newest additions.

As the men walked and got closer to the center of the city they began to draw more attention; more eyes held onto them for much longer than had been the case near the outskirts of the city. Holden could sense the apparent unease in some of the eyes that looked upon them. He wasn't sure what the matter was, but their host seemed to notice as he began to quicken his pace even more.

"Quickly, friends. We are close." He spoke under his breath as he hurried on his way to their destination.

They finally reached a home with a latticework archway overgrown with ivy. Covering the walkway to the door was a canopy of interwoven branches from several maples growing in a brief yard. Lockland stopped at the door and looked back at his new friends.

"The Gatekeeper is different than most. Though he is an old man, he is not feeble. His wits are sharp and he sees and hears more than most. In a time not too long ago he was my teacher." His eyes were locked on the Wanderer. The Wanderer nodded as if in understanding of some secret being shared. Holden had no idea what the hell Lockland was talking about. He only knew he was ready to be out of sight of any other eyes o the streets.

Lockland turned back to the door and raised his hand to grasp the doorknocker when the door slowly opened. Before them stood a young man in his early 20's. He was dressed in loose fitting clothing, light green cotton pants and a light brown cotton shirt. The man greeted them warmly enough.

"Welcome Commander Lockland and friends. My master has been awaiting your arrival. Please, come inside." The young man stepped aside as he opened the door fully. Lockland quickly stepped inside and the two travelers followed.

The young man closed the door behind them and barred it shut. He then began down a brief hallway and made a turn to a doorway that opened upon a deep set of stairs. He walked ahead of the men as he descended down the stairwell which doubled back on itself several times as they seemingly descended several floors beneath the surface before reaching the bottom. At the bottom of the stairs was another hallway. Their young host began walking down the hallway toward the end. He passed several closed doors before reaching the door at the end of the hall. There he stopped and turned to face the three men.

"My master has been awaiting your arrival for some time now. He bids you enter and speak with him. He also advises that time is of the essence now. You and many others are at risk of ruin should you tarry." He was looking directly at the Wanderer as he spoke, but he also turned his eye to Lockland at the last. With that he opened the door and stepped aside.

The three men entered a large chamber. Lockland led the way.

Holden was astounded at the size of the chamber itself, but the number of books on the numerous shelves was almost too much to take in. He was nearly lost as he began to stray away from his companions.

"Please do not tarry." The soft words of the young man behind him brought him back to their current predicament. He caught up to his friends as they continued forward. The Wanderer only looked back at him and smiled briefly as they continued walking to the center of the grand chamber. They reached the center and found their host waiting. He was seated at a rather large table with several books strewn upon it. He was seemingly preoccupied with his head bent over one particular tome. Lockland and the Wanderer stopped on the opposite side of the table and waited. Holden joined them. The young man circled the table and stood near his master.

The Gatekeeper slowly looked up and smiled at his guests. Holden thought the man looked ancient. The lines on his face were a veritable roadmap to the wisdom and knowledge he likely possessed. His smile was warm and inviting. There was knowledge, understanding, and so much wisdom in that face. Holden was drawn to this man much as a child is drawn to a grandfather. He found himself smiling back at the face before him.

"Well, well, well. You finally made it. I've been waiting for a time, and here you are. Well, well, well." The gatekeeper continued smiling as he looked into the face of the Wanderer. The Wanderer only looked back stoically, an amused look on his face.

"Do I know you?" The Wanderer asked of the Gatekeeper. Their host smiled a bit more broadly and showed a great many white teeth.

"Maybe you do, maybe you don't. But I know you. I know who you are, whose you are. I know much that you would likely want to remain hidden." The Gatekeeper continued smiling as he spoke. "But, alas, we don't have time to speak in detail of what I know."

"No, we do not." The Wanderer seemed on edge but not as he had been before. There was no undertone of pending violence. There was something else. Apprehension. The Wanderer was hoping to avoid some truth this man had knowledge of. Holden was almost sure of it.

"The commander brought you here to me for a reason. Do you know what that reason is?"

"Yes."

"Does he know who you are?"

"Not truly, though he has s very good idea of what I am."

Holden was doing his best to keep up. Something important was taking place here. He was sure of it.

"I know exactly who you are. Alexander Horatio Sloane. I knew your father and his father and his father's father. I know the true name of your house. I know of your ancestors and their relation to the Elds. I know of the blood flowing in your veins. And I know of your quest."

It seemed every hair on Holden's body was standing on end. A severe chill coursed through his body and he could not help but shiver slightly. He looked away from the face of the old man and looked into the face of the Wanderer. He saw the plea there for the old man to stop, but the old man continued.

"You are indeed of royal blood. You are of the old line. You were thought dead and gone from this world. You were assumed lost to us. But I knew better. She talks to me too."

Holden looked back into the gatekeeper's worn visage. The old man was looking directly at him and smiling again. Holden smiled and nodded. He could feel tears forming at the corners of his eyes. This was not a chance meeting. None of this was chance. She was even here in this place. He could sense her presence. He smelled the flowers and felt the warmth of her presence.

"I know what it is you desire, Wanderer. I know what you hunt. You must abandon that quest for a time. The boy needs you to mind her for now. You must. If you would see it done, you can restore greatness to this land if you would simply take what is rightfully yours."

"No." The Wanderer spoke harshly. More harshly than Holden believed he should have to the man.

The gatekeeper but smiled and nodded slowly. He stood up from his seated position. His young servant stepped forward to assist him as he stood. Once standing he looked upon the three men before him and spoke.

"You need to retrieve the young ones from the castle proper. They are indeed in danger. If she finds out more about the boy, she will kill him. And she is capable of it. He is the key to all of it. Whether you should fulfill your own destiny or not, he is still the key. Do not fail him, knight."

"I will not." The Wanderer bore a grim look upon his face as he spoke.

"Oh I know of your resolve, man. That much is apparent simply by your appearance here. But choices will need be made before the end. You must each choose the path of your heart. Light or dark, you must choose. I would like to be there for it, but alas this body of mine is grown too weak."

The Gatekeeper began to walk from the table. The young man walked with him, guiding him with the use of an offered arm.

"There are secret ways into the castle, old ways forgotten by many. Many were closed off in times long since passed. But some remain. Some of us have kept them for times such as this. There is a great storm brewing. War comes as it has not come to us in a great long time.

Wanderer, knight, you are part of a great and terrible secret that will come to light. The evil to be unleashed upon the land must be stopped and this city must not fall."

The old man stood before a large bookshelf on a nearby wall. He nodded to his servant. The young man released his master and pulled several books from the shelf in a particular order. He then pushed aside the bookshelf as if it were on casters. It moved with a deep rumbling. Uncovered by the moved bookshelf stood an old oaken door with a great set of locks in a grand archway. The young man returned to his master and led him to the locks. The gatekeeper removed a large ring of keys from his robes, and after a moment of searching he chose several keys and began to unlock the locks one after the other. Once done, he gave the keys to the young man and turned to face the three men.

"You must leave me now and continue on your journey. Ah, that we might have had more time to sit and speak in earnest, knight. You are not the last of your kind, but you are by far the most intriguing. Good travels, young men." He then grasped the large handle on the door and gave a push. The door opened on a dark hallway.

"Aaron will lead you from here." The young man left his master's side and stood in the doorway. He had produced a lamp from a nearby shelf.

The Wanderer and Holden entered the hallway. Lockland remained with the old man.

"There are more men in the city who follow the old crown, knight. We will aid you in any way we can when you choose to make known your intent to lead. I am in your service." Lockland looked into the eyes of the Wanderer as he spoke. The Wanderer simply nodded at the man in return.

"Take care, my son. Be sure of foot and get them to safety." The Gatekeeper spoke to the young man holding the lamp.

244

"I will father." The young man turned and began down the hallway. The Wanderer looked one last time upon the old man before turning to follow the young man. Holden quickly followed suit.

Holden heard the large door close behind them as they walked swiftly down the dusty and dusky hallway. He had no idea where they were headed or what dangers awaited them. He knew only that he was exactly where he was supposed to be and with exactly the right person.

He thought he smelled a slight hint of roses in the overwhelming muskiness of the dark hallway. The scent was short lived as they found their way into catacombs that led directly to the active sewers of the castle. The young man moved with surefooted swiftness deeper into the catacombs. He occasionally paused to unlock large doors into more hospitable hallways. After a time he began to slow his pace, and he eventually stopped and turned to face his companions as he cautioned them to be silent throughout the remainder of their travels.

"We have entered the domain of the castle proper. The hallways we now travel are still in use by some members of the castle staff. Be as silent as you can and we may yet enter the castle without notice." The young man gave a brief smile at the last moment before turning and continuing on his way.

Kat looked at herself in the mirror trying to steel herself for what she was contemplating. She was not sure she would be able to do it. The consequences were dire if she failed, but she felt the weight of destruction if she should not make the attempt. Evil was astir. She could feel it seeking to destroy everything. The very air of the castle was rife with it. It tickled her nerves like an electrical charge in the air every time she was in the Queen Mother's presence. She could not avoid its presence. She was compelled to act.

She wore her small pack on her back as she left her quarters. She hurried down the hallway toward her new friends. She thought of what was to be. She was so very unsure of the future now. She had been in the care of this place for so long. She did not know what to think. She knew only she had to act now. There was no time left. The days had led to this. She was sure that the boy was key to something enormous. She just could not fathom what that really entailed.

She was excited.

She smiled as she reached his door. She noticed that there was no guard in the hallway outside the boy's chambers. The first stirrings of worry began to gnaw at her. She entered without knocking and noted the room was empty. There was no sign of the boy, Evan. The room had been made up as if it had not been used for some time. Everything was in order.

Panic chewed at her nerves. Her heart rate increased. She stretched her sight as far as she could but was unable to sense him. Something was very wrong. Where was he?

She hurried out the door and began to walk towards the chambers of the brother and sister, Finn and Kiran. She passed a few servants in the hallway. She purposely slowed her pace and tried to smile at them. They quieted their conversation at the sight of her and quickly passed her. The servants had always been afraid of her, thinking her a witch. They were right in some regards.

Her thoughts tripped over one another in her mind. She tried again and again to locate the boy, to feel his presence. Fear was taking hold of her. Her heart

246

hammered in her chest by the time she reached the door to Kiran and Finn's chambers. She noted two guards in the hallway outside. That brought a bit of relief. At least these two were still safe. She knocked softly before slipping inside.

"Why hello there, my dear girl." The Queen Mother greeted her cheerily. She sat upon the bed in the room. In her lap sat the young boy, Finn. He was smiling at her as well. Kat did her best to smile as well.

"Your grace. I was checking on our guests. Hoping to speak with them and glean some more regarding their intent." She looked briefly about the room as she entered. Kiran was not with them. Alarms shrilled in her head. Oh there was something very wrong here.

"Oh, I know exactly why you are here, child. My new friend was telling me all about your earlier visit. It would seem you have been very busy lately, child." The Queen Mother smiled very broadly at that, looking deep into Kat's eyes. The world began to drop from under Kat's feet then. Her head began to spin and darkness took her. The evil smile was the last thing she remembered before falling into deep sleep. Rough hands caught her before she hit the floor.

The Queen Mother placed the boy on his feet and took his hand.

"Come, Finn. Walk with me and tell me more of your new friend. Tell me more of Evan and how magical he is."

They then walked out the door and toward her chambers. Kat was carried out the room and in a different direction by a castle guard. As she slept she dreamed of dark things she hoped she would forget upon waking. She would not be so lucky.

Evan and Kiran sat on the floor on either side of the girl, Kat. The guards had brought her into the small cell and abruptly placed her on the cold floor. Kiran looked at her worriedly then at Evan.

"What's wrong with her? Can you help her?"

Evan did not know how to tell Kiran that he had no power in this place. He wasn't sure what power he had at all, but whatever it was he was bereft of it in here. He could not even see into the girl to know what was wrong with her. He simply shook his head as he looked at her.

"I don't know what's wrong with her. Kiran, I don't know anything anymore." Evan was on the verge of breaking down. He looked at Kiran and felt a surge of strength flow into him. It was from her. She was still looking upon their new friend. The girl remained still for a long time before she began to stir.

After a time she abruptly sat up and looked at her cell mates.

"Oh no!" She was looking deep into Evan's eyes as she spoke.

Without warning she hugged him tightly. A brief stirring of jealousy crept into Kiran's heart almost instantly, but she brushed it aside. She knew Evan was special to any who met him. For his part, Evan seemed taken aback and looked startled. He looked at Kiran with a surprise evident on his face. Kat began to weep quietly as she held onto Evan. She very slowly released her grasp, remaining close to him as she spoke.

"I am so very sorry. I have failed you. I had hoped to get you away from here before she found out. But I have failed."

Evan and Kiran were not sure exactly what was happening, but they both asked almost simultaneously regarding Finn.

"The Queen Mother has him. She has taken him and is learning much about you. As much as he knows.

248

She will piece more of it together. She will know who you are soon. Then, I fear, she will come for you both. Perhaps she will come for me as well. I sought to betray her, and she does not take well to those who go against her will." Kat shed a few more silent tears as she spoke.

"Oh Evan, whether you came too soon or too late I do not know. But somehow I fear it was not the right time. I had hoped to be wrong, but my sight was not of the type to know for certain."

Evan and Kiran looked questioningly at one another.

"What are you talking about?" Kiran grasped the girl's shoulder and spun her around a bit more roughly than she intended. Kat nearly fell over as her attention was so focused on Evan. She looked intently and somewhat irritatedly at the girl who had dared touch her so.

"Foolish girl! He is far more than you could know. He is power incarnate, though even he does not know it. She will kill him now or seek to turn him. He bears a power no manchild has borne since the times of the old kings. He is power incarnate! And she cannot allow it to come to fruition. Cannot. She will kill him if she even suspects. And I fear your brother is giving her more than enough to suspect."

Evan stood up as the girl spoke. He was afraid and thrilled all at once. Power was something he had never craved but at times of weakness had wished for. He had wished for it so that he could defend those he had loved. Those he had lost. He had lost so much for one so young. He had wanted to protect those who could not protect themselves. And lately he had wanted to avenge those same ones he had lost. He was bereft of it now, but he recalled the thrill of the power as it had come to him. The absolute power that had shown itself in the cavern. It was overwhelming. It was inexplicable. It was fantastic.

He was looking at the girl who still sat upon the floor between him and Kiran. Kiran and Kat both were looking up at him. They each had a puzzled look upon their faces. Each for different reasons.

"Evan?" Kiran softly spoke his name. He was lost in his thoughts and unable to respond to her. He felt a smile upon his face as he stared at Kat. She was like him, and she knew what he was feeling. She knew what was coursing through him. He needed to keep her close. He needed to save her. He reached his hand out to her.

"Evan!" Kiran spoke more forcefully this time. He looked at her and for the briefest moment she did not believe he recognized her.

He seemed to shake off some veil from his mind as Kat pulled herself to her feet using his outstretched hand for help. Evan then offered the hand to Kiran who after a quick frown grasped it and stood at his side. She looked distrustfully at the other girl who stood before them. Kat seemed nonplussed at the glare given by Kiran.

"We must get out of this cell." Kat was speaking directly to Evan. He understood why their escape from the cell was important. Neither of them had any power in this place.

"There is no way out that we could find." Evan spoke to Kat while looking at Kiran. Kiran was still looking intently at their new friend. Evan thought he sensed some anger. Or was it resentment? He was not entirely sure. He shook it off. Their current predicament was a bit more important than the hurt feelings of Kiran. He would have to deal with that later. If there was a later.

Kat began to search the cell more intently. She walked around checking the walls and corners. There was old bedding on the floor. She moved it about and checked various crevices before finally giving up. She looked at her new friends who only looked at her as she searched.

"I suppose you have already done the same?" Kat asked as Kiran gave a brief sigh of disapproval.

"Of course we have! We aren't stupid. We were trying to find a way out long before those guards brought you here." Kiran was visibly upset. Her voice was shaking as she spoke, and she was beginning to shake as well. She was angry. She was afraid. She was losing hope. Her brother was alone. Her father was dead. And she felt she was losing Evan to this strange girl.

Evan held her hand and pulled her to him. She looked into his eyes and saw the concern there. She took a deep breath and hugged him tightly. She began to cry in earnest. She let loose as he held her. He did not speak. He knew that she did not need words from him. She only needed him. Kat was perceptive even without her powers. She too remained quiet as Kiran embraced Evan. She sat on ruffled bedding and tried to think of a new course of action. There had to be a way for them to get out of here. She just had to keep thinking.

Evan was trying to do the same thing. But his mind was now so very clouded with images that came to him. Images of him saving so many of his friends. He could have saved them. He had this power in him. He should have saved them. Guilt began to seep into him at this thought. Guilt and a desire to avenge, a desire to make men pay for their wanton destruction and theft of the lives of his friends. Some men deserved to die. He thought he knew a little of the mind of the Wanderer as these thoughts entered his mind. A warm spot began to grow in his heart. And a small smile played at the corner of his mouth as he imagined taking the lives of those men who had made a life of killing innocent people in the land.

The young man, Aaron, continued leading his two companions through hallways and locked doors. They eventually reached a well-lit hallway that was obviously in recent use. Lamps lit their passage. Aaron cautioned them not to speak to any they should pass. He told them he would get them as close to the children as he could before the need for any violence. Both men nodded their understanding.

At some point the trio entered a large kitchen. The young man bade them remain in a corner while he made his way to a pair of women nearby. They appeared to be preparing a platter of fruit and cheeses. The young man slipped them each a coin as he finished speaking with them. He returned to his companions with a grim look upon his face.

"We must hurry. I know where your friends are. They are in danger but we may yet get to them in time." Aaron turned and made his way to the door. The Wanderer looked at the two women who had not taken their eyes of him. The older woman smiled and bowed her head slightly as she took note of his gaze. He bowed his head in return. He kept close to the young man who led them.

After a time winding through some twists and turns the young man entered a particularly dark hallway. He put out his own lamp and spoke quietly to the two men.

"We must make our way to the dungeons. Your friends are being held there. They have not been there long, but there is apparently some intrigue surrounding them. They are definitely in danger. We cannot use the lamp from this point on. We must not draw attention to ourselves. Any who might note our passage from this point on must not get word to the crown or the Black Guard."

The three waited for a brief while longer as their eyes adjusted to the gloom. They then continued on. They made more turns down even darker hallways. As they descended a dank set of stairs, they heard a brief bit of conversation between a pair of guards. The men sat at a table just out of sight of the stairs. The three men approached silently. Holden and the Wanderer quickly subdued the men and had them tied up and gagged. They had not killed the guards, but the two unfortunate souls would awaken with horrible headaches and very sore bruises. Holden thought he might have broken the arm of the guard he had accosted.

Around the next corner they spied two guards outside one door. There were several other doors unguarded. It was apparent to the trio that the children were most likely in that particular cell.

"How quickly can we be out of the castle once we have the children?" The Wanderer quietly asked the young man.

"Our escape is nearby, in the bowels of the castle. We will move straightaway to the escape as soon as your friends are secured."

"Good. Stay here until I call for you. Pay no heed to the sound of gunfire. Wait for me to call you." The Wanderer waited for each man to nod his understanding of his command.

The Wanderer then smiled and stepped into the hallway. He immediately began walking toward the men standing guard outside the cell. They were clothed in the dark garb of the Black Guard. Both men immediately drew pistols and challenged the Wanderer. He continued walking forward. The Wanderer knew they would fire as soon as he got close enough. He knew they would hit him and take him down. He knew all this and was counting on it. The two guards opened fire simultaneously, striking the man in the chest. Each man fired two shots. Four rounds found their mark. The Wanderer fell to the ground. He lay face first on the cold floor of the hallway. He heard a scream from the other side of the door the men had been guarding. The two guards approached. One of them holstered his weapon as the other circled to maintain cover. The Wanderer was roughly turned over.

A single shot tore through the throat of the guard covering the Wanderer with his weapon while a knife found the throat of the man who had turned him over. The Wanderer stood, maintaining his hold on the knife embedded deeply into the throat of one of his would-be killers. He slowly holstered his own smoking pistol as he waited for the guard to expire. He helped the man against a wall of the hallway. As the guard began to slide to the floor the Wanderer removed his blade from the man's throat. He then called for his companions.

Holden and Aaron moved quickly down the hallway to join the Wanderer who had already moved to the door of the cell. He was trying several different keys in the lock before Aaron took the keys from him and immediately located the correct key. The door was unlocked and the Wanderer stepped inside. The boy ran to him and embraced him hard. So too did the girl, Kiran. The Wanderer looked into the eyes of the strange girl and noted the slight shake of her head. Where was Finn?

12 Escape

The Lady gave no words or visions to either of them. Holden and the Wanderer stood in knee-deep, dirty water along with the three children. Aaron worked on an old lock that held shut a small grate through which the water traveled. It was their escape. The Wanderer's mind seemed far away. He was not facing the others. He peered back in the direction they had come. Holden knew what he was contemplating. Evan was staring at his protector waiting for the man to look at him. Waiting for the words he knew to come.

"A-ha!" Aaron had gotten the lock undone. He began to work to loosen the grate and get it open. It was very badly stuck. He was struggling fiercely. Holden turned and began to help him. The two made some leeway as the grate began to open slowly toward them. The Wanderer turned back and faced Evan. They had not spoken much as they had run from the dungeons back into the catacombs beneath the castle. Although Evan's percipience had never been able to breach the Wanderer's interior he knew what the man had been contemplating, and he saw the determined look upon his face.

"You are going back for him, aren't you?" He asked the question though he had no need to do so. The Wanderer surprised him by smiling genuinely and tussling the boy's hair.

"We cannot continue without at least trying. I cannot."

The others were now listening intently. The two men had gotten the grate open enough for them to squeeze through the opening.

"But you only just found me." Tears were forming at the rims of Evan's eyes. He tried his best to be strong, but he was so very tired and so very afraid. He felt like such a child, but at the moment he did not care. "You only just came back!" He violently wrapped his arms around the man and the tears poured freely as he openly wept.

The Wanderer let him be for but a moment. Time was not their friend. They needed to hurry. He needed to hurry if he was to have any chance at all of escaping with Finn.

"I cannot leave Finn here to die. Terran kept you for me. He died protecting you. His family is now in my care. All of his family. I must do all I can to bring him back. Protecting him is the same as protecting you. I must do this." The Wanderer slowly but forcefully pushed Evan from him and gazed directly into him. Evan saw a glint of fire in the gray orbs.

"Promise me you will come back. Promise you will find us again."

The Wanderer smiled his crooked smile as he stepped back from the boy and the company.

"I promise, Evan. I will find you again."

"We must hurry." Aaron was urging them to enter the drain. Holden took the boy by the shoulder and guided him to the opening. As he and Evan entered he looked back at the Wanderer and gave a brief nod. The Wanderer took it for its meaning: Holden would do his all to protect the boy until they should meet again. Kiran blew the Wanderer a kiss as she silently wept. She stepped beyond the grate as well. Aaron was waiting for the other girl, but she only stared at the Wanderer.

"Hurry child. We must be on our way. I do not know how long before they find us here." Aaron spoke to the girl but she did not acknowledge him. She continued looking at the Wanderer until he finally took his gaze off the others to notice her.

"You will need my help if you want to find him."

"Is that so?" The Wanderer looked deeply at the girl. She was slight and young, but her eyes held ages upon ages of secrets. He nodded briefly. At that she turned and began back the way they had come. The Wanderer followed quickly on her heels.

"Oh great." Aaron muttered under his breath as he stepped through and pulled the grate closed behind him. He had no way of locking it, and it likely did not matter. Soon every inch of the castle above and below would be scoured looking for the escapees and their accomplices. He hoped to have his charges far from the city before their escape route was located.

As he took the lead and began into the cramped passageway, he removed a glow stick from a small pack he carried beneath his cloak. He activated it and continued forward wordlessly. The children followed and Holden brought up the rear. None of them had any words regarding the Wanderer or the strange girl. But all of them were holding onto hope for their reunion some time soon.

The girl moved quickly and quietly back into the hallways of the castle proper. The Wanderer followed as quickly and nearly as quietly. He realized she was barefooted and her steps barely made a sound as she sometimes ran from corner to corner and sometimes slinked down long hallways between open doorways. On several occasions she turned and held her finger to her lips as if he were being too loud. His hiking boots were not nearly as stealthy as her soft feet. He many times darted into empty storerooms behind the girl. A few times they listened as voices hurried by the rooms in which they hid. The alarm had been sounded.

He kept pace as they continued on and he paid close attention to the rooms they passed and the corners they turned. Many times she would turn and smile into his stern face. He felt her mind probing his exterior looking for a way into his mind. After a long stretch in a servant's quarters she spoke evenly to him.

"If we are lucky he will be attended by only one or two guards. And she will be elsewhere directing the search for us."

"And if we are unlucky?"

The girl only shrugged as she took a very deep breath and slowly exhaled. She crept back into the hallway and the Wanderer followed closely. They eventually made their way into what appeared to be something of an antechamber. Several columns lined the walls and a massive tapestry covered the far wall. Comfortable benches were strategically placed between the columns. The room was empty.

The girl quickly crept toward the tapestry and stood at its edge near the farthest column on the left side of the room. She looked briefly into the Wanderer's face, a hint of worry and doubt barely contained in her own. She then turned, pulled at the edge of the tapestry, and stepped behind. The Wanderer followed. In the dim light of the brief space in which they stood he saw her manipulating several stones in the wall. After only the briefest of moments a doorway opened before them. The stonework of the door was impeccable. It fit perfectly into the work of the wall and would not have been noticed by any who had no previous knowledge.

They stepped into a dark and narrow passage. The Wanderer again stayed close to the girl as the passage wound this way and that. More than a few times they reached T intersections and the girl made sure judgments in her choices turning left, right, left again. The Wanderer mapped the turns in his head, doing his best to keep his bearing as they travelled through the maze of passages. They eventually reached a narrow flight of spiraling steps. At the top the girl paused. She took a deep breath and steeled herself before stepping through an actual door with a bronze handle.

The Wanderer stepped into the large closet with the girl. Through the entryway between the large closet and the room beyond there was a great deal of light entering. The girl stood still and held her finger to her lips. The Wanderer could hear voices in the next room. More precisely he heard one voice. It was the boy. Finn was singing an old lullaby under his breath. It was an old one his mother may have sung to him when he was much younger. The Wanderer moved slowly and quietly out of the closet and into the room.

The guard standing between the boy and the door on the other side of the room had no time to act. The Wanderer drew his 1911 and fired one shot into the man's face just as his face registered surprise at the appearance of the Wanderer from the closet. Finn screamed and jumped from the bed on which he had been seated. He turned in time to see the Wanderer holstering his weapon. The body of the guard falling to the floor was an audible thud behind the boy.

Finn immediately ran to the man. He grasped him tightly and held on as if for dear life. The girl stepped out of the closet then. She walked beyond the Wanderer and stood before him. Both she and the boy screamed almost simultaneously. Finn nearly went limp as he put his hands to his ears. The Wanderer felt a crawling sensation on almost every inch of his body but could not discern what was causing it.

He felt a rush of power come from the girl then as she regained herself. The boy still held his hands to his ears but he looked fearfully at the door to the room. The girl, Kat, turned to face the Wanderer. Her face was pained as she struggled to hold some external power at bay.

"Take him now. Go find your friends."

"No." The Wanderer began to reach for her but was unable to grasp her. A force emanated from her and repulsed his hand.

"Go now! She is nearly here. Go!"

A million ants crawling over his body now, the Wanderer grasped the boy's hand and made his way back into the passage. He hurried back down the stairs into the darkness. He could not move as fast as he wished with Finn in tow, but he moved as fast as he dared. He also had to be sure of his turns as he made his way back through the passage traveling in reverse the path he and the girl had taken there. The crawling of his skin lessened almost as soon as he and the boy began down the steps. Once deep within the passages it all but disappeared.

On and on they traveled. Then Wanderer picked the boy up and held him in his support arm. He held a pistol in his strong hand, his right hand. He kept it tucked close to his body, beneath his left arm that held the boy close. Finn held on so tightly he likely would have stayed attached to the Wanderer without the arm of the man beneath him. They traveled much more slowly once they exited the tunnels. The light of the large anteroom was a welcome sensation for the boy, but the Wanderer liked it less. At least in the dark they would not be so easily detected. He hoped they could make it out the castle and to their friends without the need for any more death.

Surprisingly, they were only noticed by one member of the Black Guard as they made their way through the castle proper. The Wanderer was able to dispatch him without the boy seeing it. The soldier had been surprised by the pair as they quickly rounded a corner, and the Wanderer had placed the barrel of his pistol less than an inch from the man's eye just as he pulled the trigger and emptied the man's mind of its final thought.

At one point the duo had hidden in a large kitchen area as several other guards had passed, headed in the direction they had just come from. There were considerably more servants in the kitchen than the Wanderer had hoped. One of the women slowly held her finger to her mouth and shook her head. She walked evenly to a hanging curtain and held it open, revealing a small storeroom. The Wanderer quickly darted inside with his little companion as the woman let the drape fall behind them. A passing guard paused and looked inside the kitchen. The workers paused as he did so, looking questioningly at him. His gazed panned the room before he shook his head and joined the other guards.

The old woman stood stolidly as the Wanderer exited the small storeroom with Finn attached. Her head was bowed slightly as she looked up into the Wanderer's face. She almost seemed to want to speak, but instead she bowed even more when he looked at her. Several other servants in the room joined her at this. The Wanderer seemed a bit perplexed, but he nodded briefly in return.

"Thank you... May your kindness be returned ten-fold." The Wanderer spoke the words of thanks he had learned as a child. As he turned to leave he almost did not notice the startled expressions on a few of the older servants. One of them even gave an audible gasp.

He quickly exited the room and continued down the hallway to the hidden entrance to the catacombs. There were no discernible voices beyond the entrance, but the Wanderer stayed put for a while longer than possibly needed. Something was terribly wrong. He was not sure what it was.

And then he felt it. The rushing sensation of the insects. His skin crawled as a shudder overcame him. Nausea nearly took him as well. It was the piercing wail of the boy he held that kept him focused on the task at hand. Whatever power had been kept at bay by the girl was no longer so held back. It was loosed upon the castle, above and below. And it was in full force.

The Wanderer held the screaming boy a bit more tightly and began moving as he fought the urges pulling at his body. The urgings of the evil power screaming for him to lie down in surrender. Eventually he made it to the grate and got it open. As he entered the drainage tunnel and closed the grate behind him he felt an enormous push of power and thought he heard a scream in his mind as well. The evil sensations stopped altogether then. He wondered about the girl who had given herself for them. He steeled himself for what might lay ahead, and he continued forward into the darkness.

Kat stood still and defiant in the room. She was in the back bedroom of the Queen Mother. She had been in this room before. On more than one occasion she had found her way here via the secret passageway. She had hoped the evil woman had not known of her finding the passageways. She had also hoped the woman had not known about them. She had hoped for a great many things in the years she had been held captive in this gilded prison. And now her hopes were dashed, gone from her as a dream leaves upon waking to reality.

She pushed back against the power on the other side of the door. She used all her ability to keep it at bay. It was growing nearer and its strength was something she had never felt at such a level before. Its wielder was more powerful than she had imagined. The door was a good way across the room. There was a rise up to the entrance from the bedroom proper. On the other side of the door was the anteroom, an outer room for entertaining guests and meeting with servants. Several sitting chairs and a dining table were there as well. The Queen Mother's quarters were quite austere and full of many splendid fineries. Kat had been witness to a great many of them.

Her thoughts were not of the outlay of the anteroom, nor were they of the exquisite tomes on shelves, nor of the fruit and fine cheeses on the dining table. Her thoughts were of the being who approached her, the being who carried such tremendous power, the being who caused her such pain at the exercising of her own defenses.

Sweat beaded on her forehead and covered her entire body in a sheen. Her every nerve was alive as she fought the power that approached. She pushed as hard as she could and felt the being out there test her defenses. Though her eyes had closed she could feel her own aura extended outward, passing beyond worldly physical boundaries such as walls, doors, and floors. Its hue was a bright yellow. It was as fierce as it had ever been, possibly even more bright than ever before. She was drawing on every bit of strength she had within her. The being on the other side was pushing in a very direct manner, testing the boundaries as prescribed by Kat's own bright and fierce shield.

Kat saw in her mind the argent tendrils of the being seemingly caress the bright yellow of her aura as it extended outward. At the points that touched her yellow shield a shudder went through the entirety of the aura. Fierce sparks of electricity sprayed the air and the aura bent inward at the touch. It was unable to grow beyond the touch of the tendrils. The being moved forward ever cautiously, testing each slight step for any possible harm. Kat pushed as much as she could, reaching into her core and drawing upon the faintest bit of reserves. She was so very tired from her capture and the draining power of the Listless Cell the Wanderer had found them in.

The being continued forward ever closer to the door of the bedroom. Kat's aura of power continued to give way to the argent power of the being. Seconds, minutes, hours, all time was a thing unknown to Kat as she became lost to all she had within her. She focused her energies on the being coming closer and tried to increase the energies of her mind in order to concentrate the aura protecting her from the approaching thing. Its virulence was so potent. She saw within her mind's eye as the many sparks of spent energy from contact of her aura with the approaching tendrils became a heavy black ichor falling to the floor of the anteroom leaving pockmarks in their wake. This being was too powerful!

It was just outside the door now. Kat became lost to her own swirling sensibilities. Her power was at its peak now. She had never before expended so much of her energies. Still it was not enough. The creature was slowly opening the door. It was entering the room. The pressure became so great upon her that Kat fell to her knees. Her head was beginning to swoon. She hardened herself and her power transformed. It began to harden around the creature as it entered the room. Kat's eyes remained closed as she knelt upon the carpeted flooring of the Queen Mother's private bedroom.

She focused every bit of energy she had at her disposal. She had to hold it for as long as she could. The children and the strange man needed her to hold on as long as possible. This thing had to be held at bay. She had to hold it. Kneeling and with her head bent under the weight of the debilitating expenditure of energy, Kat continued concentrating her energies around the being. It paused just within the door to the bedroom proper. It held its ground. Its argent tendrils flared and came together. They melded and slowly formed a large spike of deep, dark crimson. The spike of virulent energy moved forward and began to steadily pierce her hardened arc of power. Large splashes of power-laden ichor continued to fall upon the floor, marring the carpeting and searing farther into the stone beneath.

The creature steadily moved forward one slow step at a time. Kat was all but spent, yet she continued to fight for her new friends and for the future she had briefly glimpsed. After a time she lost her fight and fell fully forward onto her face. Her breaths came in ragged gasps and a profound sweat covered her entirely. Her damp hair cascaded around her bowed head and hung down to the dark purple carpeting. After some time she gathered herself enough to look up into the face of the being she had fought so valiantly against.

Atop a flowing black robe of rich crushed velvet were bright, green eyes slightly aglow with an argent power. Those eyes looked upon her with a real hint of urgent danger as they remained steady in the face of her longtime captor. The Queen Mother smiled unevenly as she took a deep breath.

"Oh dear child, what have you done? You've been awfully naughty of late, haven't you?" The woman knelt before the exhausted child then and gently placed her hand under the girl's chin. She tenderly brushed Kat's damp hair from her face. Kat was so very taken aback. All this time she had not been aware of the power residing in the woman. She had hoped to hide so much of herself from the Queen Mother, but she now wondered how much had already been known by the evil woman crouched before her.

"Oh dear little one, do not worry. Everything will become so very clear to you very, very soon." With that she released the girl's chin and let her head drop once again to the carpet. Not-so-gentle hands then helped Kat to her feet. She was carried out of the bedroom. The voice of the tall, beautifully evil woman carried her to sleep.

"You will be the key to my victory. You will help me rule them all."

The guards left her chambers, and the Queen Mother stared into her closets. She sent a blast of prescient energy beyond the hidden doorway into the passageways and farther into the castle. It was directed at the two who had escaped, the boy and the other who had come with Kat to rescue him. She could not sense who the other was. But she felt his presence. He was a powerful one too. She sent her prescient power directly after them and though it took some time she found them far beneath the castle in the sewers. She hit as hard as she could from such a distance but it was but a brief sting. After only a few more moments they were gone.

The Wanderer exited the sewer at another grate. This one was smaller than the one in the castle sewers. He had to crouch low to get beyond and out the grate. It had been left unlocked by Aaron as he had escaped with the two other children and Holden. The Wanderer stepped out into the starlit night. He was in a shallow valley well outside the castle proper but still within the city itself. A moderately steady creek ran through the slight valley. The runoff from the sewer joined the creek and flowed into a larger adjoining flow that later joined the Northland river. This river flowed westward before joining the greater Divider in the far west.

The Wanderer remained as hidden as he could in the starlight that seemed so stark compared to the darkness of the drainage pipe he had just traveled. He felt so very exposed and unprotected. He discerned the presence of the men before they made themselves known.

"Hail, friend." A voice called out in the slight darkness. From a nearby copse of tall shrubs stepped a soldier. He was clothed in the garb of the city soldiers. His colors were those of Lockland. Several others stepped forward from their own hiding places. None of the men held weapons in hand. The Wanderer stood fully erect with the boy still in his arms. He noted only half a dozen men in addition to the initial soldier. The men approached him then, the one who called out in the lead. Holden noted the gold leaf on the man's shoulder and took him as a lieutenant.

"We are sent by our captain. He prays you heed my direction, but should you not he bids me serve you as best I can." The young man spoke with confidence though an air of deference belied each word. The Wanderer saw an honest face looking upon him in the soft light of the early night stars. A diminishing glow remained ghostlike from the west. It barely filtered into the shallow valley they inhabited. The Wanderer saw a truth, an honesty, in the face before him. He nodded slowly and distinctly at the man.

"We will follow you if you can get me to my companions." The Wanderer spoke quietly and surely to the fellow before him.

"Your friends should likely be near the city wall by now. They are safe. It is you we must protect the night." The lieutenant looked around nervously.

"Speak, man" The Wanderer voiced the words in hushed tones, following the lead of the young man standing before him, not wanting to raise his voice for fear of them being discovered.

"News of your escape has spread beyond the castle. The crown searches for the boy. And you, of course. But..." The lieutenant paused and looked intently at the Wanderer. His head bowed slightly and he seemed to be at odds with himself.

"But what? I somehow don't think we have so very much time for any hesitation at this point, Lieutenant. Do we?"

"No, of course not. But it is now so much more dangerous to travel the route taken by your companions. And I have been tasked with taking you a different route. A route that requires a stop for the night."

The Wanderer was cautious, but he felt no true deceit or danger in the lieutenant or his men. They were all stealing looks at him, each doing his best to maintain his demeanor, but each stealing glances of him when they thought him not paying attentions.

"Well then, Lieutenant, lead on. I will follow you to whatever end your captain has set for me. Know that I will not forego my friends. I will get to them as soon as I can. With or without your help."

The lieutenant nodded and motioned for his men to move out. He fell in with them, and the Wanderer followed. Finn, his body, mind, and spirit depleted, was fast asleep in his protector's arms. Moving slowly and cautiously the small party made its way through a thick woodland to a large home. The men did not approach the front entrance, but instead they circled around to the rear of the home and entered an unlocked door without announcing themselves.

The Wanderer was led quietly to a small bedroom where he deposited the boy. Finn fell into the bed without any hesitation. He awoke slightly and grasped the Wanderer's hand for a time until he fell back into a deeper sleep. The Wanderer sat in a nearby chair after the boy returned to slumber. Several moments later the door to the room opened slightly and the lieutenant peered inside. The Wanderer quietly stood and exited the room.

"There is someone who would speak with you this night." The young man spoke with his head slightly bowed. His tone remained one of deference. The Wanderer was bothered more than he cared to be at this. He nodded at his new companion.

"Lead on then." He spoke the words and knew he might regret this meeting long before he arrived. He hoped he was wrong, but it was likely he was not.

The two men walked toward the rear of the house and eventually entered the kitchen area. Seated at a small table was a lone man dressed in a plain brown robe. He was clean-shaven and bore no resemblance to any soldier the Wanderer had ever seen. Yet he still seemed somewhat familiar.

The Wanderer approached the table and noted the lieutenant had retreated and exited the kitchen. The man looked deeply into the Wanderer's face before he smiled and took a deep breath.

"Welcome, traveler. Please have a seat and speak with me for a while." The man motioned to the table. There were three additional chairs at the small round table. The Wanderer took the chair opposite the man. He sat down and looked deeply into the face before him. How did he know this face? He was not sure, but he was certain it was familiar to him.

"Alexander Horatio Sloane. That is a name I had not thought I would ever hear again. A name I had little reason to believe was still present in the land. And here you sit in my home, at my table, at arm's length from me." The man beamed a genuine smile then. He looked into the eyes of the Wanderer with something akin to hope. The Wanderer saw it and was unsure what it meant.

He had left this great city so long ago. And his departure was as an exile. The crown had exiled him! He did not understand this reception at all. He was unsure of some of what had transpired upon his return to the North, what had once been Avalon. This was outside the realm of what he had expected. The man was waiting for something. He was waiting for Alex to speak.

"How is it you know me, stranger?" The Wanderer asked very deliberately.

The other man straightened up and cleared his throat.

"Oh my, where are my manners? I have not even introduced myself. That is s very unacceptable." The man abruptly stood and straightened his robe about himself. The Wanderer also stood and remained facing his host.

"I am Reginald Thorson, son of Thor Haarkenson, son of Haarken Horsevaal, once known as Haarken Ashbringer, Knight of the Realm. I am a grandson of the knights of old."

The Wanderer looked upon his host anew. How was this possible? How had he not known of this? His host smiled broadly though there was not the least bit of malice there. Instead there was joy, deep and ebullient. Thorson's smile was nearly ear-to-ear, and in his eyes tears welled up and threatened to fall freely from the rims of quivering eyes.

"I know who you are, my friend." The man spoke conspiratorially to the Wanderer. "I know the portents you fulfill and the portents you make anew."

The Wanderer was unsure of exactly what the man spoke.

"I am not sure I am all you make of me. I suspect I am little more than you in the grand scheme of things." The Wanderer spoke as evenly as he could though he felt the air growing thicker and the atmosphere more and more heavy. Soon he believed he would find it very difficult to breathe in such confines. An unknown weight was settling upon him. A weight borne of knowledge. The man before him knew things he had either forgotten, never been told, or had chosen to put out of his conscious thoughts. Either way, things continued to grow beyond what he had hoped they might.

Where in the hell was that lady when needed?

"Oh no, friend. You are much more than I. You are something lost to us, something returned, something so very needed." Thorson paused and looked for the longest time into the face of his guest. The man was breathing deeply and evenly. The Wanderer was nearly loath to ask what his host was talking about. He somewhat feared the answer although he was certain it was coming.

"You are a promise kept. Many have awaited your return. I am included in that group. You are not only that which you know of yourself." Thorson spoke very evenly and when he finished he motioned for the Wanderer to take his seat at the table again. Both men sat down.

"Sir Alex, I must sincerely apologize. I learned of your arrival a bit late. I was not available for the news until after you had already made some preparations to rescue your companions. Had I known I might well have been able to make a difference in the man's fate. I was present when he was struck down, the father of the children, that is. I was at court. I had business with the crown, and the Queen Mother requires all callers sit through the day's proceedings prior to granting any audiences. I was there and I saw the man die and the children get whisked away. One of the children was quite peculiar though I know not how to describe it. The one boy." Thorson had been speaking for a time and had wandered mentally to the previous day's events. When he looked back into the eyes of the Wanderer, he found his guest looking intently and intensely back at him.

A brief silence passed.

"You are not exactly as you think you are. You are not exactly who you think you are." The Wanderer heard the words spoken by his host, but he was unsure how to take them. Discernment had ever been his friend. The Lady had likely granted him that gift some many years hence. He could discern no falsehood in his host's words. But a troubling voice of warning began to tug at his sub-conscious. It was not borne of the supernatural. It was an old thing borne of years of experience and life. He was not accustomed to such things as doubt, and it was doubt now entering his mind.

"Your exile was not as you may recall. You left this place a long time ago. A very long time ago."

The Wanderer heard his host's words as he peered off into the distance, looking through Thorson and into his past. He listened as the man spoke of things from long ago and he saw things in his mind he had hoped to forget. Some things he had mercifully been able to truly forget. His life prior to leaving the city and service to the North had been so very different to the life he now led. Everything had changed due to his choice. He was unsure how much time had passed since he had been exiled. He had trouble remembering certain things, but he remembered one face as clearly as if the man were in the room with them. It was the man he meant to kill before the end. It was the source of his bargain with the Lady, why he followed her lead in some things so that he could be assured of his chance to end the life of the man who had carved such a great hole in the his heart.

13 Dreams

Fire. It burned fiercely in the distance in all directions. Lady Heather stood upon the peak of a high mountain. In every direction she looked an inferno blazed in the distance effectively surrounding her mountain perch. It crept closer and closer. She could smell the stench of death as it grew nearer and nearer. Its heat was not yet upon her, but the air was still and the blaze pushed the air in about her. In the distance she also could see various fauna rushing this way and that, looking for an escape. Many would begin up the mountainside and upon noting her they would turn and run back into the forest toward the inferno. *Why would they do that?* she wondered.

She knew she was dreaming but it seemed so real. The sights, the sounds, the smells. She even felt the closing air on the flesh of her exposed arms. Everything felt real. Closer and closer the fire crept toward her. The air began to rush up the mountainside more fiercely. She could feel heat beginning to sting her eyes. There was the slightest bit of smoke in the encroaching air as well. The scent of the flames was none too pleasant either. The seared flesh of many a forest animal came to her. Death was within the flames.

She began to cry as she dropped to her knees. The young princess was overwhelmed by it all. Death was out there. It was in full effect within the flames. It was prowling and devouring. And it was voracious. She wept freely and openly. There was no one to see her weakness anyway. She gazed into the creeping flames as they grew closer to the mountainside. Eventually she would be alone in the desolation, the mountain the only thing saving her from the blaze.

In the time it took for the flames to reach the base of the rocky mountainside, Princess Heather thought of a great many things. She remembered her home and thought to herself she would never see it again. The beautiful towers and stonework would be but a distant memory. She would be trapped atop this mountain the rest of her life. She would not see her few friends, her servants, her family (even them). She would die alone here with none to protect her. Oh dear Girard! What had become of him? Her protector had been with her since she was but a child. And now? What had they done to him?

The fire had reached the base of the mountain. It held there, though it did not lose any strength. Heather came out of herself and her thoughts, and she realized that the flames that had approached had consumed the forest in its entirety all around her. But even though there was no fuel for the flames the earth itself was now ablaze. The very ground of rock, sand, dirt, it all was now afire. How?

In the near distance Heather saw a brightness approaching in the scorched and still-burning earth. It blazed its own path directly toward the mountain, toward her. As it reached the base of the mountain, Heather realized it was a man. He was dressed in all white clothing, and in his right hand he held a sword. The sword is what shone so brightly. The blade burned as if afire. Flames licked at the edges of the blade and played along the hilt. It was a beacon even in the fires that now held the earth about the man. The young man was looking up at her. His features were plain to her though he was some distance away as only things in dreams can be.

"My lady, if you would please come down and join me." He was holding his left hand up and out toward the mountain, toward Heather.

She looked all about and felt the beginnings of panic settle upon her. She could only shake her head at the strange man.

"But, my lady, there is no place for you to go. None except with me." He was smiling up at her now.

"No." Heather whispered to herself as she shook her head more violently this time.

The pale man then took a tentative step forward. The earth at his feet singed and smoldered, and the flames in which he had been steeped also moved forward. Heather stood, and panic took hold. She began to look all around the mountain then. The flames on either side seemed to have inched forward with the step of the stranger. She looked at him as he stepped forward again. The flames followed.

"No! Stop it! Stay away!" She was screaming at him now. Her heart pounded in her chest and her breath came in gasps. She was sweating profusely and her eyes were wide with fear.

Thunder rumbled in the distance. A storm grew quickly and severely in the near distance. A heavy rain began falling. The scorched and burning earth was now beginning to smolder. Steam was rising in the distance as the storm moved fiercely forward. And at the forefront of the storm an iridescent figure led the way. He moved as quickly as the man in white had moved. His path brought him nearer and nearer the man in white. The stranger turned his attention from the princess to the approaching interloper.

Within moments the two stood facing one another, a mere ten paces separating them. The new stranger was clad in a flowing, red, hooded robe. He faced the stranger in white without speaking. The man in white raised his sword before him and smiled at his foe. The two stared at one another for a brief moment. Heather was spellbound. She watched the two intently, waiting for what might come next. She continued to breathe heavily, her heart beating fiercely within her breast.

Without warning the stranger in white rushed toward the robed figure, a primal scream issuing from his open mouth. A flourish of red was all she could see as the robed one escaped the swing of the attacking man's blade. With another flourish of robes he stood behind his attacker and raised his hands one after another in quick, fluid motions.

The man in white had turned quickly enough for another strike, but he was unable to move. With each motion of his hands, the robed figure was directing the earth. Almost immediately the feet of the attacker were mired in newly released earth, living earth. It had come from beneath the scorched land left in the wake of the now extinguished fire. The storm of the robed one continued to billow in his presence, and the earth was coming back to life. The mire at his feet continued to advance upward and to consume the legs of the man in white. He snarled at his foe and began to flail at the mire advancing up to his knees now. The sputtering blade did no damage to the living and powerful earth.

"No! It cannot be! No!" He snarled at the robed figure as he tried lunging at his enemy. The red robes were just out of reach of his blade. The sword's flames remained though it hissed audibly in the constant downpour. The earth continued advancing up the man in white as the robed figure continued his hand motions. As the flowing earth reached mid-torso he dropped his hands to his side. He then removed his hood and looked into the face of the man in white.

"You! You will not win, boy. My master rules now and will rule ever more. You will see." He looked up at the princess and smiled. "You will all see."

The dark-haired figure in the red robe then raised his hands high above his head and slowly brought them down in front of him. The earth began to swallow the man in white. He sank slowly, all the while struggling defiantly.

Finally there was nothing left of him but the sword, its flame now fully extinguished. The robed figure stepped forward a few paces and picked it up. It flared briefly in his hands then went back to sleep.

He turned and looked up into the face of the princess. Smiling up at her was the face of a boy. His olive complexion complemented his almond colored eyes. His smile was warm and comforting. The rain had stopped. The earth about the boy was returning to life and green sprouts of grass grew at each of his footsteps as he approached the mountainside. She was unable to contain her own smile as she started down the mountain.

Heather awoke with a hint of a smile on her face. There was even hope in her heart. Several days had passed since her capture. The old man and his young accomplice had been sure to take good care of her. She had not been harmed during her imprisonment. She was even granted a very nice room in the home of the mayor. The older man (Brickman was his name) had been very genteel, but his mannerisms and choice of words belied a very evil presence. She was very wary of him and very afraid.

But the dream had refreshed her. To a degree. She had lost so much hope. Her men had been slaughtered. She had seen their bodies being gathered in the streets for the townspeople to see. And the number of marauders in the town was incredible! She had never heard of so many of them acting in concert. It was unheard of. Who was this Brickman that he could control such a large host? There had to be several hundred in the town itself.

She sat up in her bed. It was still a few hours before dawn. Two days had passed since her capture. She was unsure of her future, but she had been granted some slight bit of hope in that dream. She had not dreamed at all in the days before. She wanted so very much to believe there was some hope to be had, even if only in a dream.

Girard's body lay broken upon the floor of his cell. He was clothed in filthy underpants only. He had soiled himself on more than one occasion. He was asleep, barely. He had been in the cell for so long, it seemed. The days were a blur. He had lost all track of time. Every couple of hours he had been awakened for a new round of torture. He was constantly beaten with various devices. His fingernails had been pulled from his hands one at a time over the period of an entire day. Every few hours, in order to wake him, he was doused with freezing cold water. Then the new session would begin. He had just completed one such session and had fallen into a sleep akin to unconsciousness. His mind wandered to dreams.

Girard stood in full battle regalia. He was whole and unbroken. His armor was immaculate. The midday sun reflected off the exposed portions of his polished plate. He was adorned in an argent cape. A shield with an unknown crest featuring a griffon devouring a dragon was in his left hand. His right hand held a great sword, one he could not imagine swinging with one hand. He lifted the massive sword easily with one hand and swung the blade in easy looping arcs. A smile came across his face. He was without pain, he was whole, and he was at the forefront of a great host.

Behind Girard stood, at the ready, a legion of men. His own army, ready to be led to war under his lead. Girard looked back at his men. They were all there, ready for him to lead them to victory. He saw faces of men he had never seen before. They looked upon him with love in their eyes. They awaited his command. They were his to command if he would but give them his orders.

A voice spoke to him then, slyly and in whispered tones

"You are destined to lead, my soldier. Do you not feel it? Do you not feel the power at your command?"

Girard was almost drunk with the power of command. He was ecstatic to have the use of his appendages. To be so strong. To have men ready to follow him to whatever battle he might lead. He was ready to be that man, that leader, that hero.

"You will lead my army, Girard. You will be my greatest general. You will lead, and they will follow. You will achieve victory after victory. And you will be known as the greatest soldier to have ever lived."

Girard's swollen lips smiled as he lay on the floor of his cell. He was missing several teeth that had been violently knocked from his mouth during earlier torture sessions. His nose remained at an odd angle, as it had also been broken. He was forced to breath through his open mouth due to the damage done to his nose. His jaw was also out of place. He had several broken bones in his hands and feet as well. His body remained in constant pain, and during his torture sessions he was in absolute agony as new means of injuring him were exhibited.

But for this brief moment he was happy. As his mind dreamed the dream of power, of wholeness, of might. The old man watched Girard through the bars of the cell. He smiled his own smile as he continued to whisper to Girard. "Yes, my great Girard, you will indeed be the greatest of my accomplishments, the greatest of all my generals, the mightiest of my defenders. You will conquer the enemies of the realm of the new land. And you will be hero to us all."

"Hero." The broken man muttered as he lay sleeping on the floor.

The old man turned and walked away. He passed the two marauders who hauled a large bucket filled with ice water as they approached the cell to begin the next prescribed session for the soldier.

Holden was somewhat loath to sleep out in the open under the clear night canopy. He watched over the children as they slept in a dense copse of low-lying trees. They had traveled for a considerable time once they had escaped the walls of the city. Their trek had taken them through some of the less desirable neighborhoods within the Northern Realm. He had seen places similar in his prior travels. Slums were slums, no matter where in the world they might be found. Aaron had led them for a long time into the night and deeper into the forest to the west of the city. He seemed determined to get to a certain location before stopping. Finally they had to stop because the children could go no farther.

Aaron sat slightly away from the children and Holden. The Gatekeeper's apprentice was looking intently at Evan as the boy slept on ground they had cleared for a brief rest. The young man then looked into Holden's heavy-lidded eyes. Holden was somewhat surprised at the light smile that played on the lips of the man from the North.

"He is very special, this boy." Aaron spoke softly and directly to the man looking at him. Holden simply nodded. He was nearly too tired to speak. He continued to struggle to keep his eyes open as Aaron looked back at the boy momentarily before looking off into the darkened distance.

"Rest, friend. I have been preparing for this for a long time. I am well rested, and I will maintain watch until such time as we must again be on our feet."

Holden barely heard the last of the young man's words as he drifted into the sleep of exhaustion. Almost immediately he slipped into dreams.

Fire burned everywhere. Holden's mind showed him images of places he had traveled in his recent past and places he had known from childhood. They were all engulfed in angry flames. He could smell the stench of burning bodies. The heat of the flames and stinging smoke overcame him, and he felt himself coughing violently even as his corporeal body remained inured in sleep. He traveled to many places in the south. Every home he had ever known was aflame. Every person he had ever known was dead. Every hope he had ever known was dashed.

He then traveled east and saw a great host of men. Entire cities thrived and machines were operating. Weapons were being amassed and armies being built. A force was preparing to head west. South. North. Everywhere. Another apocalypse was brewing.

Through the heat and flames that were always present, Holden saw a man in highly polished armor. He stood speaking to the men assembled before him. He was armed with a great and menacing sword. He had a great shield upon his back. His face was covered with a helmet, but Holden heard his voice well enough.

"We prepare for our greatest march, our greatest victory. The deceivers of the Northern Realm will fall before the righteous and rightful ruler of the land. We shall ever be his right hand! Follow me, brothers. To victory!"

The man raised the great sword high into the air as the host of men erupted into a long, sustained cheer. A chill passed through Holden at this sight. The man turned from his host and began forward as the men followed eagerly.

Holden abruptly sat up from his brief slumber. Aaron was about the business of waking the children as quietly as he could. Evan was getting up on his own. He paused for a brief moment and looked intently at Holden. The man was lost in his thoughts for a moment and did not at first realize the boy was scrutinizing him. When he noticed Evan's gaze upon him he tried to smile, but he knew it was probably not enough to put the boy at ease. Evan simply smiled back slyly and held his finger up to his lips slightly shaking his head. Holden frowned a bit, but Evan only gestured with his eyes at Kiran and again shook his head as he peered back at Holden. Holden nodded understanding.

The boy gathered himself and what little belongings he had at this point. So too did Holden begin getting up. Aaron helped Kiran to her feet. Though he had seen the brief exchange between Evan and Holden, Aaron kept silent and gave no indication he knew. The small group began to move in the pre-dawn darkness.

"What time is it?" Kiran was rubbing hr eyes as they began anew their trek into the woodlands.

"Two hours before sunrise. We must continue to our destination and hopefully arrive before our path is discovered." Aaron spoke authoritatively. He looked at Evan as he spoke. Evan only nodded understanding. The boy had not spoken since waking. He seemed deep in thought.

Holden was so very troubled by his own thoughts resulting from the dream. Or vision. Or whatever the hell it was he had seen as he so briefly slept. He did not notice the boy's somber mood. The whole company seemed on edge. Kiran had her own pain and horror to keep at bay as they marched on. Her father had been murdered before her very eyes. Now she was in the company of those she hardly knew. Her love of Evan was all that maintained them.

282

Evan was lost in his thoughts as well. He, too, had dreamed. He had seen much he could share with no one. Even the Wanderer would be unable to help him with the Evil he had seen in his mind's eye. The Lady could not keep him from it either. He was lost to the images playing over and over in his mind.

Evan had traveled in his sleep. He had gone so much farther than ever before. And the distance had seemed so great he had feared he would not ever return. But he had. And a part of him wished he had not. He had seen death infinite and indefinite. He had been forced to endure hatred, despite, murder. Murder, the horrific choice men seemed so eager to embrace. He had seen it multiplied to such a degree he thought he would die from the exposure.

Choices would become so very important to the company. They all had choices to make. But he knew now he would need to make choices for them all to ensure their very survival.

Alex stood silently, watching Finn sleep peacefully in a bed too big for him. The boy was swallowed in soft bedding and huge pillows. He looked as if he would sleep for some time. Alex wondered if he ever would be able to sleep like that again in his life. He stood staring at the boy for quite some time as his mind turned over his options. He was filled with the knowledge given him by Thorson and so very troubled by it. The lady had not given any indication as to whether he should follow the lead of this new ally.

Damn, too many people were becoming too many complications. He was so much better at following his path when he was the only one on it. His mind played impending events to their natural conclusion should he fail to act on the information he had just been given. The Kingdom was in peril, and a great many people were somehow dependent upon him for guidance. How had this come to be?

And how was it he had such incomplete memory of himself relative to the Kingdom? How had he not known his true lineage? It was much to ponder. And so he pondered. For much of the night he stood in the room looking upon the sleeping boy, thinking of another boy he had been tasked with protecting. There was much still unanswered even in the wake of the many revelations from Thorson.

Two hours before dawn was to break, the wanderer stepped out of the room and left the sleeping Finn. He walked into the kitchen and was greeted by Thorson, Lockland, and the Gatekeeper. The three men had been speaking in hushed and urgent tones. They quieted and looked inquisitively at the knight as he entered the kitchen. Alex made eye contact with each of the men before speaking.

"Destiny, it seems, has led me back home, after a more considerable time than I had known. I am unsure of exactly what I ought do, but my heart tells me that I must do what I can in the face of the evil entrenched in my home." He paused and again looked each man individually in the eye. The words he then spoke seemed to come from some other as they left his lips.

"Let us now plan the overthrow of the crown."

Ω

Following is an excerpt from the forthcoming
Argent: Knight.

The various energies of earth, fire, love, despair, heat, cold, wind, rain, and all between, all of these magics swirled about as Evan faced Bradley. The latter held the former at bay. The two were locked in a terrible and powerful exchange. Their auras were visible to all standing upon the battlement. Holden looked upon them and tried his best to get closer. He was held in check by the marauders who constantly fired on him. Occasionally one would present himself and Holden would fire his own shots taking their number down, but it was far too slow a decrease for him to advance close enough to assist the boy.

Just beyond the battle of magical wills of Evan and Bradley, the great swirling energies of the mage continued. Brickman maintained his posture. He was full of dark energies that swirled upward and outward from him. His arms raised with red and black tendrils reaching towards the heavens, he commanded his men onward to battle against the forces of the city. The soldiers were putting up a great fight, but they were being slaughtered slowly but surely by the berserk marauders and ill creatures at the command of the mage.

More and more of the soldiers fell to the marauders, to the horrid beasts roaming and looking for the flesh of men to consume, to the demons awakened from the dark and forgotten recesses of the earth. The mage continued to pour out his malice and evil into the early morning air.

Then a rallying cry was heard in the near distance. The Knight stood below the parapets. He looked up into the heavens and saw the dark power pouring into the sky, darkening the light of the early day. He grimaced in pain. His wounds were many, perhaps even mortal. But he had strength left to confront his foe. He had lived a long time for this moment. He pushed forward and countless soldiers followed. He fired his weapon at any enemy who got in his field of vision and was within his range. The 1911 was fired repeatedly until empty and then quickly reloaded.

Various men fell before him. Headshots, shots to the throat, the neck, any exposed weakness was found by his rounds. He dropped most of them with only one shot, while some took two. His mission was to have enough rounds to make his foe suffer at his hands. He wanted as many rounds as possible to put into Brickman before delivering the final shot to his enemy's brain.

On and on he fought into the keep and his soldiers followed. They were emboldened by their captain. The Knight had sparked a fervor in them. They were determined to maintain the North in all its glory. They were loath to let it fall. They would march onward with him to their doom if there were the barest hope of saving their home. And so forward did they go.

Holden continued to fight his own battle upon the edge of the battlement. He still was making his way closer and closer to the boy. But he feared he would be too late. Evan appeared to be losing the battle of wills with the mage's apprentice. Bradley was smiling as he drew strength from his master. He pushed his blood red virulence upon Evan's waning blue luminescence. Evan was so tired. He had fought so hard. Sweat poured down his face as he struggled to fight through Bradley's onslaught. He had to stop the mage. He had to save them.

He saw her face then. Kiran came to him. Her innocence was in his mind now. Unbidden, her innocence and beauty filled his vision. He had to win. He had to stop the mage! Evan reached into the powers hidden within the stone at his feet. He drew upon the deep-rooted power of the earth. He glared at the mage's pupil. A fire crept into his eyes and his own face bore the beginnings of a smile. The power came upon him in a rush, and his aura displayed the cascade in stunning colors. Reds, blues, yellows, bright oranges, dark purples, all these colors rushed in and exploded in magnificent displays. Many of the marauders turned their attention and attempted to intervene. Some fired shots at Evan, but the rounds could not penetrate this new barrier. He was beginning to win his battle.

Bradley's power was buckling under the newfound immensity of Evan's. The red virulence that had before been pushing against Evan's blue aura was now decreased about him in a steadily shrinking protective bubble. Evan was overpowering him. Evan stepped forward, prepared to finish his foe. Holden tried to get to his charge, but again was held back by intermittent gunfire from the entrenched marauders on the battlement.

Then a commotion from the south tower entrance changed the game altogether. The Knight and a small contingent had broken onto the battlement and were even closer to the boy and the two powerful enemies than Holden.

The Knight saw his lifelong foe, arms raised to the sky. He saw his opportunity so clearly before him. He brought all his will to bear on killing the evil man for whom he had dedicated his long life to hunt and destroy. He brought up the weapon and was about to fire when he saw the boy standing over the mage's pupil. Evan was enveloped in a multitude of colors and smiling with murderous intent. In his hands he held a short sword wreathed in flame. It shone brightly and with an evil light at its core. It was hungry for blood. It cared not who wielded it so long as it tasted crimson life waters and spread death.

Damn!

The Knight called out to the boy, and for a moment the boy hesitated to look upon him. There was the briefest moment of recognition, but the smile never left the boy's face. He turned back to the mage's apprentice and raised the sword high above his head. The Knight took aim and fired several shots.